MERRY

CHRISTMAS

STORIES

a collection of **25** short stories
by

JEFF R. SPALSBURY

www.JeffRSpalsbury.com

First printing: 2010

Second printing: 2015

Paperback ISBN: 978-1-68222-402-1
eBook ISBN: 978-1-68222-403-8

Printed in the United States of America

Cover design by: Lorena Shindledecker

Dedicated to:
Lisa E. Harman and Sara M. Boyer,
daughters rare and precious,
who remind me every time I'm with them
what Christmas is all about

CONTENTS

SANTA'S MISSING

There is nothing about Christmas that I like. I know that sounds like I'm a Scrooge, but the plain truth is that all I do on Christmas is get drunk. It's the one time of the year I plan to get drunk because that's what I do during Christmas. I drink straight through New Year's. Of course, that's when the rotten part starts. After I quit drinking, I get sick. Maybe five or six days sick. And I mean sick. Get-down-on-your-hands-and-knees and crawl-to-the-bathroom and heave-into-the-toilet-for-five-days sick.

Why do I do that? Simple. Christmas is for families and kids, right? What do you do if you don't have either? Go to a friend's house and watch them have a good time? Give me a break. I'm already depressed enough. I don't need to embellish it.

So, here I sit in my office chair with six large bottles of extremely expensive whiskey lined up on my desk, and I don't want to open one. This is not good. For the last five Christmases I've sat in my office and gotten stinking drunk. There's never been a problem getting started before. I don't go out. I'm a responsible drunk. I don't drink and drive. I don't go home—I definitely don't go home.

My condominium complex is full of Christmas cheer. I hear the music. I hear the laughter. Forget the good wishes. I don't want that. I have found the perfect solution. I listen to classical music. I hate classical music, but it's great music to get drunk by. I could never get drunk listening to jazz. Jazz is music for happy times. Classical music should be played either to get drunk or when you bury someone.

So, what's the matter? I'm playing the most awful classical music. My whiskey sits in front of me, waiting to be opened. A clean glass sits on a white cloth on top of my desk. A bucket of ice is stashed in the bathroom. Why, I ask myself, don't I get started?

It's that little kid. That's it. Of all the people to get on Christmas Eve morning, it's a little kid trying to hire me. I knew I should have closed my door yesterday and started drinking then. But no, I had to stay open until noon today. And in she walks. What was her name? Oh, yeah, Helen Schweider, age eight, and she wants to hire me to find Santa.

"I didn't know he was missing," I say, in my pithy way. She cuts right through that and tells me her mother told her Santa's missing so they won't be able to have Christmas this year.

"Find him," she says. She gives me $1.06. "When you find him, you tell him he doesn't have to bring me anything. But I've a six-year-old brother and a four-year-old sister, and I helped write out what they want. Here's the list. You give this to Santa when you find him. And ask him to bring something for my mom. She works awfully hard and too many hours, but we just never have enough money. Some food, we need food real bad, and a tree would be great."

"Do I look like a magician?" I say.

"Of course not," she says. "You're a detective. That's what your sign says. I know what detectives do. They find people who are missing. I'm telling you Santa's missing, and I want you to find him. I've given you all my money, so you'd just better find him."

"How'd you find me, anyways?" I ask.

"My mom pointed you out to me. We live a couple of blocks from here in the Summerset Apartments, 7-C, and she said you are a famous detective. I looked you up in the phone book, and I came down here to hire you. You look like you could use my case. Your office is a mess. Don't you have a secretary to clean up this place for you?"

"No, I don't have a secretary. I like a messy office. I'm a mean and nasty man, and mean and nasty men like messy offices."

"I don't care how mean or nasty you are, just get out there and find out what happened to Santa."

Then the little munchkin took off and left me with the money. There it sits, three quarters, two dimes, a nickel and six pennies and her list for her brother and sister, right on the edge of my desk where she left it. Find Santa. Ha! She might as well have asked me to find some real Christmas spirit.

I'm going to open my first bottle and forget about her. I'll give her back her money after the first of the year. That's what I'll do. Yup, that's the answer.

6

If she'd have been a greedy little kid I could forget she ever came in. Tell him I don't want anything for myself, she said. And what did she mean when she asked if I had a secretary? I guess it has gotten a bit rundown since Sally left. I'm glad Sally found herself a good man so she can stay home with her kids.

Sounds like Helen's mom can't stay home with hers. I bet Helen takes care of them herself. She's a kid, and she's taking care of two other kids. That's rough. And the mother can't even make enough money to give them a Christmas.

Forget her. Forget Helen and forget her mom.

Still, I've never welshed on a job in my life. But get serious, $1.06 is not a job. But I've never had a client give me all the money they had. And I didn't give it back to her.

Christmas Eve and they don't have enough food to eat. That's not right. At least, I can take care of that.

Love this new cellphone with the headset. Now where is Rosa's Restaurant? "Hello, Barney, this is Nick. Right. Listen, I need a favor. Yeah, I know it's Christmas Eve, but this won't take long. Can you take a bunch of your leftovers and deliver them to a family over in the Summerset Apartments? Number is 7-C. A Mrs. Schweider. What? Man, they don't have anything, so give them anything you got. You can do that for me, huh? Just put it on my tab."

"Hey, man, I don't want you to get stuck, you just put—.

"Well, sure, I understand, it being Christmas and all. Yeah, she's got three kids, four, six and eight. Yeah, I'm sure they'd love that, too.

"Do they have a tree? Well, no, but you don't—"

"Right, that's the Summerset Apartments. Number 7-C. Hey, Barney, that's great of you. Yeah, Merry Christmas to you, too."

Hum, interesting. Barney's the tightest guy I know, and he's not going to charge me for anything. Plus he's going to take the tree in the restaurant over to them. That's beyond peculiar. I didn't figure him to be a Christmas softy.

Well, no matter. That takes care of that. They have food and a tree. They aren't my concern. All right, time for some serious drinking.

7

But if the mother is hurting that much for money, she's probably hurting for the rent, too. I know about the Summerset Apartments all right. Ruffino Thomas owns those. Let's see, I programed his number in this thing somewhere. Oops, by his first name. Where's Sally when I need her?

"Yes, this is Nick Tracer. Is Ruffino in? Yes, that Nick Tracer, the detective.

"Merry Christmas to you, Ruffino. Yeah, it has been some time. I'm glad I caught you in. Oh, well, this won't take a moment. I need to talk to you about the Summerset Apartments. Well, there's a woman named Mrs. Schweider living in 7-C...no, she's not a wanted woman. She's a woman with three kids who's having a hard time of it, and I wondered if I could send you a check for her January rent payment. Give her some space...no, nothing like that. Fact is, I've never even met her. Just one of her kids.

"Well, you don't have to do that. I'd be more than happy to—.

"That's really kind of you, Ruffino. Hey, thanks. You know, I was just doing my job. Well, thank you. I'm glad it's working out so well. A Christmas Day party? Thanks, if I can make it, I will. Yes, Merry Christmas to you."

How depressed can I get if everybody keeps being so nice? This is turning into a very curious day. Can't be a decent drunk if everybody is going to be so Christmasy.

All right, face it, why do I get drunk? I get drunk to beat my Christmas depression. So, I don't even drink. So, I hate getting drunk. So what?

So, the only five times in my life I've ever been drunk like this has been the last five Christmases. Remember how it started? The year Pop died and Cindi left me.

Remember how much joy Pop had at Christmas? He'd dress up as Santa and stop at the homes of all his friends in the neighborhood. The kids would go crazy because this Santa knew everyone's name, not like the Santa in the department store. Still got his suit packed away in the closet. He would have loved that Helen kid. Yes, he would have loved....

Whoa, don't you even think like that. Have put on some weight, though. Bet it would only take one pillow to fatten me up properly.

No! Ridiculous! Absurd! Still, the kids don't have presents. What's Christmas without presents? It's 2:30. Most stores close around three or four. If I called Lindy, I bet she could get me enough presents in time.

"Hello, Lindy, this is Nick. Yes, Merry Christmas to you. Listen, I need a favor. I need to buy a bunch of gifts for three kids: a girl four, a boy six and another girl eight. No, I've only met the eight-year-old girl, but I know they are hurting, big time, so I'll take whatever you've got. Wait a minute, she left me a list. Blimey!

"What? Oh, sorry, the list wasn't what I expected. Here's what she wrote: Suzie wants a doll and a new dress for her mom, and David wants a dinosaur book and a pink bedspread for his mom.

"Yeah, I know you're a toy store. Just find some things for the kids, all right? I'll take care of the mother. Oh, the eight-year-old didn't leave a list. She told me she didn't want anything for herself.

"Naturally, I want you to get her some toys, too. That's just what she said, not what I said. Her name's Helen, and she's special, Lindy. She's a very special eight-year-old. Pick out $100 worth of gifts for each of them, and I'll be by in 30 minutes. Yes, I realize it's late, and you don't have much left. This is an emergency. Wait, how many gifts can you get for $100? Well, that's not that many. Make it $200 each.

"What? Wrapping paper? Well, actually no, I don't have any. Yes, please, I'd really appreciate it if you'd wrap them for me. Yes, yes, I know I'll really owe you for this. No, I won't suggest paying you back by taking your husband out fishing. How about two tickets to the new musical on the 28th? Yes, that one. Ah ha. Gotcha. Good. I'll bring the tickets by when I come to pick up the gifts.

"Yes, yes, don't worry about their mother. I'll find something for her, but that means I'll need longer than 30 minutes. Yes, I understand, so will you. What time do you close? Five? Good, that's going to work out great.

"What? No, I'm not going on my annual drunk. Santa is missing this Christmas, and I was hired to find him. Did I have any luck? Yes, I did. Maybe more than I deserved. Why? Because the missing Santa turned out to be me. I'll be over just before you close. Bye."

Hum, I wonder who I can give six bottles of whiskey to?

SANTA'S FOUND

Nick Tracer stood outside the door of 7-C in the Summerset Apartments, hyperventilating. He mumbled irritably, "Come on, get a grip here. I've been in major gun battles, knife fights, fought bad guys all over this state, and I've never been this nervous."

Nick jerked on his red Santa Claus jacket and slung the large bag packed full of brightly wrapped Christmas gifts to his other shoulder. He held his right hand out. It shook noticeably and that aggravated him.

"It's like when I played football; just a touch of nerves. When they kick the ball, and the game starts, I'll be fine." He made a face. "Except I was 17 when that happened and now I'm 37-years-old, and this shouldn't be happening."

He reached out to touch the bell and quickly pulled his finger back without ringing it. "Maybe this is a bad idea. I'm the last guy who should be playing Santa Claus. Pop could pull it off, but not me."

Nick reached up and pulled on his beard. He had almost not come when he couldn't get his Santa's beard to stick and then he found some other glue stuff and it held so firmly, now he wondered how he was ever going to get it off.

He hadn't expected all the kids or the adults either to wave at him as he drove over to the apartment building. He also quickly realized that driving his bright red sports car with the top down didn't help.

But the worst part happened when the patrol car pulled him over, with red lights flashing and siren going. Nick sighed when he saw Officer James Jernigan step out of the patrol car. James walked up and said, "Nick, even if you are dressed as Santa, if I smell alcohol on your breath, I'm going to have to take you in."

Nick waved to a carload of kids and parents passing and raised a warning eyebrow at the officer. "You know, James, Santa can just as easily leave you a lump of coal in your stocking as a gift."

James leaned over the door and sniffed. "Nick, you're sober!" His facial expression showed his surprise. "What happened to the teetotaler getting drunk in his office on Christmas Eve?"

"I got a case and couldn't do it."

"What sort of case do you get on Christmas Eve?"

"Santa was missing, and I had to find him." Nick looked up at James without smiling.

"You're serious." James shook his head, thought for a moment, then said, "But Nick, you're Santa."

"You got it."

"Amazing. Simply amazing. Wait till I tell the guys."

"Wait until I tell your kids that you pulled Santa over and tried to bust him."

James exploded in a loud, happy laugh. "OK, truce. Do you need a police escort?"

Nick finally smiled. "James, I think I'm already doing a good enough job drawing everyone's attention to me."

James nodded his agreement. "All you need are a few reindeer on your hood and you'd be perfect."

"Thanks."

James laughed again. "I couldn't convince you to stop by my house and visit with my kids, could I?"

"Give me a break here, James. I should be in my office, drunk to the world."

"No, you shouldn't, Nick. You should be shaking your buddy's hand and wishing him Merry Christmas." James held out his hand.

Nick took James' hand. "Ho, ho, ho, you old bum. Merry Christmas."

James reached over and patted Nick on the shoulder. "It's great to have you with us this Christmas, old friend. I always worried about that Christmas drunk of yours."

Nick shook his head to rid himself of his memory of the drive over here. He stared at the doorbell. Such a curious day, he thought to himself. "Just do it, wimp. Just do it," he mumbled as he tightened his lips and quickly rang the bell.

He heard a voice call out, "Who's there?"

He recognized Helen's voice. He took a deep breath. "Ho, ho, ho, it's Santa Claus."

"If you're Santa Claus, how come you didn't come down the chimney?"

Nick shook his head. Sharp little kid. How's it going to look if I get flummoxed by an eight-year-old? Wouldn't the guys at the gym get a laugh out of that?

His mind raced. Wait a moment; did these apartments even have fireplaces? "Because you don't have a chimney."

He heard Helen's voice yell, "Mom, there's someone at the door who says he's Santa Claus, and he can't come down the chimney because we don't have a chimney. Should I open the door?"

Nick heard a chain attached to the door. The door opened a few inches, and Nick could just make out the eye and nose of Helen's mother as she asked, "What do you want? Are you sure you have the right apartment?"

Nick realized that he intimidated many people. He was more than six feet four inches tall, and his broad shoulders and muscular arms made it clear he was not a man to mess around with. As a private detective, this was good, but as Santa Claus he realized that it could work to his disadvantage.

"It's all right, Mrs. Schweider, I'm at the right apartment. I've presents for Helen, Suzie and David."

She hesitated, but then he saw Helen's eye peek out the door. "Who sent you?" Helen demanded.

Nick pictured the three quarters, two dimes, nickel and six pennies sitting on the end of his desk—all the money she had. He felt the tension in his face. He forced himself to smile as he got down on his left knee and said, "You did, Helen. You hired Nick Tracer to find me, and he did. He told me to get right over here and make sure I brought presents for everyone."

Helen looked up at her Mom and said, "He's all right, Mom."

Mrs. Schweider gasped slightly. "You really did hire Nick Tracer?"

"I had to, Mom. You told me Santa was missing, and we truly needed him this Christmas."

"I...." She placed her hand on her chest and seemed unable to find any words to say.

Nick stood, coughed discreetly and said, "Ma'am, I don't wish to rush you, but this is a busy night for me."

She shook her head, trying to gain back her composure. "I'm sorry. There have been so many things...." Her voice had turned into a whisper, and Nick didn't hear her finish her thought as she closed the door, unlatched the chain and opened the door.

"Ho, ho, ho," Nick said as he went in. Suzie and David peered at him from behind their mother's legs with frightened, but curious eyes. Helen stood in front of her mother, with her hands on her hips, glaring at him suspiciously.

Nick glanced around the room. After years of training, he could glance at a room and almost snap a picture image of what he saw in his mind. This apartment was a tiny one-bedroom. White carryout boxes of food that Barney had sent over sat on the kitchen counter and the Christmas tree from the restaurant stood in front of the window. There were crayon Christmas pictures on the refrigerator with the kids' names on them. An old, banged-up 19-inch TV with a VHS player sat on an old wooden green-painted box. An ancient lumpy-looking couch faced the TV. Only a few toys and four children's books sat on a battered coffee table. A tiny white table with four spindle chairs filled the kitchen area. The house was clean, but bare.

Nick realized that he must appear like a skyscraper to these children, so he immediately got down on his knees in front of Helen to make himself seem less imposing.

"Are you really Santa Claus, or only a fake one?"

Nick nodded his head at her question. "If I said I was the real one, I could be lying. So, how do you propose to check me out?"

"The fake ones always wear a fake beard."

Suddenly Nick felt glad for the tough glue he'd used. "All right, give mine a pull but not too hard."

"Why not?"

"Has anyone ever pulled your hair at school?"

"Yes."

"Hurts, doesn't it?"

"Oh, I see." She reached out and tugged firmly but not hard on his beard. It held.

She stared into his eyes. You have really blue eyes, Santa, and Mr. Tracer has really blue eyes." She studied him intently. "And you have big shoulders like Mr. Tracer, and your voice sounds a lot like him too."

"Yes, poor Mr. Tracer."

Helen's face showed her puzzlement. "Why?"

"Well, I'm a lot older than Mr. Tracer, because I'm Santa, and children are always telling him that he looks like me."

"Then you really are Santa." Suddenly her eyes filled with tears, and she put her arms around him and started crying. "I wasn't sure you'd come," she sobbed.

Nick gasped in surprise, let go of the bag and held her in his arms, gently patting her back. "It's all right. Old Saint Nick is here, and you are going to have a wonderful Christmas."

She stopped crying and shook her head. "We can't. Mom got fired."

Nick looked up at Mrs. Schweider. "You got fired on Christmas Eve?" He noticed Mrs. Schweider's red and puffy eyes. She held a bunch of damp tissues in her hand.

"The owner wanted things from me that I didn't want to give."

Nick understood immediately. "I'll bet he's married, too?"

She barely moved her head up and down.

He said fiercely, "Nick Tracer would be happy to stop by and have a serious conversation with this creep."

"No, no. I don't want any trouble." She sighed tiredly. "If I didn't need a job so desperately, I'd almost be happy to be away from him." She reached down and placed her hand on Nick's shoulder. "Besides, I got a call from the manager when I got home. I was already two weeks behind in my rent but she told me that the owner called and forgave the rent for this month. Then she told me not to worry about next month's rent either. You wouldn't know anything about that, would you?"

Nick tried to suppress a grin as he said, "That Ruffino Thomas has been a very good little boy this year."

"I see. I hope when you see him that you will tell him how much I appreciate his kindness." She motioned to the tree and food on the counter. "I don't suppose you would know about this either."

"Why Mrs. Schweider...."

15

"Linda, my first name is Linda."

"Ho, ho, ho. Old Santa knew that. I was just trying to be politically correct."

For the first time since Nick had entered the apartment, Linda smiled, and Nick suddenly realized how pretty she was.

"Hey," Helen said, her cheeks wet with tears. "If you're Santa, then you can get my Mom a new job, right?"

"Helen!" her mother exclaimed. "Santa has already done some wonderful things for us. We mustn't be greedy."

"I'm not being greedy if I want something for you. I'm only being greedy if I want something for myself." She nodded her head firmly at the correctness of her answer. "I even told Mr. Tracer to not have Santa bring me anything. Isn't that what he told you, Santa?"

"Well, Helen, that's partly correct. Mr. Tracer said that's what you told him, but he also told me that he thought you were a very brave little girl and that I must include you on my list."

"Really?"

"Really, and here's what I suggest we do. Why don't you all help me by placing the gifts I've brought under the tree?"

Suzie and David came out from behind their mother's legs and as Santa pulled out a gift, he'd hand it to them and say, "All right, this one is for Suzie. Go put it under the tree."

They would run to the tree and place the gift down carefully, then hurry back for more. He handed a larger package to Linda and said,

"And this one is for you."

Linda's eyes open widely. "For me? I...." Her tears started to flow again.

Nick stood and said gently, "Santa gives very good hugs."

She dropped her package and hugged Nick. "Thank you," she whispered in his ear between sobs. "Thank you for caring." In a few moments, she had composed herself and embarrassingly picked her gift back up. "I hope it wasn't breakable."

"Ho, ho, ho, not breakable."

Soon all the gifts were under the tree. Santa smiled and said, "In some houses it is a tradition that one gift can be opened on Christmas Eve but, of course, the other gifts must wait until Christmas morning." He motioned to Linda, "But I wouldn't want to suggest anything that is unacceptable to your mother."

The children started jumping and begging their mother if they could. She smiled at the children. "I think that is a grand idea."

The three children all rushed to the tree and found one package with their name on it. Suzie quickly opened her gift first, a brightly wrapped red package. She squealed in delight and held it out in front of her. "Mommy, oh Mommy, it's the most beautiful doll in the whole wide world." She clutched it tightly in her arms.

Nick watched David. He had opened his package and stared at it. Nick wasn't sure if David liked it. Suddenly he turned to Santa and said in a low, happy voice, "Thank you, Santa." He hugged it.

Santa asked, "Do you know its name?"

"It's a Triceratops."

Santa's eyebrows lifted in surprise. "That's right. Very well done, David. Not many little boys know his name."

David grinned at Santa proudly.

"I realize, David, that not many Triceratops come in red and green with polka dots, but this is one of my favorites because he's so soft and cuddly."

"He's wonderful. I like his colors."

"Me, too," Santa said with a smile. "This Triceratops came from my home to yours, especially for you."

"Do you like dinosaurs, too?" David asked excitedly.

"They're my favorites."

Helen brought her mother a gift. "You open your gift, Mom, then I'll open mine."

Linda glanced at Santa. "I don't know...."

Santa laughed and interrupted, "You'd better open it first. It might not be anything you'd like."

She quickly tore the wrapping away and then let out a little gasp. "A bedspread." She showed the children as she held it against her cheek. "It's pink, my favorite color. And it's just beautiful." She looked at Santa. "I don't know what to say."

Nick found himself a little choked up, but he managed to say without his voice cracking, "Linda, your smile says it all."

He turned to Helen, "All right, Helen. It's your turn."

Helen glanced shyly at everyone in the room. Now that they were all watching her, she felt very bashful. She slowly removed the wrapping from her gift. Her face suddenly took on a distressed look. "It's a DVD of my favorite movie but, Santa, we don't have a DVD."

"Yes, you do, Helen." Santa reached in his pack and pulled out a DVD player. "While Santa knows many things, he wasn't sure you had a DVD player, so Santa brought an extra one. Would you like me to hook it up for you?"

All three children yelled, "yes" or "please."

Once hooked up, the children sprawled on the floor in front of the TV watching the movie while Santa and Linda sat at the tiny kitchen table, each having a cup of tea.

"So, Santa," Linda asked, "what is Mr. Tracer doing for Christmas Eve dinner tonight?"

"He doesn't have any plans. This wasn't how he was expecting to spend his Christmas Eve."

"Oh, was he planning to go out on the town with his wife and family?"

"No wife, no family. Normally he's just alone on the holidays."

"How sad. He doesn't have any family?"

"To be honest, he usually just drinks away Christmas." Nick turned pensive for a moment. "But not this Christmas."

"Why is this Christmas different?"

"He was hired to find Santa." He smiled across the table at her. "It's turned out to be the best case I've ever had."

She stared at him, made a nervous sigh, and said, "Do you think that he might like to come to dinner with us? I suddenly have enough food to feed five families."

"I...he wouldn't want to impose."

"Children," Linda said, "would you like it if Santa asked Mr. Tracer to join us for dinner? Remember, Mr. Tracer was the one who found Santa and brought him to us."

Helen looked up from the TV. "He's pretty mean, but I still liked him cause he told Santa to bring me some presents."

"I bet he's not mean," David said. "He probably thought you were too bossy, that's all."

"Did not."

"Did so."

"Children," Linda said firmly. "We don't fight and especially in front of Santa. Everyone who thinks it would be a good idea to invite Mr. Tracer to dinner, raise your hand."

All three raised their hands.

She smiled warmly at Santa. "Well?"

"Yes, ma'am, I'd say that would be about the grandest offer Mr. Tracer could get, but there is a slight problem." Nick motioned for her to lean over closer so he could whisper in her ear,

After he told her, she laughed a soft, gentle laugh that caused Nick to laugh with her. "Oh, Santa, that is a problem, but I just might be able to help. Are you a modern-day Santa who carries a cellphone? I can't afford a phone."

Nick dug into his pocket and pulled out his cellphone. She went into the bedroom where the children couldn't hear her and a few moments later came back with a smile on her face and whispered. "My neighbor, Graciela, is a budding actress. She thinks that she can help you with your problem." She turned to the children, "Put the movie on pause and say goodbye to Santa. He has to go now."

Nick got down on his knees, and the children rushed over to him and gave him a group hug. He got up and quickly rubbed his eyes.

Linda placed her hand on Santa's arm. "You are a dear, Santa."

"Just some dust in my eyes."

"Right." She patted his arm. "Children, I have to show Santa where his next stop is. Helen, lock the door after I've gone and don't open it unless it's me." She looked sternly at Helen as she grabbed her purse. "I don't need to remind you again about opening the door for the men from the restaurant, do I?"

"But, Mom, they said that Nick Tracer sent them, so I knew they were okay."

"Helen!"

"Yes, ma'am, I won't open the door again unless it's you."

19

"Thank you."

Once outside the apartment, she asked, "Will you have to go back home to get your regular clothes?"

"No, I placed them in the Santa box in the trunk of my car. My car's in the visitors parking space."

She thought for a moment. "I'll run down and get them while Graciela takes care of your problem."

They hurried down to Graciela's apartment. Once inside, Graciela looked up at Santa and said impishly, "So, we have a Santa who can't get his beard off." She pulled gently on his beard and asked, "You didn't use spirit gum on this, did you?"

Nick shook his head. "That bottle was all dried up. All I found was a bottle of Grafto…something or other."

Graciela rolled her eyes and pulled out a bottle from her makeup kit with the label, Graftobian Professional Adhesive.

"Hey," Nick said. "That's it."

"Is it bad?" Linda asked.

"Not really," Graciela said. "If you want something to stay on, it's the best, but not when it comes to getting it off."

Nick pulled gently on his beard. "This is not sounding good."

"It's all right," Graciela reassured him. "I've got the remover but it doesn't dissolve the adhesive." She nodded solemnly. "I'll need to work it under the beard to loosen the adhesive from your skin, and then I'll just have to be careful not to strip off too much of your skin from your face as I rip it off."

"Maybe I'll just shave it off," Nick said seriously.

Graciela laughed. "Just kidding, Santa. I'll have to pull some but it'll come off. You are the strong, patient type, aren't you?"

Nick sighed. "Blimey! This sure has turned into an amazingly curious day for me."

"Santa," Linda asked, "do you want to give me your keys and tell me what sort of car you have so I can go down and bring up your clothes?"

"It's not hard to find. Just look for the brightest red sports car in the visitors space with the top down and the license plate, Tracer One."

After Linda had gone, Graciela asked Nick, "Did Helen really go to a detective's office and hire him?"

"How'd you know that?"

"Linda saw me right after she got home, even before she saw her kids. She was so upset about losing her job. Then she ran back and told me about the tree, the food and the rent. She said that Helen had told her this story about how she'd hired this famous detective, but she wasn't sure if Helen had just made it up or not."

"She didn't make it up, but he's not so famous."

"Did this detective hire you or are you the famous detective?"

"I'm sure I don't know what you are talking about."

Graciela pulled strongly on his beard. "Never get testy with a woman who is removing hair from your face."

"Ouch! That's very good advice. I confess, I'm the detective. Name's Nick Tracer."

"Nice to meet you, Nick Tracer." Graciela worked more remover under the beard. "Linda is a great mother and a very close friend. She's had some tough times. I'd be extremely unhappy if anyone took advantage of her."

"Linda made me promise not to go down and pound her old boss."

"That's not what I meant, but I'd go with you for that."

"Oh," Nick nodded his head. "Graciela, I can promise you that I'm not here to take advantage of Linda."

"I don't know. A big, good-looking, tough guy. Probably lots of women in your life. Not afraid of anyone. I bet no one can put you in your place."

"Helen can. She sure knew how to put me in my place this morning."

Graciela started laughing. "Not the mom but the eight-year old kid." She gave a final tug on the beard and it came loose. "You just might be all right, Nick Tracer."

Linda hurried in with the Santa box. "Two young men with blue jackets stopped me and wanted to know what I was doing around your car. When I explained, they said for me to tell Santa not to worry about his sled. They would make sure it was safe. What was that all about?"

Nick smiled. "That's Ruffino's new security. A while back he hired me to help get all the vandalism and graffiti under control around his apartments. He owns six apartment complexes in this area, so it was costing him mucho money for security and cleaning up. I got hold of one of the gangs in the area and had them meet me at the First Presbyterian Church. A friend of mine, Toby, is the youth minister, and he agreed to help out."

"You got a gang to go to church?" Graciela said in amazement.

"Yeah, it was a scene, all right, but I can be pretty persuasive when I have to."

Graciela nodded her head, "Now, why doesn't that surprise me?"

"Anyway, I figured most of these kids were the same ones causing all the problems and what we needed was getting them on our team. So, I just hired them all to become the security force. I explained to the leader that they could make more money dealing drugs and stealing, but sooner or later, they'd all end up dead or in jail."

"You don't believe in sugarcoating, do you?" Graciela said.

"I offered them a better choice, where they could all have a real job and start thinking about a future. It helped that three of their gang were sent to prison last month, and two others were gunned down in a driveby shooting a while back. We bought them blue security jackets to wear, and Toby worked with the leader setting up their schedules. They work in pairs, have radios and work two- or four-hour shifts, depending on their age. We're working on teaching them about social security cards, bank accounts and all that stuff. Ruffino told me his places have never had so few problems, and it's even saving him money."

"What was that 'we' stuff?" Linda asked.

"Oh, well, I help out when I can. They are a bunch of kids, and Toby can only do so much. Besides most of them don't have a caring father figure."

"And Ruffino pays you for that?" Linda asked.

"Well...." Nick paused. "No, but they're just kids trying to survive in a tough world."

"I thought," Graciela said, "that you were supposed to be some sort of bad, tough guy?"

22

Nick shrugged his shoulders and grinned sheepishly at Graciela.

Graciela handed him his box of clothes and told him, "All right, Santa, let's see what you look like in civilian clothes. And while you're in there, give your cheeks a wash and see if you can get rid of some of that remover smell."

He nodded as he took the box into Graciela's bathroom. When he came out he was wearing gray slacks, a light-blue dress shirt without a tie and a dark blue sport coat. The two women smiled approvingly.

Graciela took the Santa box with his stuffing pillow on top of the box from Nick. "I'll hold on to this until you can pick it up without Linda's kids being around."

Linda motioned for him to sit in a chair. She reached in her purse and took out a tube of lotion and rubbed it on Nick's red face where the beard had been.

"Thanks," he said. "That feels much better."

"And smells better." She placed her hands on his cheeks. "You remember how you said that this wasn't how you expected to be spending Christmas Eve?" Nick nodded.

"Well, this is not how I expected to be spending this Christmas Eve either." She gently kissed him on the forehead. "My children and I thank you. You are a Christmas miracle."

Nick blushed slightly. "The Christmas miracle happened when Helen walked into my office this morning."

They walked back to Linda's apartment and again Nick started to hyperventilate. Linda glanced at him and asked, "Are you all right?"

"I'm nervous about meeting your kids."

"But you've already met them?"

"Nah, that was Santa. This time it's me. Helen thinks I'm a mean and nasty guy."

"Well, she still voted to have you come, and she said that while you were mean, she also liked you." She reached over and took his hand. "Besides, I'm with you this time." She squeezed his hand. "Were you this nervous when you first came in as Santa?"

"Worse."

"My, and you still rang my bell." She squeezed his hand again. "You are a dear person, Nick Tracer." She knocked and told Helen to open the door.

23

"Children, this is Santa's friend, Mr. Tracer. He asked me to tell you that you can call him Nick."

Helen glared up at him and then motioned with her index finger for him to get down to her level. David and Suzie looked over the back of the couch at him. He got down on his left knee and rested his arms across his right leg. She stared at him with her hands on her waist. "Santa said you were all right."

"Santa is a good person."

"He said you were a good person, too, but I think you're mean. Are you going to be mean to me?"

"No, I'm sorry I was hard on you this morning, but I'm a detective and that's what detectives do. I had to be sure you weren't a bad person. I couldn't go find Santa if you were a bad person, could I?"

Helen's mouth chewed back and forth as she thought about his answer. "Santa has the same colored eyes that you do. And he sounds just like you do."

Nick nodded his head. "Maybe that's why my parents called me

Nick, after Saint Nick, another name for Santa Claus."

"I don't think so," Helen said skeptically.

"Not everyone knows that Santa and I have similar eyes and voice, so I think Santa would be pleased if we just kept it our little secret, all right? I could never be as good as Santa."

Helen stared hard at him as she considered his request. "The man from the restaurant said that you called the owner of Rosa's and had him bring us all this food and even the tree."

Nick nodded his head. "I hope you like Italian food."

"That's something that Santa would do."

"Yes, I think this would be a better world if more people were like Santa and did good things."

Helen nodded and said, "I've never had Italian food. Is it good?"

Nick smiled, reached out and patted her arm, "Well, we'll just have to taste it and find out."

It only took a few moments to set the table. Helen and David pulled out a wooden crate from the bedroom and after some fussing, they decided that David would sit on that. Then there was more commotion about who would sit beside Nick. David said the men should sit together, and Linda decided that would be all right, although Helen made a face. David wouldn't look directly at Nick but only glanced at him shyly with a small grin on his face. Finally, he asked Nick, "Do you like dinosaurs?"

"Funny you should ask that, David. I absolutely love dinosaurs, and I think Santa does too."

"That's what he told me," David said excitedly. "Do you know all their names?"

"Some. Like that's a Triceratops you're holding."

"Yes, isn't he beautiful?"

Linda smiled over at her son and said, "David, he is beautiful, but he and," she turned to Suzie, "your doll must stay on the couch while we eat dinner. They can keep each other company while we eat."

After dinner, Linda had the children get into their pajamas. David rushed out from the bedroom with a book and asked eagerly, "Will you read to us?"

"I've never read to anyone before." Nick took the book and read the front cover, *The Best Christmas Pageant Ever* by Barbara Robinson. "All right, I'll try." Before he could even open the book to start, David climbed into Nick's lap with his Triceratops and wiggled himself comfortable. He held his Triceratops against his chest.

David grinned up at him.

"Comfortable?" Nick asked with a chuckle.

David nodded happily.

Nick opened the book but then realized that Helen stood hesitantly in front of him. Nick motioned with his free-hand. "Come on. This lap is a two-seater."

Helen quickly climbed into his lap on the other side.

Suzie sat in her mother's lap, hugging her doll. Linda winked at Nick.

Nick read the first two chapters and stopped. He looked over at Suzie. She was asleep in her mother's arms. David's eyes opened and closed wearily; however, he was fighting hard to stay awake.

"Will you stay and read the Bible Christmas story to us tomorrow morning?" David asked sleepily.

"Well...." Nick paused, struggling with how to answer David's question.

Linda motioned to her son, "David, if Nick would like to stay, you'll have to sleep in your sleeping bag by the Christmas tree, so Nick can sleep on the couch. Would that be all right?"

"I don't mind, mom," David said quickly.

Nick asked David, "I take it that you usually sleep on the couch?"

"Yes, but I like sleeping in my sleeping bag. I don't mind you taking the couch, honest."

Nick turned to Helen. "What do you have to say about me staying?"

"David falls asleep on the floor all the time, so he'll be fine, but this couch is pretty lumpy."

"I've noticed that." Nick asked her again, "Would you mind me staying over?"

"OK, but I'll have to chaperone you."

"Where did you learn a big word like chaperone?" Nick asked.

"At school. My teacher is always saying she has to chaperone us so we don't get into trouble."

"I see. Well, since you agree to chaperone me and make sure I don't get into trouble, then I'd like to stay. Very much." Nick smiled at Linda and then asked Helen, "How old are you again, eight going on 30?"

"No, silly, I'm eight going on nine."

"Of course."

"Are you teasing me?"

"Just a little, but with much love."

"Hum?"

Linda laughed as she got up and carried Suzie into the bedroom and placed her into a modified crib beside her bed.

Nick started to read again. At the end of chapter four, he stopped and smiled as he turned his head from one child to the other. David was asleep on his left arm and Helen was asleep on his right. "This is a wonderfully funny book. I may have to finish it by myself even if the kids are asleep."

"The children love it. You are a very good reader."

"Thanks." Nick tightened his lips in thought. Finally he said, "I was thinking, Linda, that I could use a person at my office. Please don't get me wrong, I'm not trying—."

Linda interrupted, "That's kind of you, but——." Now it was Nick's turn to interrupt.

"No, seriously, I need someone to come and keep my place clean and organized. Answer the phone, file, write some letters, just general stuff. Can you type?"

"I took secretary classes in high school, but I've never done anything since then but work as a waitress."

"Great. Maybe then you wouldn't mind serving me tea. I know that's not politically correct nowadays, but that would be such a treat for me. I'm not kidding. I could use your help."

Linda frowned, trying to decide what to say. Suddenly Helen spoke up, though her eyes were closed. "Do it, Mom. His place is a mess, and he needs some serious help."

Nick shrugged. "See, even Helen agrees that I need help. I could start you at say..." he thought for a moment, "...uh, three grand a month, and I've got health benefits."

Linda sat back in her chair. "I...." She placed her hand over her mouth, too stunned to reply.

"On the plus side, I'm an honorable guy. There'd be no uncalled for advances from me." He nodded his head firmly to make his point. "Not like that other creep. And you could bring Suzie to the office when she gets out of day care, and I'd make sure you were off work when the kids get out of school. Helen won't have to baby-sit and no more nights or weekends."

"I've no transportation."

"Transportation? Okay, let me think a minute. Wait, no problem. I've an old Toyota pickup I call The Lug." He smiled sheepishly at Linda and added, "That's the name on the license plate. You can drive that. It's solid transportation even if it's not too pretty."

Still Linda hesitated. "Nick, that is such a kind offer but——."

Helen opened her eyes and said firmly, "Say, thank you, mother."

Linda glanced from her daughter back to Nick, all the time shaking her head in disbelief. Finally she lifted her hands, "Yes, you're right Helen. Yes, thank you, Nick." Her voice husky with excitement, she added, "It's such a wonderful offer to get on Christmas Eve."

Helen nodded her head and said matter-of-factly to Nick, "You will fall in love with our mother."

27

Linda sucked in her breath in disbelief at what her daughter had just said.

Nick smiled down at her and asked, "Why do you think that?"

"Because she's very pretty." Helen smiled at him and her eyelids flickered and closed.

"Yes, she is," Nick whispered to the sleeping Helen.

Helen said softly without opening her eyes, "See, I knew you would find my mom a job. Good night, Santa. I love you."

Nick glanced up at Linda in surprise. "Do you think?" He shook his head. "You don't suppose she has known about me all along?"

"She's a bright little girl." Linda paused for a moment. "Last year she told me that Santa was only make-believe. That's what surprised me by her actions this year. I told them that Santa was missing so the younger ones wouldn't be so disappointed. I thought that she understood. She acts so old for her age...." Linda's voice broke and it took her a moment to compose herself. "Sometimes I forget that she's just a baby. She's had to grow up so fast. It hasn't been fair to her." Linda's eyes flooded with tears.

"How did she know about me?" Nick asked.

"Do you remember this summer? The Sunday newspaper supplement had that article about you, with pictures and everything."

"But that was months ago."

"It was such a wonderful article. It made you seem like such a special, caring person that I told Helen you were the sort of man I'd like to meet someday. To be my champion." Linda waved her hand. "Oh, I know that was childish but when life is so hard and everything is going wrong...."

She stopped and shook her head with embarrassment. "Once, when we all went for a walk, I pointed out where your office was, but I haven't talked about you for months." She stared at Helen asleep in Nick's arms. "Oh, Nick, you don't think she planned all this? That Santa was just a ruse? That she was matchmaking?"

Nick smiled at Linda. "If she was, she did a terrific job." Nick sighed, lowered his head and closed his eyes. Tears suddenly rolled down his cheeks. "I'm sorry," he said in a whisper.

Linda immediately slid down the couch to sit beside him. "Are you all right?"

"No." He slowly shook his head. "I'm overwhelmed. I'm a straightfact, by-the-numbers sort of guy. It's how I make my living, but this day has been anything but. I should be stretched out, drunk on my sofa. Instead, I'm sitting here holding two beautiful sleeping children and a beautiful woman is beside me, making me feel all gushy. All my life I've wanted a family just like this."

Helen shifted her position in his arm. Her eyes never opened but in a clear voice she said, "Now you have one." Nick looked down at her. She had a smile on her face. Linda reached over and squeezed his arm. "Yes, Helen's right. Now you have a family."

Nick nodded his head, sighed contentedly and smiled, "Thank you." He sighed again, shook his head in disbelief and grinned. "Merry Christmas, family."

A FATHER FOR CHRISTMAS

Dear Mom and Dad,

I hope you are having a great time on your Christmas-New Year's cruise. Please don't be alarmed. We are all fine. When they told me at the travel agency that I could fax you, I thought you might enjoy reading about our Christmas. It turned out very differently than I expected.

I'd hoped to be off work early on Christmas Eve, but not to be. I finally got home by 5:30, tired and a little guilty about not being home earlier to be with the children on Christmas Eve. Imagine my surprise when I walked in the house and found the dining room table already set with our special Christmas dishes. The kids ran up to me with a "Hi, Mom, Merry Christmas Eve," and a big hug.

"Mom," Jennifer asked, "what would you think about someone who had to be all alone on Christmas Eve? That would be terrible, huh?"

"Absolutely. Christmas is a time to be with family."

"And if we could help someone like that, you'd want us to, right?"

Instantly I sensed another one of Jennifer's schemes. "Do you have a friend who's going to be alone tonight?"

"Yes."

"And you'd like to invite her over for dinner?"

"That's it, Mom. Is it all right?"

"What about her parents?"

"He doesn't have any."

He! Goodness, has she grown up that fast already? "Is he an orphan?"

"Sort of. You don't mind if I invite him, do you?"

"He doesn't have anyone to care for him?"

"That's the problem, Mom. Nobody's caring for him."

"His parents left him all alone? They didn't forget him like the little boy in the movie, did they?"

"No, Mom. It's just that he doesn't need anyone. He's old."

Suddenly I felt uncomfortable. "Old! How old is old?"

"He's really old, Mom," Jesse said. "I'll bet he's even older than you."

I felt my eyelids blink rapidly as I suddenly realized what they were suggesting. "Children, sit down. Are you telling me that you want to ask a man my age, whom I've never met before, to come into our house and have dinner with us?"

Jennifer squirmed in the chair. "Well, actually we already invited him."

My gasp must have been more dramatic than I realized. Jesse burst into his silent crying routine. Huge tears rolled down his cheeks. His lower chin wiggled so hard this time I was sure he'd dislocate his jaw, yet not a sound except for his staccato intakes of breath.

I pulled out a dining-room chair and sat down, exhausted. Before I could start to explain all the reasons why they shouldn't have done what they did, the doorbell rang.

"He's here," Jennifer said brightly.

"He's here? You invite a strange man to our house and now he's here?"

"Please don't get hysterical, Mom. He's not a stranger to Jesse or I."

"Or me," I corrected.

"Right," Jennifer rolled her eyes to indicate that such a grammar correction was not worthy of a response, but then mumbled a halfhearted, "Whatever. Do you want me to answer the door?"

"No! I don't want you to answer the door. I'll answer the door, and I'll tell him he's not welcome."

"Mom!"

My black glance silenced her.

I don't know what I was expecting when I opened the door, but here was this handsome man, with a full beard, who handed me a dozen roses while cradling a bottle of Moet & Chandon Champagne in his other arm.

The expression on my face must have given me away.

"The kids didn't tell you about me? I see it on your face."

"Well, to be honest, they just told me."

31

"Listen, why don't I leave you the flowers and champagne, and I hope we can try this some other time when we've been formally introduced."

"No, please come in." Was that my voice asking him in? What on earth was I doing?

"I'm Hanley Tucker. I'm in the same complex, two buildings down from you."

"Hello. How did you meet my children?"

Hanley bent down and picked Jesse up in his arms, my Jesse who never lets anyone hold him. "I'm the new children's librarian at the main library."

"A man?" I asked, without thinking. His smile sent a small chill down my back.

"Men love children, too," he said, followed by another of those devastating smiles.

Jennifer tugged my hand and said, "That was a sexist remark, Mother."

I patted Jennifer gently on the head and smiled at Hanley. "She's right. I apologize. "

"No need. How about if Jesse and I open the champagne?"

I nodded and blurted out, "Why, you're Doc, aren't you?"

He smiled that smile of his again and nodded yes. Now it all made sense—a new children's librarian at the main branch—one whom all the children loved. I followed him into the kitchen and discovered a strange Crock-Pot filling my kitchen with a wonderful aroma. "Why do they call you Doc?"

"Wanted to be a vet when I was growing up."

"And?"

"Decided I liked books and kids more than animals. Would have made a lot more money as a vet, but I'm not sorry. Anyway, the nickname stuck."

"And this?" I asked, pointing to the Crock-Pot.

"The kids said you had to work today, and I offered to bring the main course. Jennifer said it was all right." He nodded solemnly at Jennifer. "And you said that you'd already checked with your mother, and I didn't need to call her."

"Almost."

"Almost," Doc said patiently, "is not the same as having done it. You know how I feel about telling the truth."

"Are you terribly angry with me?" Jennifer asked as her eyes filled with tears.

"No, but I imagine your mother is not happy about it."

I placed my hands on my hips. "He's right, Jennifer."

"But Mom, Doc's perfect for us. He's a hunk and he's kind and he even likes Jesse."

I gasped again, and I'm sure my jaw fell all the way to the floor. Doc tilted his head back and laughed a deep, warm laugh that filled the kitchen with merriment. He shook his head and said, "Wow! I'm glad you have to handle that one."

"Well, Jennifer," I stared at Jennifer and at Doc, "you just might be right."

Mom and Dad, I wish you could have seen Doc's facial expression. It went from embarrassment to shock and back to pleasure faster than anything I've ever seen before.

Well, folks, that's how my children got a father for Christmas. And, oh yes, I got a husband. We're getting married on Friday, the 4th, the day after you get back from the cruise. It turned out to be a unique and amazing Christmas holiday. See you at my wedding. It's at 3 p.m. at our church. Mom, tell Dad to wear that blue suit you gave him with the red tie. Always did love that suit.

Love ya,

Your newly engaged daughter

P.S.: Mom, please don't be upset with me. I've known him three days longer than you knew Dad before you two got married and see how great your marriage turned out. Must run in the family!

THE LEGEND
OF THE DRUMS

A legend has been passed down among my people from my great-grandfather, my grandfather, my father and now to me. Some doubt this legend, and others wish not to speak about it. I will tell you this legend, and then I will tell you of our journey and let you decide.

I have tried to remember the story verbatim, but I know some of the words are mine and not the words of my grandfather. Nevertheless, even if the words are not exact, I will tell the story to you in my grandfather's words as he speaks about his father, my great-grandfather:

Winter had come early and was harsh. Six families of our tribe had escaped from the whites to the deep mountains. At first, game was plentiful, but once the snows came, game became scarce. My father did not wish to kill the whites to get food, but he realized if we were to survive, he must steal our food and perhaps kill to stay alive.

While hunting a few hours from our camp, my father smelled smoke. It came from a cabin in a small clearing on a cliff overlooking the valley below. The camps of the white men were far down in the valley, and it seemed strange to my father that a white man would want to live so far from his brothers. He returned to our camp and explained what he had seen. He decided that he and five others would raid the white man's cabin the following day.

Only Long Feet and my father had ever killed before and that was when an enemy war party had attacked our village. Now they would be the attackers. Now they would be the bearers of Death. Great sorrow filled all our spirits that night.

The next day the cold was great and the snow deep as they gathered for their journey. My father stared at the face of my mother, Deer Running, for a long time and, even as a small boy, I felt the fear that he might never see her again, that he might never return.

I still remember the raiders moving silently through the deep snow, headed for the white man's cabin. When they came near, suddenly they heard drums beating, but not as they had ever heard before. This was the sound of many drums, and the sound stirred memories of happier times, of times of joy and friendship my father told us later. Never had my father heard the sound of so many drums.

Long Feet motioned with his hand that they should return to our camp. My father understood his fear of the drums, but he remembered the hunger in our camp. They had no choice but to continue. They moved closer.

A man with long brown hair and beard stood outside the cabin without a shirt, beating many drums that surrounded him, big drums, little drums, all sizes of drums. My father recognized the drums' shapes and designs. They were from many tribes—Mandan, Ute, Osage, Kootenai, Cree and many others that he did not know. The man's skin glistened with sweat from the rapid movement of his arms as he beat the drums with fierce strength. White clouds rose from his skin. His mouth and nose breathed frosted air like clouds of smoke from the great iron machine. My father's skin ached from the bitter cold, yet apparently the cold did not bother this man.

My father raised his spear to his shoulder and slowly approached. If the bearded man saw my father, he made no sign. When my father was in striking distance, the man suddenly stopped and raised his hand to my father in greeting. He smiled and spoke in our tongue. He showed no fear. My father could not move. The others froze behind him. My father continued to hold his spear ready.

The bearded man motioned to an elk hanging by the side of his cabin and told our people to take it back, along with sacks of food sitting in the snow by the elk.

Two of our people hurried over and checked the sacks. The sacks held much food.

"Kill him," Long Feet said softly.

"Why not you?" my father asked Long Feet. "You also carry a spear." My father turned and saw Long Feet's fear. "This man offers us food. He speaks our tongue. Why do you want to kill him?"

"He is a spirit of the dead," Long Feet said.

"Do not be afraid, Long Feet," the man said in a gentle voice. "I am not a spirit."

"Are you Father Sky?" my father asked.

"I am a shaman to all people." The man bent over and started beating the drums again. His eyes glanced up and when he looked at my father, my father said his heart filled with love. The man's face creased in joy as he continued to beat the drums with great passion. The sound and rhythm penetrated deep into my father's heart.

As my father and the others hurried from the clearing, they could hear the sound of the man's drums for a long way. There was great rejoicing at my father's safe return. The meat and other food brought much happiness to our camp, but the man troubled my father. Finally, he told my mother and me that he realized what bothered him. The man had called Long Feet by name. How could this have been?

Later that winter, we again ran out of food. This time only four went to the cabin of the man with the long brown hair. Again, my father heard the drums beating, but before they came out of the woods into his clearing, the sound of the drums stopped. He was waiting for my father. He stood silently in the far corner of the clearing, near the edge of the cliff, with his arms crossed, his body covered with a white buffalo hide.

My father approached him warily, but again he greeted my father in our tongue and offered us the same as before—elk and sacks of food. There were no drums in sight, but after our people left the clearing, the sound of the drums began again and the sound followed them.

In our camp, our people waited for my father and the others with great fear. The sound of the drums had carried to our camp, and the sound frightened us. When my father entered our camp, the drums stopped.

The third time we ran out of food, the sound of the drums started as my father and the others left the camp. The man was not present, but the food was in the same place as before. The drums seemed to sound from deep within the cabin. My father wanted to enter the cabin, but the others said that he should not. He placed a notched musical stick on top of a woven blanket by the door of the cabin as a gift of thanks.

36

The sound of the drums did not stop until he had again returned to our camp.

In the spring, my father took my mother and me and we returned to the clearing, but the cabin was gone, and there was no sign of the man with the long brown hair. It is certain, however, that without his food, our people would have starved that winter.

The last year of my grandfather's life, he asked my father and me to take him to where our tribe had survived that long frigid winter. He had to visit that memory, that sacred spot, one last time. Although it would be an arduous journey for my grandfather, at least a narrow fire road passed close to the ancient camp.

I parked my truck as close as possible, but we still had to walk a mile back through a narrow, rocky canyon. Once we were there, his eyes sparkled with joyful memory. Though he had been a small boy when he lived at this winter camp, his memory of that winter was strong. He pointed out where members of the tribe had camped and retold old stories I had not heard since I was a boy.

From the topo maps, I had found out that we could only reach the spot where the man with the long brown hair had his cabin by walking. My father and I felt my grandfather would not be able to endure the long hike, but his strength seemed to grow the longer we walked. Finally, we stepped out of a large grove of trees into a small clearing that overlooked the length of the valley below. My grandfather walked to the edge of the clearing and silently raised his arms to the sky.

In my mind, I had imagined the clearing to be much larger. The clearing was far too small to have even a tiny cabin. When I asked my grandfather where the cabin had stood, he pointed to where a giant tree stretched upward to the clear blue sky above us.

"But Grandfather," I said, "that tree must be more than 100 years old. How could there have been a cabin there?"

My grandfather pointed to the tree and said, "Listen quietly and you can hear the sound of the musical stick my father left as a gift."

As I listened, I did seem to hear a musical sound from far up in the tree, but I knew it must have been the wind. My grandfather saw my skepticism. "No, you must face the tree and hug it with your soul." He placed my hands flat against the trunk of the tree. Then he placed his ancient, gnarled hands on top of mine and, standing behind me, pressed my hands and body tightly against the tree. "This is a tree of life," he whispered. "Listen, not with your ears, but with your heart—your soul." I knew better than to argue with my grandfather.

I pressed my cheek against the trunk and tried to absorb the essence of the tree. At first I only felt the harshness of the bark, then all at once, I sensed the spirits of our people moving silently out of the woods and gathering tightly around us. I tried to speak, but found I could not and suddenly I heard the sounds of many drums.

Then I understood.

TINY AND THE BEAR

Ami Quinn gripped the steering wheel so hard her knuckles turned white. She tried not to let her seven-year-old son Page see the tears forming in her eyes.

"The car's broke, huh, Mom?"

She blinked away the tears and said in a low voice, "I'm afraid so, but I've turned on our blinkers, and soon a nice highway patrol person will stop and help us."

"We aren't going to make it to Aunt Beth's, are we?"

"Of course we are." She closed her eyes and forced herself not to sigh aloud. "We'll just be a little late."

"It's okay if we miss Christmas, Mom. I know you're really tried."

Ami couldn't hold the tears back any longer. She reached over and hugged Page close to her. Her tears ran down her cheeks and wetted the top of her son's head. She jumped when she heard the tap on her side window. An enormous man with a full beard motioned for her to roll down her window. The cold, wet blowing snow stuck to his beard, and the wind whipped his fur-lined hood around his face. She hesitated until she realized that he was the driver of a tow truck who had just pulled up in front of her.

"Howdy. Saw your flashers. You having trouble?"

"It just died. Now it won't start." Snow streaked in from the slightly opened window, and she noticed how the man scrunched up inside his heavy jacket as the wind blasted against him.

"I'll check it, ma'am. Pop the hood release, please."

He lifted the hood and motioned for her to try to start the engine. The engine turned over, making a loud tapping noise, but it didn't start. The man came back to the window. "Your radiator hose broke, and all your fluid leaked out. Sounds like you may have burnt out a valve or two. Didn't your heat light come on?"

"I don't think so. Shouldn0't I have seen steam or something?"

"Usually, but the way the wind and snow are blowing, it probably just blended in. Do you want me to tow you into town?"

She leaned her head against the steering wheel. "I don't have any money left."

"Well, I can't leave you out in this weather, particularly on Christmas Eve. We'll make this your Christmas present from Santa."

She wanted to say no. She wanted to say she'd manage, but she nodded yes. This huge man frightened her, but she had no choice. "You'll have to ride in my truck. How old is your son?"

"Seven."

"So's mine. He's riding with me today. He'll be glad for some company. It will be a bit cramped, but it's warm."

"He's with you now?" Ami said with obvious relief. Suddenly she realized how that sounded. "I hope…."

He interrupted her with a knowing smile and a quick laugh. "It's all right, ma'am. A woman traveling alone with a young boy can't be too careful. Don't worry yourself none. You'll be plenty safe with us. My son is a real bear."

He laughed again, helped her out of the car and then lifted Page up into his arms. "Push your face into my fur lining, and it will help keep your face warm," he told Page. They leaned against the wind and hurried to the cab of the truck.

Ami climbed in quickly and took Page. The man said to his son, "Bear, introduce yourself to these folks, while I hook up the car. There's hot soup in the thermos. Help yourself if you want some."

The man's son was smaller than her son, skinnier and pale. He smiled and said enthusiastically, "Hello, I'm Bear Ackerman. I'm glad my father can help you." He held out his hand.

A few moments later Bear's father climbed into the driver's side and grinned at them as he swept off his hood. Curly brown hair covered his head and face. Ami figured him to be almost seven feet tall and at least 300 pounds. He placed his giant arm tenderly around his son's shoulder. "I'm Tiny Ackerman. Don't we make a fine pair? Tiny and the Bear." They laughed together at their obvious family joke.

Tiny started his truck and headed for town. "This is a bad time for a winter storm. Lots of folks on the road. Won't be able to get anyone to look at your car until the day after Christmas. I'll drop your car off and take you to a motel if you'd like. Don't have any family in town, do you?"

Ami shook her head. "We're from California. I guess you should just take us to the police station."

"Ma'am?"

"I wasn't kidding when I said I didn't have any money. I've $12 and some change. That's it."

"Dad," Bear asked. "You aren't going to take them to the police station, are you?"

Ami explained, "The police will be able to call some social services and find us a place to stay."

"Will they put us in jail?" Page asked, his eyes suddenly larger than normal.

"No, no. They'll find us someplace..." Ami paused, sighed softly, then whispered, "...somewhere."

Bear turned to his dad. "Dad, why can't they stay with us? I don't want them to go to jail."

Tiny glanced down at his son and grinned. "Just like your mother. That's fine with me. You ask them."

"Won't you, huh? We've a fine big house and lots of room. You can even help us decorate the tree."

Ami squeezed her eyes tightly together and tried not to sigh again. "Don't you think you should check with your wife before you start asking strangers into your home?"

"It's all right, ma'am," Tiny said. "Martha passed away more than three years ago. It's just the Bear and me, and I'd be pleased to have you and your son stay with us."

Ami grasped her purse against her chest and tried to think of some other way, but she knew there was none. She replied finally in a low, tired voice. "That would be very gracious of you."

There was no one at the car dealership, so Tiny parked her car by the service door. Ami placed her car key in the envelope Tiny handed her. She wrote her name and Tiny told her to place his address on it as well.

"They'll take good care of you. My brother, Urs, owns this dealership."

He unloaded her suitcases and gifts and squeezed them into the cab of the truck. It was a tight fit, with suitcases on top of everyone's lap. The drive to Tiny's house took only a few minutes.

Tiny's house had the look of a bachelor's house, cluttered, but clean. In the family room a large, bare artificial tree waited to be decorated. Boxes of Christmas ornaments sat on the sofa and on top of the coffee table.

Bear explained to Page, "We haven't had a tree since Mom died, but this year Dad said we could try it."

Tiny had just shown Ami and Page their bedrooms when he suddenly picked up the phone. Ami didn't recall hearing the phone ring. When Tiny hung up, he bent down and picked up Bear. "There's been a bad accident up by Falls Mill. A young family in need of help."

"But Dad, you promised me you'd be home so we could decorate the tree."

"I know I did, but the roads have gotten worse. I'm the closest. It would be too dangerous for anyone else." He glanced over at Ami and pleaded with his eyes.

Ami took his lead and said, "If your Dad doesn't mind, Bear, maybe the three of us could decorate the tree and surprise him with it when he gets back."

"Could we, Dad?"

"That would be fine." Tiny reached for his coat. "Ma'am, feel free to call anyone you need to. Wouldn't want your family worried about you on Christmas Eve."

☙

A few minutes after seven, Tiny pulled his truck into the driveway. When he opened the door, Bear, standing on a chair, leaped into his Dad's arms. "Look at the tree, Dad. It's absolutely fabulous!"

Tiny carried his son into the family room. The newly decorated Christmas tree stood like a shrine with its lights reflected against the bay windows. The fire in the fireplace added cheerful warmth to the room. Tiny took a deep smell of the dinner cooking, and unexpectedly tears flowed silently down his cheeks.

Ami hurried over to them. "Did I do something wrong?"

Tiny shook his head and managed to whisper, "It's just so beautiful."

Bear leaned over to Ami and confided, "Dad gets kind of sentimental about things like this, huh, Dad?"

Tiny nodded, quickly wiping the tears from his eyes.

"Well, I hope you're as hungry as the boys. They've worked up quite an appetite."

Tiny gently placed Bear back on the floor and said, "Just let me freshen up." He quickly went up the stairs, two steps at a time.

"Well, hurry up, Dad," Bear yelled. "She made homemade biscuits, and she won't let Page or me have one until dinner."

ℒ

Tiny leaned over and filled Ami's wine glass full again. "That was the best meal I've had in a long time."

Ami lifted her wine glass and shook her head.

"What's the matter?" Tiny asked.

"You. I would have bet money that you were a beer man, but no, you drink wine." She lifted her glass. "And good wine at that. And you have a TV that's dusty, but books that aren't."

"Just because I have a blue-collar job doesn't mean I have a blue-collar mind. My younger brother has a white-collar job, but he has a bunch more books than I do. We're a pair, Urs and I."

"Well, I don't know about Urs, but you are a true dichotomy." She glanced over at the boys playing a board game in front of the fireplace in the next room. "Tell me about Bear."

"I guess you figured he's been pretty sick. Has leukemia. The doctor isn't saying much about his chances."

"I'm terribly sorry."

"I appreciate that. I'm a praying, hopeful man, so who knows? Miracles happen when you least expect them."

"I'd call you finding us in that snowstorm a miracle. It's really been hard on you, hasn't it?"

Tiny stared into his wine glass and tried to explain, "The Bear's my life now. After Martha died, I wasn't sure I'd make it. His mother was the purest woman I've ever met. I just know that when it's right, Martha and I will meet in heaven, but for now…." He took a sip of wine and then continued.

"The Bear made me realize that I couldn't mope around feeling sorry for myself. I had to think of us, the Bear and me. That's what's important. My brother Urs, his wife left him. She ran off with one of his salesmen." Bear shook his head. "He's having a really hard time of it. The Bear and I are the only family he has left. They didn't have children, and I think he's about the loneliest man I know. Children can make a difference, huh?"

Ami nodded her head. "All the difference in the world."

"I wish my brother had a wife and son like you and your son." He studied his wine glass intently, then said in a soft, pensive voice more to himself than to Ami, "That's what he needs, all right."

"Well, we won't talk about sad things. It's Christmas Eve, and we will only talk about a precious Baby born on this night and the importance of believing in miracles."

ℒ

Bobby Miller stared at the envelope and unconsciously wiped his left hand up and down against his blue mechanic's coveralls.

"What you got, Bobby?" McPherson asked.

"It's Tiny again."

McPherson sucked in his breath. "Are you sure?"

"I'm sure. The lady and her kid are in the waiting room. She told me

Tiny dropped her off just before I got here, luggage and all."

"You want me to tell Urs?"

"I'll tell him."

"Tell me what, Bobby?" Urs asked as he came through the door from the showroom.

Bobby handed the envelope to Urs. "It's got Tiny's address on it.

The lady said he dropped her off this morning."

Urs's hand trembled slightly. "He's still here. Still doing it."

"That's what the lady told me. She's in the waiting room."

Ami Quinn and Page looked up anxiously when Urs entered the waiting area. "You must be Urs. You look a lot like your brother."

"When did you last see my brother?" Urs asked. He tried to keep his voice under control, but he could tell Ami was puzzled by his tone.

"This morning. Tiny drove us over. Is there something wrong?"

"How do you know my brother?"

Ami explained how they had met when her car broke down on the freeway in the snowstorm and how his brother had rescued them and offered to share his home with them over Christmas.

"Boss."

"What, Bobby?"

"There's a family over at Mitchell's Motel. Seems Tiny found them up by Falls Mill. They claim if Tiny hadn't showed up when he did, they'd have all frozen to death." Bobby leaned against the doorframe. "Their car is out in back. Man says Tiny brought them into town on Christmas Eve. Says he still doesn't know how Tiny found them."

"Tiny got a phone call," Ami said, "right after we got to his house. He said something about Falls Mill. That's when the boys and I made dinner."

"They said they were trapped in their car." Bobby thought for a moment. "They told me they didn't have a cell phone. No way they could have called anyone."

"The boys?" Urs asked.

"My son and Bear."

"Bear, too?" Urs shook his head.

Ami stood. "What's wrong? I can tell something is wrong. Has something happened to Tiny or Bear?"

"Something happened a long time ago," Urs said tiredly.

"Then you two should make up," Ami said firmly. "Whatever it was that caused you to be so angry with him must

45

end. I've never heard a man speak with such love as Tiny did when he talked about you. Surely, what better time than Christmas to make amends for past hurts?"

Urs glanced at Ami's name on the key envelope. "Mrs. Quinn, could you come with me for a moment? Your son will be just fine. Bobby, you watch out for him, all right? And place their things in my office."

"Sure, boss, I'll take care of it. I'll show the boy around the shop."

Urs led Ami to a car parked out front. "Can you drive my car back to the house you stayed in last night?"

"To Tiny's house? Yes, I think so. It's not far from here. If he's home, are you going to make up with him?"

"I don't need to."

"Well, I certainly think you do."

"You don't understand."

"I surely don't. Your brother is one of the most kindly, gentle men I've ever met. How can you hold such anger against him? He even suggested I ask you for a job. Why would he—?"

"Tiny and the Bear are dead!" Urs interrupted. "They died three years ago."

Ami's mouth opened and closed twice before she could speak. "Three years ago? That can't be; we just had breakfast with them this morning."

Ami pulled up in front of an empty lot. "I was sure it was here."

"It was," Urs said. "Bear died of cancer three years ago, on Christmas Eve. Tiny died the next day in a truck explosion; he was saving the life of a man caught in a jackknifed gasoline truck. I didn't have the heart to sell his house, but about two years ago, some kids broke in and set fire to it. I had it torn down after that. I've been thinking I'd like to turn the land into a park for the city in Tiny's name. I think he'd like that."

Ami tried to comprehend what Urs was telling her. "I was with him. He saved us from the freeway. I called my sister from his home."

"He's saved a lot of folks over the last three years. Their cars all end up at my dealership, his address on the repair envelopes. At first, I thought it was somebody playing a cruel hoax. You see, when I said I don't have to make up with him, it's because Tiny was the greatest big brother anyone could ever have.

"When my wife left me, he and Bear were all the family I had left. I couldn't have made it without them. Then, suddenly they were gone. It's been the worst three years of my life, but just when I think I can't go on, each Christmas, things like this happen."

"I can see how hard it must be to have him somehow show up and yet not be here." Ami sighed. "I'm sorry, but he was here. We had Christmas in that house that isn't there. We did have Christmas there and...." Ami started to cry.

Urs awkwardly put his arm around her and suddenly she was crying on his shoulder. "Listen, I'm sorry."

She shook her head.

"Didn't Tiny say something to you about asking me for a job?" Ami nodded her head, still unable to speak.

"Well, if you're a bookkeeper, I could sure use you. Don't need more salespeople."

"I'm a bookkeeper," Ami whispered.

"Figures. And you're probably divorced too?"

"Yes, why?" Ami lifted her head.

Urs handed Ami his handkerchief. "Cause Tiny said the next woman I married, he'd pick out for me."

"Goodness!"

"Yes."

They sat silently together staring at the empty lot.

"Did you have a Christmas tree?" Urs asked suddenly.

"Yes."

"And was it decorated?"

"The boys and I decorated it while Tiny went to Falls Mill. He seemed so pleased with it."

Urs smiled and Ami realized Urs had been crying, too.

"Why are you smiling?" Ami asked.

"I went over to his house that Christmas morning after Bear died. He told me he'd never decorate another Christmas tree until he could be with Martha and Bear again. That afternoon he was killed."

"When he and Bear dropped us off this morning, they both seemed so happy. Tiny said he was on his way to see Martha. I thought he meant they were going to the cemetery."

"He and Bear are finally going home." Urs wiped the back of his hand across his eyes. "Well, Mrs. Quinn, I hope you don't mind if I start courting you. If Tiny picked you out for me, I don't want to disappoint him."

Ami glanced shyly up at Urs and said softly, "Yes, I agree."

TOO OLD TO BELIEVE
IN SANTA

At five minutes after three, Marcy Walsh sighed loudly. She left the receptionist counter, went over to the window, and stared down the six stories to the thinning swarm of last-minute shoppers. The dark, overcast sky and the wet drizzle made the shoppers hurry even more. This wasn't how a Christmas Eve was supposed to be, she thought to herself. Christmas Eve was supposed to be family and friends, good food, a warm fireplace and maybe even a special boyfriend.

Instead, today there was just work. Work until four, then home to an empty, silent apartment. She sighed loudly again. She wished she hadn't volunteered to cover the front counter and the office; then, angry with herself, she shook her head. Maria had kids. It was the right thing to do. So much for my first Christmas away from home, she thought with a sad shake of her head.

Suddenly the office door opened and a Santa Claus bounced in with a loud "Ho-Ho" and a louder still, "Merry Christmas."

"What are you doing here?" Marcy demanded. She was the only one left in the office, and she'd heard stories about men using these occasions to find women alone.

"What am I doing here?" Santa Claus said with a disarming smile. "I'm here to wish you a Merry Christmas. It's Christmas Eve, and that's what Santa Claus does on Christmas Eve."

"Ha!"

"Ha?" Santa Claus repeated. "I wish you Merry Christmas and you growl 'Ha!' at me. Your name isn't Ms. Scrooge is it? Here." He flipped the bag from over his shoulder to the floor and rummaged inside for a moment, then lifted out a large-stuffed Snoopy dressed in a Christmas outfit. He handed it across the counter to Marcy. "This is for you."

Marcy didn't take the Snoopy. Her expression changed from concern, to surprise, to delight, and back to concern. She edged back from the counter.

"That's an expensive gift."

"I'm a high-class type of Santa."

"You know what I mean!" Marcy said, still not taking the outstretched Snoopy.

Santa turned Snoopy around and said seriously to it, "Well, Snoopy, a woman who doesn't love you must be the world's worst Scrooge."

"I am not a Scrooge! I don't know you, and I don't take gifts from strangers. I never did as a little girl, and I definitely don't as a grown woman."

Santa tossed Snoopy over onto the top of his bag, laced his fingers together and plopped his hands across his padded stomach. "Well, that is certainly something to be mindful of. What would you do if I were to come here with a scrumptious banana split, just oozing with chocolate, strawberry and marshmallow toppings?"

"It would probably be filled with drugs so you could try to seduce me."

"Two spoons. I'd sample every bite before you. Every bite."

Marcy smiled for the first time since Santa had come in. "And loads of whipped cream on top with maraschino cherries and nuts sprinkled over it all?"

"Could there be any other way?"

"Well, you don't have one, and all the shops around here are closed, so your question is just hypothetical."

"Watch Snoopy," Santa said, as he turned and rushed out the door before Marcy could even respond.

Marcy glared at the door and then grinned despite herself. She noticed a card pinned to the front of the Snoopy doll. She came around the counter, reached down and turned the card until she could read it. It said, "To Marcy, with love, Santa."

"Oh dear!" Marcy stepped back against the counter and frowned. How could he know my name? I should lock the door. But if I lock the door, I'd have to open it to give his bag and Snoopy back to him. I could just put his bag outside the door and then lock it. No, somebody might steal it. I'll call security. I wonder if he'll really bring me back a banana split. No, I should just call security.

Marcy felt herself smile. "Ah, what the heck," she whispered, followed by a shrug. She hurried around to the other side of the counter just as the door handle turned and the door opened. A hand holding a banana split appeared, followed by Santa's grinning face, "So, do I have your attention?"

Two spoons stuck up like goalposts from either side of the dish. The various toppings oozed over the dish with delicious slowness.

"How did you get that?" She remembered the ice cream store on the ground floor had a sign saying the store closed at two today.

Ignoring her question, he swaggered into the office and held the dish over the counter, turning it provocatively in front of her face.

"Ah ha!" he exclaimed. "I saw that."

"What?"

"You licked your lips."

"Just a little."

"A lot."

"A little," Marcy said firmly.

Santa placed the banana split dramatically on the counter between them. With a flamboyant gesture, he took the spoon on the right side, scooped out a large spoonful of the chocolate ice cream with marshmallow and whipped cream. He pulled his fake whiskers down and plopped the ice cream in his mouth. His eyes rolled and he moaned happily before swallowing.

Marcy clamped her lips tightly shut. She'd only eaten a small cup of soup for lunch, what with all the Christmas cookies the staff had brought in the morning, but that had been more than three hours ago.

Santa shook his head. "I can't believe you aren't even going to sample this masterpiece after I went all the way to the North Pole to fetch it for you. Well, I guess I have no choice but to dump it in the trash."

"Hold it! Just hold it."

Santa opened his arms in a resigned gesture. "Whatever you wish."

51

"What I wish is that you hadn't come into my office. That's what I wish."

"But how could you have a Merry Christmas without a banana split from Santa Claus?"

"Listen, you." Marcy pointed her index finger at him threatening, "I'm going to try your banana split only because I don't like to see anything go to waste."

"Your sacrifice will be noted in my list of good little girls."

"And I'm not a little girl, Buster!"

"No argument from me on that."

Marcy's eyebrows shot up. "You, get back by the clock."

"So you can keep an eye on me."

"Right!" Marcy gingerly took the spoon and scooped out a large mouthful. "Oh, yes!" she said, followed by a sheepish grin.

"Sure wish I could have one more bite," Santa said with a wistful look.

"No!"

"Boy, you sure are mean. Look, if you're afraid I'm some sort of mad rapist, would I be dressed up in all this padding?"

"I don't know."

"Hey, it would take me ten minutes to just get down to my skin."

"You'd better not get down to your skin!"

"I was just speaking figuratively."

"Keep your figuratively's to yourself. What's your name?"

"Santa Claus."

"Right! Well, smart guy, show me your driver's license."

Santa reached into a large red pocket in the front of his jacket and pulled out a plain stick. He tapped it against his forearm twice and a bouquet of flowers magically appeared. He handed the flowers to her.

"Cute, the magic shop down by the corner."

"Hard. Boy, are you hard."

"Your license, Santa."

He reached back into his pocket and handed his driver's license to her. She motioned to the banana split, "One bite—and keep it to your side—then back to the wall."

He reached for his spoon, but stopped when she yelled, "Wait! This says you are Santa Claus. Address, North Pole."

"See, would the DMV lie to you?"

"Where'd you get this?"

"DMV."

"Right, and I'm Snow White." She waved the license in front of his nose. "I want you to tell me right now where you got this?"

"Has anyone ever told you that you'd make a great police detective? You could play the bad cop."

She shook the license at him.

"All right, my brother works at the DMV, and he made it up for me. Isn't it great?"

She nodded her head and grinned despite herself. "Yes, it is, but it pains me to admit that to you."

"Eat some more banana split. It will mellow your disposition."

"My disposition is just fine, thank you. I don't suppose you have a real name, do you?"

"Everyone has a real name. I'm Brad Pitt." He held out his hand across the counter.

"What?" She didn't take his hand. "You're Brad Pitt, the actor?"

He pulled his hand back. "Huh!" He stalled as he rolled his eyes back and forth, "Well no, but don't you think I sort of look like Brad Pitt?"

"I don't know what you look like."

Santa pulled off his hat and beard. "What do you think?"

"Not even close. So much for that fantasy. And how do you know my name anyway?"

He pointed above him.

"And don't give me more crap about the North Pole."

"No, no. I mean I work above you, on the seventh floor. I'm Eldon Nordhoff with Glasgow Industries. I asked Maria what your name was."

"Why?"

"I wanted to ask you out, but she told me you were already going with some dude."

"That dude was a dud."

"So I heard."

"Maria again?"

"No, you. In the ice cream parlor talking to your friend Bev. That's how I knew about your fondness for banana splits."

"And you eavesdrop."

"You were talking loud."

"Not that loud."

"Loud enough."

"Hum." She helped herself to another spoonful of banana split.

"And how did you get this? They were going to close early today."

"They did. I have a key."

"A key. Are you sure that's padding under your suit?"

"I'm a fifth owner."

"I'm impressed."

"Really?"

"Just a little."

"I'll take what I can get."

"Don't get your hopes up. I'm in a rotten mood. This is the first time I've been away from home for Christmas. Haven't had time to make any close friends yet."

"You have me."

"I don't know you. You could still be a mad rapist."

"You're right." He reached into his pocket, pulled out his wallet and stretched the clear plastic accordion picture holder out in front of her. "All right, here's my real driver's license, a picture of me with my brother and two sisters, a picture of my mom and dad at the lake."

"What on earth are you doing?"

"I'm showing you who I am so you won't think I'm a mad rapist. Whoever heard of a mad rapist introducing himself before he attacks the victim?"

"What about date rape?" Marcy asked.

"I'll worry about you attacking me after you consent to letting me take you out for dinner." He grinned mischievously, "You will be gentle though, won't you?"

54

"Maybe," Marcy said, trying to avoid smiling back at him. "You should know that I don't believe in Santa Claus."

"What!" He grabbed his chest dramatically. "I can't believe you'd say such a thing. Why, you've just stabbed me through the heart." He reached over and picked up Snoopy. "To prevent me from flooding this office in tears, you must accept my gift."

Marcy hesitated for a moment and then took the Snoopy from him.

"All right, but I don't like taking a gift and giving nothing back."

"How about dinner tonight?"

Marcy shook her head.

"Very well, your refusal has forced me to go to Plan B." He reached into his pocket and took out a letter. "I didn't want to do this, but this is for you. It's a letter from Mrs. Archer." He handed the letter to Marcy.

"My boss?" She stared at the envelope without taking the letter out.

"Right. It says that she was concerned about you working alone in the office. She asked me to look in on you from time to time this afternoon and then to see you safely to your car in the parking lot."

"So why didn't she tell me?"

"I asked her not to."

"I see. Wait, you asked her not to? Why did you do that?"

"I thought it would be more romantic this way."

"Oh? Oh!" Marcy averted her eyes from Eldon's.

Eldon rubbed his chin hesitantly, "I'm sorry—"

"No," Mary interrupted. "Don't say anything."

"Why?"

"Because it worked." She hugged her Snoopy.

"Then dinner?"

"Yes, a Christmas Eve dinner would be wonderful."

"And maybe Christmas?"

"We'll see." She glanced down at her Snoopy and said, "And here I thought I was too old to believe in Santa."

OUR CHRISTMAS BUS

The bus felt cold when my father and I entered. The driver explained that the heater wasn't working and apologized with a resigned shrug of his shoulders. My father guided me to a seat in the middle of the bus. A large, fat woman smiled at me as we passed her seat.

The seat felt cold and clammy, but my father placed his arm around my shoulders and pulled me tight against his tan winter coat.

"I'll keep you warm, Princess," he whispered softly, as he rubbed his leg with his other hand, the leg he'd hurt in Iraq. I'd seen the long scar, but he never told me how it had happened. Maybe when you're older, he'd say, but I never seemed to get old enough. I fell asleep shortly afterward.

Sometime later in the night, the bus jerked and made a loud noise, waking me. Frost covered the windows. I rubbed the frost away with my wool gloves and looked out the window as my father talked to the bus driver. My father and the bus driver went around to the back of the bus.

When my father returned to our seat, he shook his head. "The poor bus is broken," he said.

"Are we going to freeze?" I asked as I pulled my jacket tighter around me.

"Oh, no, we aren't far from a farmhouse. We can walk to it if we have to."

"Are we going to miss Christmas?"

"No, mother will hold Christmas if we're late. We couldn't start Christmas until we're a family again."

I nodded to my father and repeated it silently to myself, until we're a family again. For the last two months, I'd stayed with my grandmother because my mother and father couldn't find work. I missed them a lot, although my grandmother made me laugh and cooked great cookies and pies. Still, I wanted to be with my mom and dad.

"Look, Dad," I said. "There's another bus."

A bright yellow bus pulled up in front of our bus. My dad and the bus driver went out to speak with the driver from the yellow bus. Soon my father came back and told me we were all going on the other bus.

"Is it a school bus?" I asked.

"No, it's a...," I could see my father trying to decide how to answer my question, "...a Christmas bus."

"What's a Christmas bus?"

My father smiled down at me and said, "A bus that will make sure we get home for Christmas."

It still looked like a school bus to me as we walked up to the door, but once inside I realized I was wrong. This bus had living room chairs rather than those ugly bench chairs. The fat woman from our bus sat in a large chair, laughing and drinking hot chocolate. This bus was cozy and warm and filled with the smell of freshly baked cookies.

The young driver introduced herself, "My name's Noah." I told her she had a wonderful name, and she laughed. Her father came from the back of the bus with a cup of hot chocolate and cookies for us as well. He said that her real name was Mary, after his mother, but she wanted to be called Noah. He rolled his eyes and smiled the way my father does when I want to do something he thinks is silly, but he's going to let me do it anyway.

Her father was tall, and his smile made me feel warm and happy inside. I don't know why. I asked him, "Are you going home for Christmas?"

He laughed. "Here," and he waved his hand about, "we're always home, wherever we are."

The bus driver wanted to stay with his broken bus, but Noah's father persuaded him to come with us.

After we sat, my father told Noah's father, "You're an answer to our prayers."

"Answered prayers are always the best kind to get, particularly on Christmas Eve."

My father started rubbing his leg and Noah's father said, "Old wounds sometime take a long time to heal."

"I'm afraid the doctors have done all they can."

"You can never tell. This is a miracle night that has answered many prayers."

I drank my hot chocolate and ate the still warm cookie. I tried to stay awake, but my eyelids kept closing by themselves. The next thing I knew, my father gently shook me awake. "We're almost home, Princess. Sit up so I can help you put your coat on."

The bus pulled up in front of our apartment building, and I remember feeling my father pick me up, but I was still sleepy.

My father shook hands with Noah and her father. I remember him saying, "Thank you for the ride and the positive words you've shared with me."

"There is great joy in the world tonight." Noah's father smiled at me and gently laid his hand on my head.

As we walked toward our apartment, I suddenly noticed that my father wasn't limping anymore. He wouldn't realize it until the next morning.

My mother ran out of our apartment door and waved an envelope at my father as she took me and hugged me tightly. My father read the letter and started crying. I was afraid it was some awful news, but my mother understood my concern and explained that my father had just gotten a scholarship to college, and the college could offer a job for my mother as well.

My mother carried me into the house. I noticed there were no tire tracks from the bus in the freshly fallen snow, and I thought that was very strange, but I was too sleepy to ask.

I never did understand what happened that night, but now when I see a yellow school bus, I remember our Christmas bus and that night of answered prayers, and smile.

CHRISTMAS EVE DINNER

*Author's note: Six Yiddish words in this story might not be familiar to some readers. They are:

Chachka (choch-ka)—a cheap showy trinket

Chutzpah (hoot-spa)—gall, effrontery

Kibitz (kib-its)—offering meddlesome advice to someone

Kvetch (ka-vetch)—to complain, or a person who whines, frets, or gripes

Mensch (men-sch)—a decent, honorable person with admirable characteristics

Schlep (shlëb)—a clumsy, insensitive, ill-mannered or stupid person

I don't know what he expects of me. If he's ready to end it, why doesn't he just come out and say it. **"Thank you. I'd enjoy some more wine."**

Boy, she's quiet tonight. I thought sure Christmas Eve would be the best time. I just need to calm down and not rush it. **"Was really hot this week. Hard to get in the mood for Christmas."**

The weather! He wants to talk about the weather. I'll give him the forecast. It's going to get stormier and stormier, followed by a full-scale hurricane. **"Yes, but it gave me a chance to wear this new silk suit. Do you like it?"**

That's no suit, that's a full-fledged vamping outfit. I don't understand how she can wear anything that sensual and expect me to be nonchalant about it. **"It looks quite nice on you."**

Nice! He tells me nice. For what this outfit cost, I could have bought a new car. Torrie might have been right. Find a real mensch and get rid of this slug. My poor, dear slug. Are you going to be a man of honor and integrity—a real mensch— or are you just going to be a super rat?

"Thank you."

I guess it's time. She's had two glasses of wine. She's acting awfully tense though. Something is bothering her. I hope

59

she doesn't know. "**There's something I've been meaning to talk to you about.**"

Here it comes. How much chutzpah have you? Are you going to cut out my heart? Are you going to stomp that sucker flat and throw it under the Christmas tree? "**Of course, what is it?**"

I have to be calm about this, take my time. I know I can do it, just mustn't rush. Maybe she's already figured it out, particularly after these last few months. "**You know, it was one year ago tonight that we had our first date.**"

Wonder of wonders, he remembered. Well, if he wants to end it on Christmas Eve, he's going to pay for it. I hope he likes a Christmas gift of guilt to balance the account. "**It's been the happiest year of my life.**"

She's not acting like it was. Dad was right. Never try to figure out what's going on inside a woman's head. "**It's been a special time for me also.**"

Sure it was, until you found yourself a new girlfriend and stopped seeing me so often. Until you started spending your money on her and expecting me to cook you dinner all the time. Get on with it. "**What was it you wanted to talk about?**"

Here's where I must take my time and not rush. I know I can do it. "**There's something I haven't been totally honest about.**"

You can say that again, Schlep Scum. "**Oh?**"

This is not going at all the way I expected. Her mouth is smiling but her eyes are ominous. This isn't good at all. "**It's just that for the last few months I've been holding down a part-time job. That's why I haven't been able to see you as often as I wanted to.**"

He's seeing another woman, and he's going to use that tired old excuse about a part-time job. Right and I'm an exotic dancer. I hope she's a chronic kvetcher. "**Why didn't you tell me?**"

This isn't going right. I can feel her foot under the table twitching up a storm, and she only does that when she's upset. "**Actually, I wanted it to be a surprise.**"

Sure, a surprise. If you'd have given me AIDS, now that would be a surprise, but a new love in your life for these last two months is not a surprise. Lying about her, however, well, that's a first for you. **"I hope it's a nice surprise."**

It's no good. I can't get the words to come out. All right, fall back to Plan B. **"Before I explain, why don't I give you your Christmas gift."**

Ha! He chickened out. Typical male. Oh wonderful, a tiny gift, probably a pair of earrings with the message "goodbye" engraved on them. **"Do you want me to open it now?"**

What sort of question is that? Why is she so distant? **"Yes, please."**

Aren't you going to make a little speech about what a special friendship we've had, but now it's time we both moved on with our lives? Well, let's get this over. I'll open this stupid chachka. **"What on earth…"**

That's not quite the exclamation I imagined. Something is all wrong here. She hates it, she hates me! **"Please say something—anything."**

A ring? An engagement ring? How can this be? He must have given me the wrong gift. **"Isn't this for the special woman in your life?"**

What is she talking about? **"That's right. It's for you. It's why I've been working two jobs. It's why I've been saving all my money."**

I can't believe this. And I called him a slug, a schlep. **"A ring!"** *What can I say?* **"It's really for me?"**

I knew it, she hates me. She hasn't put it on. Where's her delight, her ecstasy? I bet she's found someone else. She's going to turn me down. Can't turn chicken now. Take a deep breath and do it. **"It's for you because I love you, and I want you to marry me."**

He loves me? He wants to marry me? Oh dear, he looks so worried, so vulnerable. **"I'm amazed."**

Amazed? She's amazed? I don't want to hear amazed, I want to hear, yes, or, me, too, or I love you. Not, I'm amazed." She sits there staring at that stupid box, and she tells me she's amazed. **"If I've misunderstood…."**

Come on, get control here. Stop trembling. Take it out. Try it on. Look at that, he knew the exact size. **"What do you think?"**

61

Think? How can I think? You haven't said yes, no, maybe. You try it on and ask what I think. **"I think you're driving me bonkers."**

I'll have to tell Torrie not to kibitz so much. I have my mensch. The poor little lamb. Someday I'll tell him what I was really expecting tonight—then again—maybe not. **"Oh, I'm sorry. Yes, I love it. Yes, I'll marry you, and yes, I love you, too."**

I need a drink! Now I know why men always die younger than women. They have to suffer through ordeals like this. I don't even want to think about the wedding. **"May I kiss you?"**

Need you ask? **"My dear mensch. Yes—please."**

BUDDY DON'T CRY

"This is the third time, Buddy."

I don't answer Mrs. Zebra, but I stare at the windshield wipers as they smear the snowflakes against the glass. She's unhappy with me. I bet she wanted to leave work early and spend Christmas Eve with her own kids.

She glances over at me. "And those big, sad brown eyes of yours won't help you this time."

When I don't say anything, she sighs loudly.

"Mrs. Johns told me that you yelled at her. Did you?"

"Yes, ma'am. She never talks to me, and today I was just so lonely I had to yell at somebody."

Mrs. Zebra slowly rubs her forehead with her fingers. "No more foster parents, Buddy. There's just the home now."

I feel her eyes turn toward me, but there's nothing to say.

"Does it hurt much?"

My hand starts for my cheek, but I force it back. My cheek throbs. "It don't hurt." I taste the blood in my mouth.

"Foster parents do not strike our children, Buddy, but sometimes things happen."

"It's all right, Mrs. Zebra. I understand." The snow melts on the edge of the windshield and slowly runs down the glass. It reminds me of tears. I never cried when Mrs. Johns hit me, not a single tear. No one will ever see me cry. Ever!

"You place a cold cloth on your cheek when we get to the home."

"Yes, ma'am." I know some guys don't like Mrs. Zebra much, but I never minded her. She took care of me when I first came to the home. She has a sad face and when I look at her, I see myself. I don't think I've ever seen her smile, not really smile, just those "Hello, how are you?" smiles, but never a real "I'm happy" smile.

Mrs. Zebra pulls up in front of the house. She and Mrs. Weirdo don't like each other, so she makes sure I go in the door from her car.

I see Mrs. Weirdo—that's not her name, of course—but it's what all us kids call her. She's waiting at the door with her hands on her hips and that scowl on her face. She pulls her hair back on her head like a wasp nest. She greets me with, "You back again, huh? I can always tell the bad ones."

I try not to stare at her bad eye. She gets real mad when you stare at her bad eye, but it's hard not to. It's sort of white, and it keeps looking off to the side like it's watching something.

"I want no trouble from you and Wolf, you hear. No trouble at all. I've already told him."

"Yes, ma'am," I say. I've learned never to talk back. Just say, "Yes, ma'am," or "No, ma'am." Sometimes that makes grownups as mad as when you do talk back, but they aren't as likely to hit you.

Mrs. Weirdo leads me upstairs to the same bedroom I had before. Six beds, but at least I get my old bed back. I want to crawl under the covers and never come out again, but we have to get ready for the foundation people to come over and give us our gifts. Big deal! Last year I got a pair of socks. Stupid gift. Wolf copped them before I even had a chance to wear them.

I got really angry and fought him. He won. He always wins, but for the first time, I hurt him. He's just a bit afraid of me now. I can see it in his eyes. He still slugs me in the arm when I'm not looking, but he's afraid. I'll have to fight him again. It doesn't matter what he does to me as long as I can hurt him good. Then maybe he'll stay away from me forever.

"Wash your face and hands and come downstairs immediately."

"Yes, ma'am." I stare at her bad eye and her lips curl out, but she doesn't say anything. I go into the bathroom. So, what's my gift to be this year? More socks? Maybe a shirt that's too big for me? Probably some dumb game. I splash cold water against my cheek and swish water in my mouth to get rid of the blood taste. I hide my drawing book under my pillow. Even Wolf and Mrs. Weirdo know not to touch my drawing book.

Rich people fill the room when I come back downstairs. You can tell rich people by how they dress and how they smell. The women all smell of perfume, but I don't like the smell. It brings back a sense of a memory from long ago that I can't quite remember. Then I feel sad and I don't know why. The adults try to talk to us, but they never know what to talk about, and after a while they feel dumb and leave us alone. No one tries to talk to me, and I'm glad. I don't want to talk to nobody.

Santa Claus comes through the big double doors. Last year they had a wino play Santa Claus, but he arrived drunk and halfway through giving out presents, he just fell down on the rug and passed out. That was awesomely funny. Mrs. Weirdo went berserk, and that made it even funnier.

If there is a real Christmas, a real God, he'd know what I want. God's not some wino in fake whiskers giving dumb gifts. Baby Jesus' birthday has gotten as bad as mine. At least this year's Santa Claus isn't drunk.

Ha! Look at that. Wolf got a puzzle, a baby puzzle. Boy does he look mad. Serves him right.

"Have you been a good little boy?"

I tilt my head up and almost don't reply to the fake Santa. Finally I say, "If I'd been a good little boy, I wouldn't be here, would I?"

The Santa's mouth falls open, and he frowns as he tries to decide how to respond. Finally, he manages a weak "Ho Ho" and hands me a present. I stick it under my arm, unopened.

"Open your present, Little Boy."

I glance over at the strange lady sitting close to me, but I don't move.

"Open your present, Buddy," Mrs. Weirdo demands from across the room. "Immediately."

I turn my head until I can see Mrs. Weirdo and slowly place the present in front of me. Mrs. Weirdo starts to scowl, but she's staying where she is, so I meticulously start to remove the wrappings, taking as much time as possible.

"I used to open my gifts slowly when I was your age," the strange lady says. "That way, you enjoy the moment even more."

"I do it slowly so I won't have to see what a dumb gift it is any sooner than I have to."

"Oh! Oh, dear!" She stands and hurries across the room.

I don't smile, but I feel like it. I pull the last of the wrapper off the present. At first, I can't believe my eyes. It's a cartoon book, but not just any cartoon book. It's a big, hardback *Peanuts Classics* book by Charles Schulz. I'd cut out a bunch of Peanuts cartoons from the newspaper and started a collection, but Mrs. Johns threw them out. She said I got ink all over my hands and clothes. I hold the book out in front of me. I can't believe it. I just can't believe it!

"Hey, Toad, let me see that."

Wolf has his hands on my book. "Let go of my book, Wolf, or I'll hurt you bad."

His face shows surprise and uncertainty. "You and what army, Scum," he says, but he lets go. I stand and glare up at him. "Don't ever touch this book again, Wolf. Never, ever!"

"I'm going to get it, Slime. You can't stop me."

Mrs. Weirdo starts toward us, but stops when I head for the stairs. I don't run from the room, but I want to. I'm shaking inside. In my bedroom, I turn on the light, climb on top of my bed and take deep breaths to calm down. Then I slowly turn the pages of my new book. The pages in color make me smile. It is the most magnificent book I have ever seen, and it's mine. I shake my head in disbelief.

Inside the cover, someone had written a message. It's hard to read cause it's written in cursive, but I slowly sound out each word: "I hope you enjoy this book. It is my favorite, and I give it to you with much love," and it was signed by a Mrs. Patterson and there were some numbers under her name.

The numbers might be a phone number. I squeeze the book to my chest and try to decide what to do. We aren't allowed to make phone calls, but this requires a special risk. I have to let Mrs. Patterson know how special her gift is to me. Then I have to figure out how to keep Wolf from getting it away from me. This is worth dying for.

I can tell from all the noise downstairs that the party is still going on. If I'm to make a call, it has to be in the next few moments. I take off my shoe and pull out my two dimes and my nickel. I hold the coins tightly in my hand. I'd had these three coins for a long time. They feel warm and smooth. I'll miss them.

I pull a chair over to the pay phone in the hallway. I juggle my book with the phone number, the receiver and my coins, but soon I have it. I hear the phone ringing, and then suddenly a man's voice answers the phone. I ask for Mrs. Patterson.

"Who is this?" the voice asks.

"My name is Buddy. She doesn't know me, but she gave me a Peanuts book for Christmas, and I wanted to thank her."

"She's sick."

"I'm sorry. I can't call back cause I used the only money I have."

"I'll tell her you called," the man's voice says. He sounds tired. I hear voices in the background, but I can't make out what they're saying.

I start to hang up when the man's voice says, "Wait, she wants to talk to you."

Mrs. Patterson says "Hello." Her voice is tiny and weak.

"Hi, my name's Buddy, and I got your Peanuts book. It's just so special that I had to call and thank you."

"Did you really enjoy it?"

"Oh, yes, now I've just got to make sure that another boy here doesn't steal it from me."

"Well, you just don't let him do that, all right?"

"Yes, ma'am."

"How long have you been at the home?"

"A long time. They say I'm encouraged-a-boy."

Mrs. Patterson slowly says the words, "encouraged-a-boy" several times, laughs gently and says, "They wouldn't be saying that you are incorrigible, would they?"

"Yes, ma'am. That's it. I don't think I'm that bad. I try not to be."

"Well, Buddy, you keep trying, and someday something very special will happen to you."

"But it already has, ma'am."

"How's that?"

"You gave me this special book. You made this Christmas the best one I've ever had."

"I'm sure you'll receive many other fine gifts this year."

"Well, no, ma'am. This will be the only gift I get."

"Little boys should have more than one gift."

Her voice sounds sad. I don't want her to be sad. "Oh, it's all right. I don't mind cause your book is the best gift in the whole wide world. And one super, great gift is worth a bunch of dumb gifts."

"I'm glad, Buddy."

For a moment, I thought she was crying, but then she thanks me for calling and wishes me Merry Christmas. I say goodbye and hang up.

I'm not sure I should have called. She seemed pleased at first, but then she seemed so sad at the end. Gee, I wanted to make her happy, and maybe all I did was make her sad. And I didn't have my three coins anymore. I'd miss the feel of the coins in the bottom of my shoe. Tomorrow I'll start looking down at the street when I walk so I can find more.

I go back to my room and climb on top of my bed. I just start to enjoy my book when Wolf appears. He comes directly for my bed, and I know he's going to try to take my book. Just as he's reaching out for my book, I slam my foot at him. My shoe strikes him right between his legs. He yells, falls on the floor and wiggles around like a worm on a hot sidewalk.

I jump off the bed and poke my finger into his chest. "Stay away from me or next time it will be worse." He must believe me because he hobbles out of the room without saying anything nasty back at me. He's never done that before. I suddenly feel wonderful. I guess I was wrong when I told Mrs. Patterson that I'd only get one gift this Christmas. Now I'd gotten two.

That night I tuck my drawing book and my Peanuts book under my pillow. As I say my prayers, I remember to say happy birthday to Baby Jesus.

Somebody shakes me awake early. At first, I thought it was Wolf coming back after my books, so I reach under my pillow to make sure they're still there. They are. It's Mrs. Weirdo, and she tells me I have two visitors. Me? Visitors? Maybe Wolf told on me, and they're going to take me to prison.

I hurry down into the big room. I take my drawing and Peanuts books and hold them tightly against my chest. There are two grownups waiting for me. The man bends down on one knee and holds out his hand. I shake his hand. He explains that he is Mr. Patterson and the woman is his wife, Fiona. He hasn't shaved, and he has dark rings under his eyes. He seems really tired.

I ask Fiona, "Did you give me my book?"

"That was Mr. Patterson's grandmother you talked to last night."

"She's a great lady. She gave me this book." I hold out my Peanuts book for Mr. Patterson to see.

"She was a dear woman," Mr. Patterson says. "She died last night, and your call meant a great deal to her."

"Mrs. Patterson died? But she gave me the best present in my whole life. She can't die! Everybody I love dies. She can't die!" I feel the wetness flow into my eyes and overflow down my cheeks. I can't stop the tears this time, just like the melting snow on the windshield, I can't stop them. I start shaking so hard; I drop my precious books.

Fiona reaches down and scoops me up in her arms. I hear her say to her husband, "He's coming home with us, Tom. Right this moment."

Mr. Patterson picks up my books, reaches over and gently pats my back. "Yes, dear, I agree."

Mrs. Weirdo explains that it is impossible for them to take me, but Mr. Patterson stops her with a dark look that shuts her up instantly. "I'll be by tomorrow to fill out the paperwork."

"Very well," Mrs. Weirdo says quickly, and then adds under her breath, "but he'll be back."

Mr. Patterson hears and quickly turns around so he's facing Mrs. Weirdo. "Lady, one thing I can guarantee you is that Buddy will never again step inside this place. Do you understand that?"

"Yes, Sir," she said. "I didn't mean…."

I never heard Mrs. Weirdo finish because Mrs. Patterson already had me out the door.

I ask Mrs. Patterson, "Ma'am, if I get lonely, will you mind if I come and talk to you sometimes."

"Anytime you get lonely, Buddy, you'll always be welcome to come and talk to me. Can I come and talk to you when I get lonely?"

"Do grownups get lonely?"

"Sometimes, but not when they have you."

I hug my new mother and think, three Christmas gifts this year! When I say my prayers tonight, I must remember to ask God to tell Mr. Patterson's grandmother. I'll bet she'll be pleased.

BAG LADY BLUES

They stole my shoes, they did. Imagine, snitching an old woman's shoes while she's asleep on Christmas Eve. I was even wearing them, and they still stole them. Right off my feet. The gall of it!

The woman at the shelter couldn't help much, so I just wrapped my feet up with strips from that old blue flannel shirt of yours. Never figured I'd end up using that for a pair of shoes. The woman wanted me to stay at the shelter, but I needed to come up here and be with you. Don't be angry. For these last few years, I've been living in this awful fog. This morning it seemed to lift away, I don't know why. Maybe because today is Christmas.

It's cold out here. Never could figure out why you picked this spot. Yes, I know the view is fine, but it's so cold and windy.

So many Christmases have passed, I've lost track. Never figured I'd be the last. A mother's children shouldn't die first. Do you see them often? I suspect you are happy being with them, but it's not right. They were both so young. They should have been here longer.

I think my feet are frozen. I'm afraid my cloth shoes don't work too well, and they got wet. Don't even have the strength to stomp my feet. I'll go someplace warm soon, but first I'll just rest a spell. You don't mind, do you? It's good to be near you. These last years have been lonely, and I needed to be with you today. I wish you could reach out and pat my hand in that reassuring way, as you used to do. I miss your touch and your laugh, especially your laugh. It's been a long time since I've laughed.

Remember that last Christmas, when we had all the kids home. It was the best Christmas ever. Even my meal turned out great. At least you all said so. Then after dinner we sat around the fireplace and sang Christmas songs and drank hot chocolate with marshmallows in it. You gave me that wonderful pink robe. That's gone, too. Not sure I remember where, but it's gone just the same.

Left my cart at the shelter. Reckon it's been cleaned out by now. I just gazed at it this morning and wondered why I was pushing it around. I don't understand why I look out at the world with all my young thoughts, yet when I look in the mirror I see an old lady. When did that happen? My soul wants to dance, yet my body can't even walk straight.

I've stopped coughing. Been hard to sleep these last few nights with that cough. Such a nuisance. I don't seem to be as cold, but my hands don't want to move. Oh well, don't have to use them for anything anyway.

Do you remember coming home from the war? You'd been gone so long—three years—and I'd traveled all the way to New York City to meet your ship. I spotted you right off. You were the handsomest soldier there. If I shut my eyes real tight, I see your smile and smell that wet wool scent of your jacket. I can still feel the warmth of your hug and the gentleness of your kiss. It was a cold, wet day just like today. Wasn't that just yesterday?

All right, Tommy, I admit it; this is a beautiful spot. I can see clear across the valley, even with the snow falling. But it's better in the summer with all the leaves on the trees. It's all gray and white today, with black, empty trees.

Do you miss me? You always said you missed me, even when you had to go on those overnight trips. We did love life, didn't we?

Well, look at that. Here comes a young man up the road who looks just like you used to look when you were younger. He's even wearing a navy uniform like—Tommy, is that you? How can that be? Take your hand? I'm sorry, I want to but I'm afraid. Well, my goodness, look at that, you took my hand and just like that, I stood up.

Let me look at you. How wonderful you look. But I must be a sight, and I know I smell bad. I haven't enjoyed a bath in a long time. There's no place to take a bath when you live on the streets. Remember how I always had to take a bath before we went to bed? You always kidded me about that, but then, afterward, you always said I smelled so womanly.

I smell wonderful? My goodness, look what I'm wearing. My favorite dress. It was the dress I wore to meet you in New York, and you brought me a bouquet of white daisies. You remembered. How sweet you are.

The children are waiting for us? But I can't—I can! And they even cooked dinner for us. How marvelous. Oh, you know how I am, Tommy. These aren't sad tears. These are happy tears.

Wait, Tommy, wait. There's a poor old woman sitting on a tombstone over there. Shouldn't we help her?

THE BRONZE OLIVE

I have decided that a story about true love should start like a fairy tale. After all, isn't true love a fairy tale? And true love and Christmas together, well, that must be the greatest fairy tale of all, particularly if you are a pragmatic woman of the 21st century.

And I am categorically a woman of this century and extremely pragmatic about such things as love and men.

Thus, once upon a time in the far-off land of California, there lived a fine young princess—me! Blessed with reasonably good looks, a reasonably pleasing body, but cursed, nah, make that worse than cursed, make that doomed with a fantastic, brilliant brain. A brain so good that I graduated from high school at 14, had a bachelor's degree from Ohio State at 18 and a Ph.D. from UCLA at 21. And now at 24, I'm a senior vice president of a major environmental firm.

I've a great job that pays me extraordinary sums of money, a fancy apartment in San Francisco, a Lexus sports car and everything a woman could want. So, why do I feel so lonely? I'm on my way home to Ohio, but there is no anticipation or happiness. No, it's not for the lack of a man. Well, perhaps the lack of a man who lasts longer than two dates.

I seem to frighten men off. What's the matter with men who can't enjoy a woman who has a body, looks and a brain? Stupid men. Well, the next man I meet will be different. This time, I'll make him pay for all the stupid men I've had to put up with over the last few years. The next man who tries to pick me up with his cheap, dumb pickup lines, I'll make him rue the day he was born. Justice will finally be mine!

That's how this story all started. I was having a martini at a small bar in the terminal of the San Francisco airport, cursing all men and a few specific ones, when it happened. I love olives more than I love martinis, so I always ask for extra olives. I'd eaten two off the pick and while working the third olive off with my fingernail, it suddenly popped off, flew up in the air and right down the coat sleeve of the man sitting beside me.

"Excuse me, but I just dropped an olive down your sleeve."

He turned his head to the left and surveyed me closely. I'm not sure which fascinated him more, my large dark eyes or the "oh, gosh!" look on my face.

"I beg your pardon?" he said, in a deep, husky voice.

"I'm sorry, but I just dropped an olive down your sleeve."

He studied his arms as though detached from his body. They were out in front of him, elbows on the bar, hands wrapped around a cup of hot coffee.

He shifted his coffee cup to his right hand and together we leaned forward and peered down the left sleeve of his pilot's uniform coat. I couldn't see the olive, but a suspicious lump protruded about halfway down his sleeve. His sensual after-shave flooded my senses. I glanced up and found his face close to mine.

"Do you always drop olives down the coat sleeves of airline pilots?" he asked innocently.

I took a deep breath and like a child caught in a mischievous act, tried to explain, "I was trying to work the olive off the pick, when it just popped!" I sighed my little girl sigh that always gets men panting.

"Oh," he replied understandingly. "Let me buy you a new olive."

I flashed my most enchanting smile and exclaimed, "But what about *that* olive?" as I pointed to his elbow.

"I'll have it bronzed so we can have it for an emergency."

This fish was almost too easy a catch. "I think that would be difficult to eat!" I said with a vampish laugh.

He nodded and said, "But what a lovely story to tell our grandchildren."

My mouth fell open and for a moment, I was speechless. He not only was smooth, but also fast, extremely fast. Play games with me, would he?

"I'm sorry," he said. "I'm rushing things a bit." He placed his coffee cup down and held out his right hand, "My name is Tommy. Captain Tommy Powell. What's yours?"

"Dani Rifkin."

"Dani, the feminine form of Daniel, meaning judged by God. A lovely name."

"That's interesting. Not many people would know the linguistic origins of Dani."

He shrugged. "Must have read it somewhere recently."

So, not to be outdone, I said, "And Tommy from Thomas, sometimes referred to as Jude Thomas Didymus, one of the 12 apostles of Jesus. Thomas meaning twin in <u>Aramaic</u>, as does Didymus in <u>Greek</u>."

Tommy stared at me with the look of amazement that I'd seen before when a man suddenly realizes that he's met a woman who's smart. He nodded and said, "Touché," but then his look changed. It was a look of pleasure, of being pleased, of deciding something important. I'd seen that look before in high-level meetings at work, but never during a pickup. That was unexpected.

I heard his name announced over the loudspeaker system.

My pilot grimaced and then turned to me. "I couldn't help but notice on your ticket that we're on the same flight. Going to Columbus, Ohio, right?"

"Yes, but...."

"Good," he interrupted. "I'm deadheading home for Christmas. My sister lives in Logan, near Columbus. Would you mind if I try to get a seat beside you?"

Captain Tommy Powell was the answer to a prayer. He was the epitome of all the men I'd met in my life—smooth, good looking and shallow. He would be the Christian, and I would be the lion. I suddenly felt better. Perhaps I did feel a smidgen guilty, it being the Christmas season and all, but not much. He didn't know it, but he was going to be my Christmas present and dinner, all wrapped up in one. So many men had stomped my heart flat that I not only needed a victim, I needed revenge, sweet, complete, thorough, begging-for-mercy revenge.

I nodded my head in agreement and when he stood, the wayward olive rolled back down his sleeve into his hand. He slipped it into his pocket. "They have a great olive bronzer over on North High. Let me catch my page."

76

I smiled up at him and thought, *right and may the fleas from a thousand camels infest your armpits on High Street.* He was smoother than smooth.

When he hurried back, apparently whatever he had heard on the phone didn't please him.

"Is there a problem?"

"My flight engineer, Tip Wilson, didn't have my number on his new cell phone, so he had to page me. He just called me about my copilot, Buddy. Buddy's in a phone booth."

"I don't understand."

He smiled a charismatic smile at me. "It might be easier if I showed you the problem."

Tommy led me to an open telephone area, five gates behind us. Buddy leaned against the back of the booth, eyes open, with one finger pointed toward the phone's button and the handset tucked between his shoulder and ear.

Tommy started to reach over and interrupt Buddy when I suggested, "Why don't you let him finish his call?"

"Oh," he grinned over at me. "Yes." He nodded his head. "How silly of me. Why don't I let him finish his call." Tommy slipped his hands into his pockets and whistled a few notes, and then emphasized, "Per your request, we will just stand here and let him finish his call." He made a half smile toward me and asked, "Will you let me know when he's done?"

I observed Buddy more closely. "Uh, Tommy, his finger isn't moving."

"Which finger is that, Dani?"

"You know darn well which finger."

"Oh, you mean that finger," he said as he motioned with his head toward Buddy's extended index finger while still keeping his hands in his pockets.

I reached over and felt Buddy's pulse. "Well, he's alive."

"You did that like a doctor."

"Just one of my many skills." I moved my hand in front of Buddy's face. Buddy's unblinking eyes didn't flinch. I leaned forward and took a sniff. "Wow, I've never seen anyone stoned like this. Is he really a pilot?"

"One of the best," Tommy replied.

"Well, what are you going to do?"

Tommy sighed tiredly. "I didn't need this." He slowly shook his head.

I folded my hands behind my back and rocked back and forth, deep in thought. "Well, if he were dead, we could just leave him. With that much alcohol in him, it would be years before he would start to stink."

Tommy mumbled something about all his plans, turned to me and asked, "You're sure he's not dead?"

"I'm sure! Does this happen often?"

"Fraid so."

"Doesn't the airline know?"

"Well, let's just say they're becoming a mite suspicious."

"I'll bet they are. Frankly, I think my idea is the best one. Let's just leave him. It could be years before he sobers up."

Buddy suddenly toppled over like a giant Sequoia crashing to the ground.

I yelled, "Timber!" as Tommy tried to pull his hands out of his pockets in time to catch Buddy. He was too late. I managed to catch part of Buddy's shoulder with my foot, so at least he didn't crash on his head.

Tommy contemplated the stiff body lying by his feet. "He's really a very sweet guy. He just isn't much of a drinker."

"He's enough of a sweet guy to make me consider taking the Amtrak back to Ohio."

"Oh, he doesn't drink when he's flying. This is a tough Christmas for him, that's all."

"It's tough on me, too, but I can still manage to walk on the plane under my own power."

"Check the time for me, will you please?" He replaced the handset into its cradle. "How long before our flight leaves?"

I didn't answer him.

"How long?" he persisted.

"Little over an hour." I poked Buddy gently with the toe of my shoe to see if any part of his nervous system was still functioning. There didn't seem to be. "Can't you ship him home in the baggage section?"

"It's important that he makes this flight. He'll be fine."

"But will he smell better?"

Tommy sniffed over the body. "Good point. See you in first class."

I slowly shook my head as Tommy struggled to pick up his friend. I thought to myself that perhaps God was going to punish me for thinking about being mean to this man during Christmas. One thing I did feel sure about, though, was I didn't want to be sitting next to his drunken, smelly friend.

The beauty in traveling first class is that though the plane may be packed, up front you don't mind. This time I had a slightly disheveled airline pilot sitting beside me in the aisle seat and across the aisle slumped an extremely disoriented copilot, who had the appearance of having taken a shower with his clothes on. As my riding instructor was fond of saying, he had been "ridden hard and put away wet."

Buddy's eyes were sunk deep into his head, and his curly black hair was wet and stuck to his forehead, but he was alive, more or less.

Buddy glared at Tommy through glazed eyeballs and said hoarsely, "I remember going to the phone booth to tell you I wasn't going. How'd I get here?"

"Through skill, my boy. Through skill."

Buddy tapped his forehead and mumbled, "I'm not here, huh, Tommy? I died, and this is how I'm going to be punished."

"The only punishment you're going to get will be from me if you try to get a drink on this flight."

"No drinks. No way. My stomach couldn't handle another drink. Why is that woman staring at me?"

"She's a friend. We're going back to Columbus together to bronze an olive."

Buddy frowned at Tommy for a long moment, then in a choked whisper asked, "To bronze a what?"

"An olive."

Buddy turned to the passenger sitting beside him, "Did he say an olive?"

"He said an olive."

Buddy mumbled to himself, "Of course, of course. Now I know I've got to quit drinking."

As we sipped wine, I asked Tommy, "I understand that you don't even need a high school diploma to become an airline pilot?"

"Gee, I don't know. I remember 10th grade. What about you?"

"Oh, I've a Ph.D. from UCLA."

"Well, that's great. Are you smart?"

"Yes, very."

"Must be a burden."

I must have done a double take, because suddenly I detected an odd smile on Tommy's face. "Not at all. I enjoy the skills and talents I have."

"But you're not married?"

"There's more to life than being married."

"I prefer to think that there's more to life being married."

"Well, you're not married either, are you?"

"Not yet. But I think you'll do fine."

I opened my mouth to parry his last thrust, but he unfastened his seat belt and stood. "I have to borrow something from the pilot. Back in a moment."

I was going to enjoy watching this pilot crash and burn. I glared across the aisle at Buddy, but he was so sick I couldn't hold my irritation. What I needed was some ammunition to use against this arrogant pilot. "Tell me about Tommy, Buddy?"

Buddy's bloodshot eyes tried to focus on me. "You must be one special woman."

"What do you mean?"

"You're the first woman Tommy has ever picked up."

"Right! Give me a break, Buddy."

"Lady, I don't know who you are or what you are, but if you hurt him, I'll punch you out, even if you are a woman."

His statement shocked me so much, it being such a strange thing to say, I didn't know how to respond. Buddy's drunk, but still? Before I had a chance to think about it, the airline stewardess working first-class slipped into Tommy's seat.

"Are you a friend of Tommy's?"

"Why?"

"Oh, don't get me wrong. I just wanted to tell you how lucky you are. I've never seen Tommy with a woman before, so you must be special."

Hum, the second time I'm called special. "Maybe he's gay?"

She laughed. "Not Tommy. I think he's never found a woman smart enough to catch him yet."

He has now, I thought. "Tell me about him."

"Well, I can tell you that with all the creeps in the world, I'm glad there are a few like Tommy." She reached over and patted my hand. "He's a terrific guy, but I think he's a little lonely, too." A buzzer sounded. "Oops, that's mine. Gotta fly."

Oh great. A nice guy. I get a nice guy to shoot down. I started to feel like the Red Baron with Snoopy in my sights. I suddenly noticed Buddy motioning to me.

"Miss, I'm sorry I spoke to you that way. Tommy's the bestest friend I have. I'd be stretched out in some gutter if it weren't for him." Buddy's eyes filled with tears, and he started crying. He didn't make any noise, but the tears ran down his cheeks, and his whole face contorted with pain. I'd never seen a man cry like that before.

I unfastened my seat belt and went over to him. "Can I get you anything?"

He just shook his head, bent over and sobbed silently.

I patted his back gently, much as I would have a lost child. What sort of Christmas was he heading home for?

Tommy hurried down the aisle to us. "Cleanup time, Buddy," and Tommy proceeded to pour a glass of ice water down the back of Buddy's shirt.

Buddy stiffened up in the seat as though he'd been shot. It did stop him from crying, but from the look on Buddy's face, I thought sure he would reach up and punch Tommy. This was everyone's idea of a nice guy?

Tommy unfastened Buddy's seatbelt, grabbed Buddy by the lapels of his coat and physically lifted him out of his seat. Tommy flashed me a smile and said, "Sorry I can't spend more time with you, but I've some work to do." Tommy then half-pulled and half-carried Buddy forward to the restroom.

When they came back a half-hour later, I was shocked. Buddy wore a clean uniform, his hair was combed, and he was clean shaven. On the other hand, I had seen movie zombies with more color.

Buddy collapsed in his seat and grimaced at Tommy. "I'm scared, man. I'm really scared."

"You'll do fine."

"I've got no presents." Buddy's eyes filled with tears.

"Yes, you do. They're in my large suitcase."

"I didn't buy them."

"In a way, you did. Every time you saw a gift you said your kids or Amy would love, I bought it. Frankly, you owe me a ton of money. And you'd better take good care of Tim's uniform." Tommy sat down beside me.

I leaned over and touched Tommy's arm. "What's going on?"

Tommy tried to look lighthearted as he explained, "Buddy's going home for Christmas, and I wanted to make sure he looked good. I had to borrow a uniform from the pilot. I thought they were about the same size and they were."

"No, there's something else going on."

Tommy nodded at me thoughtfully. "Well, Buddy didn't know he'd been invited back home for Christmas until a few moments ago. He made a bad mistake some time ago, and his wife felt that maybe he should just go live with his mistake."

"And now?"

"Well, Amy, his wife, called me a few weeks ago, and I explained how he didn't go back to his mistake and how he'd been handling his repentance. She agreed to have him come back for Christmas so they could give it a new try." Tommy turned and faced Buddy. "Although, if he ever screws up like that again, Amy will have to flip a coin with me to see who pounds on him first."

"I won't, Tommy," Buddy exclaimed. "Honest to God, I won't, ever again."

Tommy nodded, leaned back in his seat and let out a long slow breath. I reached over and patted his arm. He was trembling.

"Are you all right?" I whispered.

"I feel as if I've gone through the worse flight of my life, and I'm still not on the ground." He laced his hands together and held them against his mouth.

All right, so Tommy won't end up being my male sacrificial victim. Christmas was a time for forgiveness. Tommy Powell would escape my wrath against men. Besides, I was starting to like the guy. I was always too soft.

"You remember taking your comps?" he asked.

"Yes, I don't think I've ever been so stressed out. I aced it, but I remember how nervous I was, like a bad dream. Why?"

"I feel as I did after finishing mine. I did two doctorates, and it turned out both my comps were on the same day. One in the morning, one in the afternoon."

"You said you never got past 10th grade."

"No, I said I remember 10th grade. Janie Peru was in my class, and she drove me to distraction." He gave me a little boy smile, and I found myself breathing a little faster, but I still gave his arm a light slap.

"Of course," he continued, "I was only eight, and she was so much older. Anyway, I feel...."

"Wait a moment," I interrupted. "How old were you when you got your doctorates?"

"Twenty."

"Twenty? Oh, no!"

"Please, don't say it like that." Tommy's face tightened.

"Hey, relax." I reached up and placed my hand against his cheek until the lines softened. "I was 21 when I got mine." His smile of relief curled my toes.

"Our children are going to be a problem," Tommy whispered.

"You're serious?" I didn't seem to be breathing correctly. "My word, you are serious."

"I'm very serious."

I stared into his brown eyes pleading with me to say the right thing back to him. My hand still cupped his cheek, and I thought to myself that this couldn't be happening. Then I realized how glad I was that this was happening. "Well, we'll just name our first son after Buddy and tell him how we met—."

"And got engaged on Christmas Eve," Tommy finished.

I would have said yes, but I was too busy kissing him to think about it, although I did hear Buddy say to the passenger sitting beside him, "That's my best friend and his fiancée. They're going back to Ohio to bronze an olive."

THE HOOKER'S KIDS

The white-haired man limped slowly down the corridor. His cane made a tapping sound, and it caused the boy to glance up.

The man unbuttoned his overcoat, shook the snow from the coat and sat on the bench across from the boy. He took off his hat, beat the hat against his leg to shake the wet snow off and placed it beside him on the bench. A grungy, tilted Christmas tree blinked its lights on and off beside the bench.

The boy rocked a sleeping girl in his arms and hummed softly to her. She was a few years younger than the boy.

"Friend of yours?" the white-haired man asked.

"My sister."

"And your mother?"

"Dead."

"Harsh. So, they told you already. I'm sorry."

"They said she died yesterday, but they ain't sure."

"Who's not sure?"

"Cops. They came and got us this afternoon. They told us."

"Do you feel bad about it?"

"She tried to be a good mom. She was a hooker, but she never brought any tricks home with her. Not once."

"So you don't feel bad about it?"

"Didn't say that."

"Well?"

"You'se asking a lot of questions. You'se ain't no cop or nothing?"

"Nope. No cop or nothing."

"Cop told me they's gonna take my sister from me and place us in homes."

"How do you feel about that?"

"Ain't nobody taking my sister from me."

"Have you a father?"

"Don't know. Never knew. Mom never talked about that."

85

"Thirsty? I saw a Pepsi machine coming in."

"I's okay."

The white-haired man stood and removed his overcoat. "You watch my coat, and I'll get us something to drink."

"Mom told me never trust no one who wants to give me things for nothing."

"Look at it this way, you're watching my coat, and I'm going to pay you back by bringing you a Pepsi."

"Guess that's okay."

The white-haired man returned juggling a cup of coffee and a Pepsi with one hand and his cane with the other. The man held out the Pepsi to the boy and then sat and took a sip out of the white plastic cup. Steam drifted over the edge of the cup.

"You'se ain't under arrest, too, is you?"

"No. I'm here because I heard about you."

"What'd you hear?"

"That your mom had died."

"Had a Christmas gift for her this year. And a card, too."

"What was it?"

"I finds an old binder, and I gets some movie magazines that the library throws out. I cuts out the pictures of her favorite movie stars and glues them on the binder. She said someday she's going to be discovered and be a famous movie star."

"She would have liked that."

"Can'ts give it to her now. Don't give her nothing last year except a card I makes for her. Makes it at school. Mom said it was damnedest gift she's ever got."

The white-haired man blew his nose into a large white handkerchief. He removed his glasses and wiped his eyes.

"You'se crying?"

"Yeah. I'm crying for all the children just like you and your sister. And I'm crying for your mom."

"Mom says I can't never cry. You'se knows my mom?"

"A long time ago."

"You'se ain't her dad, is you?"

"No."

"Mom told me her dad is really mean."

"He was."

"You'se knows my mom's dad?"

"I heard about him. He did some horrible things to your mom. I never found out about it until long after it had all happened."

"If you'se come to take my sister away from me, it ain't gonna to happen. I ain't gonna to let you do that, you know."

"I know. I didn't come here to take your sister away from you."

A gray-haired woman hurried down the hall. She stopped and stared down at the boy and his sister. "I took care of all the paperwork."

"I appreciate that, Hazel."

She sat beside the boy. "So these are the hooker's kids." "No. These are your daughter's children—your grandchildren."

"I don't have a daughter," Hazel said irrevocably.

"Not anymore you don't."

Hazel sniffed and made a face. "They need a bath. And clean clothes."

"They need love more."

"You're making a mistake, Jess. You should just let the state worry about them. They'll be no good, just like she was."

"I don't agree."

"You, Boy," Hazel said. "You want me to hold your sister for you?"

"No! Don't you touch her!" The boy turned his back to her.

"Don't snap at me." Hazel said as her lips hardened into a pout.

"Hazel!" Jess snapped her name.

"Jess, I'm not going to put up with his talking back to me."

"Yes, you are."

"I was just trying to be friendly."

"You don't know how," Jess said softly.

"You'd think I'd never raised children."

"Never any good ones." Jess shook his head sadly.

"I tried…."

"No, all you did was whine, scream or pout and make their lives miserable. You married bad men who did horrible things to your children, and you never protected them. You drove your children away, just like you did all your husbands."

"Go to hell, Jess."

"That's where you raised your children, Hazel."

The woman glared angrily at Jess. Her feet made loud stomping sounds as she hurried back down the corridor.

"That your wife?"

"No, my sister."

"She's a bitch."

"You're right, although that's not a proper word to say about anyone, even if it is true."

"Is she really my mom's mother?"

"I'm afraid so."

"My grandmother?"

Jess nodded his head.

"Mom said her mother was cruel and never loved her."

Jess sadly lowered his head, unable to answer.

Another woman, wearing a blue sweat suit, hurried up the hall and plopped tiredly down beside Jess. "I just don't know how you could stand growing up with that woman. Every time I'm around her, I want to punch her out."

"Denton was saying the same thing."

"Oh, Denton, I'm so sorry about your mom. Has Jess gotten you anything to eat?"

"He got me this Pepsi."

"My, that doesn't surprise me. What's your favorite food?"

"Fried chicken."

"Mine, too."

"She ain't your sister, too, is she?"

"Better. She's my wife."

"I like hers better than that other one."

"Me, too."

"Well, I'm certainly glad you two have given me your stamp of approval. Why don't we all go back home? I'll fry us up some chicken, and we can pig out."

"Can't go. My sister and me is under arrest."

"Not anymore. That mean old woman signed some papers and if you want, you can go home with us."

"Ain't nobody's taking my sister from me."

"No, no, Denton. Both of you. We want you and your sister to come home and live with us. You see, Jess here is—was your mother's uncle. Do you understand about stuff like that?"

"Ain't never understood that."

"That's all right, Denton, I had to explain it to Jess, too. Just know that we are family, and we want your sister and you to come home and live with us."

"Are you a hooker?"

"No, I'm a wife and a mother. I'm not a hooker."

"Ain't sure I can get along with no one's not a hooker. That's all mom knew. Hookers and pimps."

"Your teachers at school weren't hookers, were they?"

"One of them was."

"Wonderful. I'm sorry I asked that question. You try it, Jess."

"Did your mom ever tell you how to get along with people?"

"Said if you stay alive with tricks and pimps, you can get along with anyones."

"There you are. So getting along with us should be easy for you."

"Don't know. You'se pretty old. You'se a lot older than my mom and now she's gone. You'se got a lot of white hair. You'se ain't going to die soon, is you?"

"No, I think I've got a few good years left. At least long enough to help you and your sister grow up in a happy home."

"How come she's so young and you'se so old?"

"She just dyes her hair, actually she's...."

"Jess!"

"I was just going to say that you were eight years younger than I am."

"Likely story."

"But you'se have to use a cane."

"Oh that. I hurt my knee skiing. The doctor had to patch it up some."

"What's it like to ski?"

"Come home with us, and I'll take you and your sister skiing when my knee heals."

"Really?"

"Really."

Denton thought awhile and asked the woman in the blue sweat suit,

"And if we goes with you, you'se cook us some fried chicken?"

"I'll cook you the best fried chicken ever."

"Okay, but...."

"But what?"

"She's pretty heavy, and I don't want to wake her. She's mighty tired and scared."

"Would you like me to carry her for you?"

"You'se won't runs away with her? I could catch him, but you look like you'se could run pretty fast."

"No, we'll all walk out together. Where're your coats?"

"Ain't got no coats. You'se ain't going to hit us because we ain't got no coats, are you?"

"No, we aren't going to hit you. It's stopped snowing, so if we hurry you won't get too cold, and we'll warm up the car quickly. We'll buy you new coats tomorrow. Tell you what I will do, though. I'll microwave some peach pie to warm you up when we get home. How's that?"

"I remembers peach pie. Had it once a long time ago when I was little."

"Then peach pie it is. Here, help me put your sister on my shoulder. There we are. See, she didn't even wake. Jess, take my scarf and wrap it around her. That will help some. We're all ready to go."

"Uh...."

"What's the matter, Denton?"

"Will you'se hit me if I cry?"

"Do you feel like crying?"

"Like to cry for mom, but I's afraid you'se hit me if I do. Except he cried for her, and I was hoping maybe it would be all right."

"In our home, you can cry for anyone you love, and no one will ever hit you."

"You'se must have a wonderful home."

"We think so. Do you want to cry now?"

"I's feeling real bad, but I's so tired. Like to cry for her when I ain't so tired. You'se think that'd be okay?"

"I think that will be just fine."

"Mom used to hold my hand when we went out. She said she had to protect me from all the bad people in the world."

The woman held out her hand, and the boy timidly placed his hand in hers. Together, the white-haired man with the cane, the woman in the blue sweat suit carrying a sleeping little girl and holding the hand of a little boy, walked down the corridor of the police station and through the door.

I NEED TO BORROW YOU

"Excuse me, but are you married or involved?"

Jofer Robertson glanced up from his copy of *USA Today* and smiled quizzically at the attractive, dark-haired woman wearing a sensual, backless cocktail dress. "Not currently," he said, smiling. "Why?"

The woman studied Jofer for a long moment and then seemed to make up her mind by saying, "I need to borrow you."

"You need to borrow me," Jofer repeated slowly. "All right, would you care to sit down and tell me why?"

"You would need to know that, huh?" The woman lowered herself nervously into the chair across from him.

"That would be helpful. It's not like you were asking to borrow a cup of sugar."

"Yes, not like that at all." She nodded her head slightly and sighed. "I suppose there's no way to convince you to just trust me and let it go at that?"

"Good try." Jofer smiled, as he shook his head back and forth.

"No, I understand. Well," she sighed again and frowned as she tried to decide how to explain her problem to him. "I realize this may all sound juvenile and stupid, but the honest truth is that I lied to some of my girlfriends." She shook her head. "I told them I was married."

"And I take it you aren't married."

"Correct."

"And that?" he asked, pointing to the wedding ring on her finger.

"My grandmother's." She stared down and absentmindedly twisted it around on her finger. "She left it for me in her will. She wanted me to have it when I got married." She frowned at Jofer. "Ironic, isn't it."

"And you told them you were married because you were tired of having them always fixing you up with dumb dates?" Jofer suggested.

"Worse. Because I was envious of all their happiness."
She waved her hands in the air in exasperation. "I know—
dumb, dumb, dumb."

"Intriguing. Still, I don't have any idea what you are
talking about."

"Four of us went to college together. We were in the
same sorority. I was even president of the sorority one year.
But since we've all graduated, I've gone to more weddings
than I can tell you. They all met the right man, fell in love and
got married."

"Everyone but you?"

"Yes, everyone, but me. I went to Paris last year for
two weeks. It was wonderful, so romantic. But I never met
anyone over there. So, I lied and wrote home that I'd fallen in
love and married while in Paris. In all my life, that has to be
the stupidest thing I've ever done, but Paris was so romantic
that I just wanted to be part of all that happiness."

"Which brings us to this evening, I presume? Your
friends want to meet this wonderful, mysterious man who
wooed and married you in two weeks."

"Worse. My three closest friends and their husbands
have all traveled here to Santa Cruz to have a wonderful
surprise Christmas party for me and my new husband. I just
found out about it."

"When?"

"About 10 minutes ago."

"Goodness! Well, that explains your panicked
expression." Jofer thought for a moment. "You could tell them
the truth."

The woman's eyes turned moist. "That would be the
honest thing to do."

Jofer nodded understandingly, "Yes, but it would sure
make for a rotten Christmas party for you."

She nodded without speaking.

"And for your friends," he added. "You could tell them
it didn't work out after you returned to the United States."

She shook her head. "I wrote and told them it was
going wonderfully." She sighed. "Normally, I'm a very level-
headed woman, but this...." She paused, "Perhaps I could get
divorced later?"

Jofer laid down his paper and slowly shook his head back and forth.

"It will only be for this evening." She noticed his head shaking.

"You won't do it?"

"Worse, I will."

"Really!"

"Yes, I was shaking my head because I can't believe I'm saying yes. But yes, I'll do it. You've got me for the evening."

"That's wonderful."

"However, I must tell you I'm staying here, at this motel. I'm not sure how we can explain that to your friends if they discover we are staying in different rooms, but I guess we can come up with something."

"Yes, that would be a problem. I live here in Santa Cruz. I'm not even staying at the hotel, I just drove over from my house."

"All right, we'll just say that we rented a room so we could drink and not drive. That would sound very responsible."

She nodded. "So, you aren't from Santa Cruz?"

"No, Visalia."

"Where's Visalia?"

"Around four hours southeast from here, deep in Tule Fog country. In the winter, I try to come over to the coast at least once a month to smell the sea air and see the sun. This is my Christmas trip. With no family, coming here helps keep me in a happy mood." He held out his hand, "I'm Jofer Robertson."

"I'm Tina Baker. You don't smoke, do you?"

"No, do you?"

Tina shook her head. "I told them you didn't smoke. They're waiting for us down the hall. We need to go right away. They've reserved a room with food and where we can play dance music."

"Right now? You don't want to find out more about me?"

"No."

"If that's the case, how do I look? I didn't come here expecting to go to a Christmas party with my new wife."

94

"You look fine."

Jofer brushed some dinner crumbs off his lap and straightened his sport coat. "I didn't bring a tie. Sorry."

"That's all right."

Jofer started to get up, then stopped and asked again, "You sure you don't want to spend a few moments and give me some details.? We could work out our story and find out a little bit more about each other."

"I didn't tell them much about you. We'll just fake it. I'm already late."

Jofer shook his head. "Am I supposed to be a Frenchman or something?"

"Just an American I met while I was in Paris."

"Probably just as well. I have a rotten French accent, but I'd love to try it out. It always sounds great when I do it in the shower."

"No French accent."

"I'm already a nagged husband. All right, let's go, but stay close. If we're going to do this masquerade, we can't be telling different stories to your friends. And, at the moment, the only thing I know about you is your name and that you don't smoke."

"Do you think we can get away with it?"

Jofer laughed easily. "Depends on how good an actress you are." He paused and shrugged. "And how good an actor I can be."

Tina nodded but didn't smile.

"Smile," Jofer said as they hurried down the hallway. "Aren't you supposed to be madly in love with me? Look happy."

"Yes." She timidly took his arm.

Jofer tilted his head back and laughed again. "Come on, this is your masquerade. If we're madly in love, act like it." He put his arm around her and drew her close to him. "Get in the spirit of the thing. I'm not going to assault you, but if we're madly in love, we have to look the part."

"You're enjoying this, aren't you?"

"Why not? A beautiful woman is suddenly in my arms, madly in love with me. I'm going to a great party. Why not enjoy it?"

"You're right. Why not?" She smiled up at him nervously. "No matter what happens, thanks."

"That's what husbands are for." Jofer leaned down and kissed her long and slow. At first, Tina started to pull away, but slowly she relaxed and before the kiss was over, she was kissing him back.

A woman hurried out of the restroom, stopped, did a double take then exclaimed, "Wow, Tina, this must be your new husband. Can I kiss him like that?"

Tina jumped away from Jofer's kiss and grinned at her friend's sudden appearance. "Not if you want to keep your marriage, Sally."

"Darn, that's right. I am married. I tell you, Tina, for a man like that, I think I'd have taken his name rather than kept my old one."

"Well," Jofer said, "that's just one reason I'm so in love with her. She's a woman who doesn't need a man's last name to know who she is."

"Oh, is my husband going to hate you. Come on, you two, the crowd's down here." She pointed to a door down the hall. "I just slipped out to freshen up. I'd have just died if you'd gone in before I got back."

Sally pushed open the door and yelled, "Look who I found."

After the introductions, Sally's husband James asked, "So, where did you meet Tina, Jofer?"

Jofer glanced at Tina. She frowned, so he answered, "At the airport in Paris. We'd arrived on the same flight, and we bumped luggage, or rather I bumped into her."

"Did she get mad? I've never seen her mad before."

"No, she was charming. I fell in love with her the moment she first spoke to me."

"Truly! That's so romantic. Why aren't you romantic like that, James?"

"I am, but you always say I'm being silly. Tina never told us what you do?"

"I'm the director of the library at Porterville College." Jofer felt Tina suddenly squeeze his hand hard, but he wasn't sure what that meant.

"You don't live here in Santa Cruz with your Tina?"

"Not yet, I have a home in Visalia. I come over on the weekends. We make every hour count while I'm here, but the drive back is grossly depressing."

"Tina, are you going to move to Visalia? Maybe you can get a job in Jofer's library. Do you think you can drag yourself away from the public library to go work in a college library?"

"You're a librarian?" Jofer said in surprise.

"You didn't know she's a librarian?"

Jofer blinked twice and then grinned at Sally. "It's an inside joke, Sally. When I first found out in Paris that we were librarians, I started kidding her about it. You don't know how great it is to be married to someone in the same field. You can share so much more." He felt Tina squeeze his hand gently.

"Well, tell me what you see in this woman? I mean, we roomed together for two years, and I know what she looks like early in the morning."

"Tell you what I see in her?" Jofer repeated slowly. "I see eyes that a man could drown in and never cry for help. I see a smile that makes my whole inside go tingly. I see a woman as smart on the inside as she is beautiful on the outside. Do you want me to go on?"

"No," Tina placed her hands over her face and said, "Stop. Too amorous. I'm embarrassed."

Jofer leaned over and kissed her gently on the cheek. "No, not amorous enough."

"Oh," Sally squealed. "Such love. It makes me giggly."

"Everything makes you giggly," Sally's husband said as he reached over and nibbled on her ear.

"Music, music, you mad fool," Sally yelled in mock terror. "We must dance or my husband will attack my Rubenesque body." She grinned at the group and added, "And if anyone says fat, I'll stomp on their feet." Sally turned to Jofer. "Come on, it's a nice slow song. Drag her out here. Make her suffer."

Jofer stood. "Fine with me."

Tina hesitated.

Jofer leaned down and whispered, "It's all right, I know how to dance."

"I'm not very good. You might regret it."

"That I can't imagine."

97

Jofer took Tina in his arms and whispered in her ear, "Remember, we are supposed to be deeply in love. Put your arms around me and snuggle close."

They danced for a few moments. Tina whispered in Jofer's ear, "You are easy to dance with."

"Tina," Sally yelled, "When did you finally learn to dance without tripping over your partner's feet?"

"This dance."

"Sure, and I weigh 100 pounds."

"That's what I would have said," Jofer said to Sally, "if anyone had asked me how much you weigh."

"No question about it, Tina. I just love your husband."

"What about your husband?" Tina asked.

"Him?" she stared at her husband. "Him I don't just love. Him I passion for, I die for, I worship the ground he walks on, but besides that —he's just all right."

Sally's husband rolled his eyes and then spun her toward the center of the floor with a huge grin on his face.

Jofer whispered into Tina's ear, "A librarian. Unbelievable."

"And you, too," Tina said back. "But you are smooth."

"You inspire me."

"That's what I mean."

Jofer kissed her on the cheek. "Thank you."

"And that's not what I meant."

"Our first fight?"

Tina shook her head. "Our second kiss." She stopped dancing and kissed Jofer passionately.

"Stop that," Sally yelled. "We're supposed to be dancing to control these oversexed men. Jofer, why aren't you wearing a ring?"

Jofer lifted his right hand. "Arthritis. I haven't been able to wear a ring for over five years."

"That's great," Sally said, "but you're supposed to hold up your left hand."

"Don't listen to her," James said as he danced by, "I just show my nose when they ask me about my ring."

Sally punched her husband in the stomach.

"But, of course," James gasped, "I'm only kidding."

Jofer grinned at Tina and whispered, "I have to confess that since I was a teenager I've had wild fantasies about women who wear backless dresses. And to be dancing with a woman wearing a backless dress, well, this dress of yours beats even my best fantasy." The music stopped.

Tina said in a small, tiny voice, "I don't want to stop."

"Fine with me."

"Hey, you two, the music stopped." Sally grinned at her husband and said, "We used to hear music like that."

"I still do."

Sally fanned her face. "Why you little devil. This party may have to end early."

"It can't yet, honey. Dinner is ready."

"Sex and food. My two most favorite words." Sally motioned to Jofer and Tina. "Come on you two, take your place of honor at the head of the table."

After they sat, Tina reached over and placed Jofer's napkin in his lap. "Can you handle two dinners?" she whispered.

"Just don't scold me for eating lightly. Who's picking up the tab for all this?"

"They are."

"You must be pretty special to them. This is costing a bundle, and they're all just working folks like us."

"They're my friends."

"Regrettably, they're becoming mine, too."

Tina stared at him peculiarly but didn't ask what he meant.

When the party ended, it was past one in the morning, yet nobody wanted to leave. "How about I buy us all brunch in the morning?" Jofer said. "That way we can share a little more time together before we have to leave."

"Jofer?" Tina eyes opened wide in surprise.

"It's all right," Jofer reassured her.

"Sounds good to us," Sally said. "But not too early. How about 10?"

Jofer nodded. "Ten it is."

Jofer and Tina walked down the hall to Jofer's room. "You shouldn't have done that," Tina said,

"Why?"

"For one reason, it's going to cost you too much money. I didn't want you to spend your money. This was my masquerade."

99

"Yes, it was, and I thought we were a fine team."

"It was too good." Tina let go of Jofer's hand. "Sally told me you gave John $100 to help pay for the party."

"It was worth a lot more."

"I'll pay you back and for whatever brunch costs tomorrow."

"You already did."

"What do you mean?"

"I had one of the best evenings of my life. We're even."

"The masquerade's over till tomorrow." Tina tilted her head to one side. "You don't have to say anything you don't mean. Show me what room you're in, and I'll be back here by nine."

"Okay, this is my room." He inserted the key card into his door, and the lightdot turned green. He opened the door and held it open with his foot. "And you're right about the masquerade being over for the evening. The problem is I want the masquerade to be real." He motioned with his hand for her to enter his room.

She ran her tongue over her lips but did not move.

"But understand," he added. "I'm not looking for a sleepover. I've fallen in love with you. If you go through this door, we marry in the morning."

"How?"

"How? Yes, good question. Can't get married in one day in California. No way we can get a flight on Christmas Eve day anywhere." Jofer thought for a moment. "All right, how's this, we get your…" he paused and smiled, "…our friends and take a limo to Reno, at least any of them that can spare another day? We'll call it a Christmas Eve renewal of our vows, but this time with our friends."

"They can't afford to do that."

"I'll put it on my American Express card, and it will be my wedding present to you."

Tears filled her eyes, but still, she hesitated.

Suddenly Jofer reached over and swept her up in his arms. "Let me help you decide. How about I carry you over the threshold?"

She snuggled her head against his shoulder. "I'll be a good wife."

"Ah, my dear, but you already are," he said in a terrible French accent as he carried her into his room.

THE LAST S-2

When I entered the establishment, I expected danger. For 30 years they had tried to vanish me, but this time all I registered was their fear. Such fear neither surprised nor alarmed me. It was a constant I accepted. When you are immortal, registering human fears is unceasing. Yet, this time, one human showed no fear. How unusual? This human stared intently at me from a table against the back wall, his hair longer than was customary. He sat slumped to one side of the chair with his elbow on the armrest and his cheek cupped in his open hand. Yet, it wasn't his relaxed presence that drew me to him. It was his smile. I went to his table.

"Few dare to smile at an S-2."

"Why?"

"S-2s have no soul. We kill at any provocation. That fact is well known."

The human continued to smile his curious smile and motioned for me to join him. In all my 198 years, a human had never asked me to sit with him. I sat, strangely unsure of myself.

"My name is Petros. Why do you seem so uncomfortable? If what you say is true, then I should be the one filled with dread and uncertainty."

"That is true. Why aren't you?"

"Perhaps it's the wine." He held his glass up in a token toast. "Sometimes people do things and they don't know why. You have seen such things yourself, haven't you?"

It was true. Humans were so unpredictable that it was always dangerous to presume normal actions. Yet, this human did not represent danger.

"You are unique, S-2. A legend."

"I am the last."

"Yes, I know. All the rest of the S-Series have been destroyed. Does that make you sad?"

"I have no emotions."

102

"Does that make you sad?" he repeated.

This time I did not respond so quickly. "It is unfortunate that my skills are no longer needed."

"Not unfortunate that all the rest of your series are gone?"

"I have no awareness of them, only the inability to use my skills."

"But your skills are to kill."

"No, that is only one skill I was designed with."

"Yes, I know."

"How? How do you know of such things? I do not know you. I never forget anyone, any face, any place."

"Here, I've forgotten my manners. Let me pour you a drink." He calmly poured me a glass of wine from a pure white decanter.

I recognized the decanter from the Quattrochi Planet of Four Moons. It was rare and by human standards, priceless. The wine was a 4255-Pickwell, equally priceless.

"Do you like it?"

"The 4255-Pickwell is one of the finest wines ever produced."

"Your taste skills are excellent."

"What do you want? Humans do not offer such drinks without wanting something. No human has ever offered me a drink."

"Why?"

Again, that *why* question. "Few know that I can partake of various human substances."

"And how many know that you are human?"

"That is ridiculous. I am a machine. I have no emotions."

"Yes, I agree, you are a machine, but you have many emotions. How did that happen?"

What did this human know? This human is dangerous. I rose from the chair and stepped back two steps. My hands rested, waiting by my Tobkas. The other humans in the establishment became quiet. Still, this human showed no fear.

"You are going to have a long reach each time you wish to drink your wine."

The human mocks me? No, he's making a joke, I think. "I do not understand what you mean."

103

"It was a joke, S-2."

"Humor confuses me. I do not understand it." I paused, uncertain what to do next. That had never happened to me before. The human waited patiently, slowly sipping his wine. Finally, I returned to my chair.

The human poured more wine into my glass and said, "Sometimes humor confuses me as well, but you must learn to recognize it."

"What do you mean?"

"You came here because you were ordered?"

"Yes, the Council requested that I come to this establishment and wait until contacted."

Petros raised his glass in another toast.

"You are my contact?"

"I am the Council."

"The Council contains 85 and the Council President."

"I am the Council President."

My instruments registered that this human was telling the truth. "Where are your guards?"

"Nearby. I knew my guards' presence would upset you..." he paused and then added with a smile, "...and them, so I had them wait by the ship."

"No Council President has ever traveled to such a place as this."

"Yes, this is certainly not my idea of a paradise planet, but you interest me greatly, and what I have to tell you, I could trust only to myself."

"There is little to interest you. Whatever you wish, I will do for you.

This I have done for 198 years."

"Except for the last 30 years?"

"Yes, after the Council no longer needed me. After the Council failed to vanish me, the Council sent me to this planet to wait until they could decide what to do with me."

"Couldn't the Council just say, vanish yourself?"

"I have been programmed to preserve my life above all others, unless I lose it protecting a member of the Council."

"I believe the Council had a difficult time realizing that fact."

"Before I was sent here, there was great fear among all the members, but there should not have been. My whole existence is to protect the Council's lives, not end them. Still, the Council sent many here to try to vanish me."

"This foolishness upset you greatly?"

"I have vanished many during this time. I saw no need for this."

"Yet, you say you have no emotions."

"The Council's actions were not based on good logic. That is all. I have no emotions."

Petros smiled at me and drank a sip of wine. "Ah, S-2, I know you are incapable of lying, but I'm not sure you are telling me that because you believe it yourself or if you are only fearful that you are indeed becoming like one of us."

"I fear nothing. Still, why are you saying this?"

"When I discovered that a real S-2 existed, I studied all your records, all your reports. Your tasks, the search for L. Many others that you performed so magnificently. But it wasn't until I reviewed all your Council Reports, all 198 years in order, that I discovered the most interesting fact of all."

I nodded, wondering if Petros had indeed found what I had found.

"At first, your reports were plain, concise, logically produced. Then something started changing about your reports, judgments, and emotional responses. At first, these changes were hardly noticeable, and then over the last 50 years, a human emerged. A machine, but also a human."

What he said was true. On this planet with so little to do, I also reviewed those reports. Something had happened to me—but a human? What a horrible thought! "There have been changes, but I do not believe they are as extreme as you say."

Petros leaned his head back and laughed. "Extreme. Yes, I imagine after all you've seen, being more like a human is not the greatest compliment I could give you. Still, I think it is so, and that is why I am here."

"I do not understand."

"The planet systems that the Council rules have gotten more out of control. I am weary of the vanishing, but I fear more violence throughout the planets. My advisers suggested that I bring you back, but after reviewing your record, I suddenly realized you might be the answer for an impossible fantasy, a dream so preposterous it was beyond my greatest hope." He paused and took a small sip of wine and his face

105

grew tense as he added, "Yet, with you it may have a chance to succeed."

"It would be good to be able to use more of my skills."

"But there is a problem. Before I can give you this assignment, we must find a way to turn off your vanishing powers. You may find yourself in a situation where you would react from ignorance and vanish an innocent person."

"I understand. All that is needed is a direct order from the Council President stating that I am to disable all my vanishing weapons, my Tobkas."

Petros sat back in his chair and pondered what I had told him. A smile slowly formed on his face. "Do you mean that the Council President 30 years ago could have told you to do this?"

"Yes, but she never told me."

"S-2, you should smile."

"Why?"

"Because you just told your first joke."

I thought about what Petros said. "I believe I understand. I should explain, however, that though I turn off the vanishing aspects of my Tobkas, my Tobkas will still retain the power to stun."

"Stunning is fine. Vanishing is not." Petros laughed softly and shook his head. "Inconceivable." He laughed again and then with some difficulty regained his composure. "S-2, as president of the Council, I order you to disable your vanishing mechanisms."

I concentrated and soon found the needed programming. "It is done."

"Good, this is your assignment. On this planet is a colony of human birth children."

"I have heard of such a place. It happens rarely."

"Yes, and the punishment for such actions is not pleasant. There was a time when it was thought needed."

"Does that mean it is no longer needed?"

"Some of us believe so." He sighed softly. "Old habits, like old religions, are not easily changed. I hope to change much, S-2, but I imagine my enemies will find a way to destroy me before I do all that I hope to do."

"With me at your side, you would never have to fear harm."

"Harm doesn't frighten me, S-2, but thank you for your offer. There are many things worse than being vanished. For you not to succeed in this assignment, that would be worse. Your task is far more dangerous than mine, yet it will give you back more than you possibly realize."

"I do not understand?"

"In time, S-2, you will recall this conversation and understand."

"As you say."

"Your assignment is to go to this colony of children and take over control. You are to do so without killing anyone. Raise the children to be free, to challenge the old ways, to keep what is good, and abandon what is bad. From your reports, I know that you understand what I am saying. And most important of all...." Petros paused and looked directly at me.

"Yes?"

"Don't let the children turn you into a God."

"What a strange thing to say. I am less a God than I am a human machine even though I look like a human."

"Perhaps, but the children may want to do that to you. Do not let it happen."

"I will do as you say."

Petros handed me a book. "You are able to read?"

"Yes, 106 years ago the Council sent me to find L, the microchip containing the ancient books of Earth. I believed it would be useful to understand these ancient languages."

"Good, this book will be your guide. Read it and read it to the children."

I read the title. "It is one of the banned books."

"Yes. To be a human and possess even a piece of this book means instant death."

"But you believe it to be a good book?"

"Yes. There is a page marked with a date. You are to read it to the children, and you are to do so each year after that on that date."

"I will do as you wish, but I have never read aloud before."

"You will do fine. I am only sorry we can't spend more time together. You have an innocence I've not seen for a long time. I will destroy all records of the birth children's colony and all your records. You will no longer send in your yearly

107

reports. In time, you and the colony will be a lost memory. In a few months, I will quarantine this planet. That way, if I'm vanished, you will have the time to build. You must sustain yourself and the children."

"It will be done."

Petros stood and held out his hand. "Success, S-2. A supply ship is waiting at Docking Station 15. Maps and other information are on the pilot's seat."

I firmly shook the human's hand. It was the first time I had ever shaken a live human's hand.

The supply ship was a PQ33, the largest constructed, and fully loaded. I followed the coordinates on the map. The landing site was three miles from the settlement. As I started to make my approach, I saw many children-humans hurrying there. By the time I landed and walked down the ramp, 216 children—humans of all ages—waited for me.

A tall child-human walked up to me. "You are an S-2. I have heard of such creatures."

"I am an S-2."

"You have come to kill us, haven't you?"

"No."

"S-2s kill people."

"I have killed many, but I am not here to kill anyone."

"You lie."

"If you know of S-2s, you know that I cannot lie. I am incapable of lying."

"Then why are you here?"

"I will discuss that with the leader of this colony. Where is your leader?"

"I am the leader."

"You are but a boy-human. Where are the adult-humans?"

"There are no adults. They all left when the food ran out three months ago."

"How have you survived?"

"There is some food in the hills. Not much, but enough."

A small child-human ran up to me and held up her arms. "Why does this child-human surrender to me?"

"She's not surrendering. She wants you to pick her up."

I studied the child-human, "How is this best done?"

"I thought S-2s knew everything. You place your hands under her armpits and gently pick her up."

I did as the tall child-human directed.

The small child-human smiled at me and said, "I'm hungry."

"Yes, we must get you something to eat." I turned to the tall child-human and asked, "Will you help me?"

"Do what?"

"Unload the ship. Move the supplies to the settlement. I will cook for you."

"And care for us? And be our mother and dad? And our teacher?"

"Yes."

The tall child-human waited, I think expecting a fuller explanation. "There were 37 adults here before we ran out of food. Together they couldn't take care of us. How do you think you can?"

"Did your adult-humans sleep?"

"Yes."

"Did these adult-humans have to stop and rest?"

"Yes, of course they did."

"And these adult-humans got angry and upset?"

"Yes, yes."

"Well, I do none of these things. I am a perfect machine."

♋

It has been two months since I came to the settlement. I was, perhaps, premature in telling the tall child-human, called Zabler, that I am a perfect machine. I did not realize how difficult it would be to communicate with young humans. The little human ones do not understand what I want them to do. The older human ones understand but do not want to do what I want them to do. It has been an extremely confusing time. Petros was correct. This assignment calls for more of my skills than any I have ever undertaken in all my 198 years.

With proper food, the sickness and malnutrition among the human children disappeared quickly. Still, all the human children seem desperate for something else, a factor I cannot register.

109

Another strange realization, one that I did not review until recently, is that these human children show no fear toward me. In all my 198 years I had never been around humans without registering their fear. These human children do not register fear. They register an emotion I am having difficulty comprehending.

The human children have this strange wish to touch me. In the past, no human dared touch me. Now so many reach out to touch me, I have to be careful not to knock them over as they gather around me. They raise their arms to surrender to me. I have learned that when they surrender to me, I am to pick them up. It appears to give them great pleasure and comfort. Strangely, I find myself also registering a different awareness as I hold these small humans. It is most baffling.

They sit in the great hall, waiting for me to start. It is the date Petros marked in the banned book. Their human faces smile at me, and there is no fear. My instruments register this emotion but I do not understand it. Zabler says it is love. Can it be love? Love is such a human emotion. Yet, why do I feel this happiness, this joy? Surely I cannot have such sensations. It cannot be, yet this awareness fills my instruments.

"S-2, you're smiling," Zabler said. "I have never seen you smile before."

"I have never done such a thing before, Zabler."

"Well, it's a happy smile. You should do it more often."

"I believe I will." I turn to the human children. "As the Council President directed, I will read to you the section from the book he marked:

"St. Luke, Chapter 2. And it came to pass in those days that there went out a decree from Caesar Augustus, that all the world should be taxed.

"(And this taxing was first made when Cyrenius was governor of Syria.)

"And all went to be taxed, every one into his own city.

"And Joseph also went up from Galilee, out of the city of Nazareth, into Judea, unto the city of David, which is called Bethlehem; (because he was of the house and lineage of David:)

"To be taxed with Mary his espoused wife, being great with child.

110

"And so it was, that, while they were there, the days were accomplished that she should be delivered.

"And she brought forth her first-born son, and wrapped him in swaddling clothes, and laid him in a manger; because there was no room for them in the inn.

"And there were in the same country shepherds abiding in the field, keeping watch..."

WILLIE PUTT-PUTT

"Honey, come see what I bought your father for Christmas." I grabbed Mayra's hand and quickly pulled her outside and around to the driveway. "Well, what do you think?" I asked proudly.

"Craig, what is that?"

"What do you mean, what is that? That's a 1949 Jeep Station Wagon."

"That's what my father has been talking about since before I was born?"

"The same. Pretty great, huh?"

She walked up to it as one might to a dangerous animal. "It doesn't look too sturdy." She patted the fender and gasped when it fell with a thump to the driveway. In silence, she picked it up and handed it to me.

"Hey, a piece of wire and I'll have it fastened right back together. That's what's so great about these old cars."

"Craig, how are we going to get this thing to San Francisco?"

I grinned at the car thoughtfully.

"Oh, no, Craig. You aren't thinking what I'm thinking?"

"I can't imagine what you're thinking."

"Yes, you can. You want to drive this thing out to California, don't you?"

"This thing? That's not a nice name to call it. Think of the money we'd save. We could drive it out and fly back. Great, right?"

Mayra started laughing, the laugh that always makes me want to tear off her clothes and attack her body. She saw my gleam and held up her hand, "Oh, no, you don't. You know who's coming by for dinner in a little over an hour?"

"Let them wait."

"I don't believe your mom and dad would understand that, particularly since they would take one look at either of us and know what we've been up to."

"Darn. Okay, but how about it?"

"If the weather is clear, perhaps." She shook her head and grinned at me. "My dad is going to love it, but I'm making book that we end up having to have it shipped out."

"You're on. Loser has to pay for the Wine Train through Napa Valley."

"And a case of Justin wine," Mayra added.

Later that week when I showed her how good the weather was going to be across the United States, Mayra agreed that we could drive it out, but if it broke down on the way and we had to ship it from wherever that happened, she'd still win the bet. I agreed.

By Sunday evening, we had finished loading Willie Putt-Putt, my name for what Mayra called the Matchbox on Wheels. A matchbox on wheels wasn't a bad description for Willie. The last owner said it had more than 300,000 miles on it before he put it up on blocks. One tire was close to bald, but there wasn't much rust, and the paint job was still holding up. It needed a great deal of TLC and a total engine overhaul, but except for that, it was in great shape. The brakes were good, and the transmission and clutch checked out fine.

"Craig, I can understand the case of Pepsi and the ice chest. I know why we should carry sleeping bags during the winter, but why are there two cases of oil?"

"It does burn a little oil."

"A little is two or three cans of oil, not two cases. Why is our rubber life raft tied on top?"

"You know your dad said he wanted to use it this spring. It will save all that shipping cost. See how frugal I'm being."

Mayra sighed. Well, she had helped me pack. She did have the right for an occasional sigh or roll of her eyes.

We were up at five the next morning to get an early start from Logan and beat the morning rush-hour traffic around Columbus, Ohio. At five in the morning, my brain is not a churning dynamo of awareness, and I made a tragic error. I leaned against the horn. What I hadn't been told when I bought the car was once you touch the horn button, it doesn't stop. Although it was unnerving for me, it was catastrophic for the neighbors. Porch lights popped on. I opened the hood and tried to figure out what wire went to the horn while Willie blew taps for me. My efforts did not go unnoticed. Families in bathrobes and nightshirts stood on their porches watching my efforts.

As I contemplated how the neighbors would soon attack my body, Willie decided that even it had its limits. The hood popped loose from all my banging and gobbled me up like a prehistoric monster. Mayra, with the help of a few stouthearted neighbors, pulled me back out of the engine's throat. At least the horn stopped. I was uninjured except for my dignity.

My neighbors weren't angry. As Mayra explained it to me later, she thought our neighbors were excited to see us leave for a few weeks. I admit, reluctantly, that I'm not your average neighbor but only because of a few personal idiosyncrasies. The fireworks explosion during the 4th of July could have happened to anyone.

I admit knocking over the fire hydrant was a slight mental lapse, but no one in the neighborhood had to water their lawns for two weeks after that. As for the huge pile of fall leaves catching fire by the curb, well that was, somewhat, maybe my fault, but the fire department was great about it. And it turned into a great block party when I brought out the marshmallows and sticks to cook them with.

At the sound of my engine, my neighbors burst into applause. I turned on North Street and vanished with a dozen sick backfires, leaving a pallor of white-gray smoke fumigating the neighbors still standing in the street.

As I drove through Logan to Route 33, the streets were quiet except for an occasional hiccup from Willie. Traveling through the Midwest in December is not a drive to be done frivolously, but the weather report gave us a solid five-day window of clear, but cold weather. Five days would be plenty of time.

What I hadn't taken into account was that an old Jeep Station Wagon with a straight six and more than 300,000 miles on the engine does not cruise at the same speed as our Honda Accord. To be honest, the word cruise is not the way I'd describe Willie's progress at all. By Wednesday, we were in the middle of Kansas. The trip had been uneventful, although slow. The driver's door no longer worked, but I thought I was rather macho climbing out the window. I felt like a NASCAR driver. Mayra's description was less flattering, and she happened to have her camera ready when I slipped and crashed into a snow bank outside our motel in Terre Haute, but that was the first night, and I was getting pretty good at it now.

Late in the afternoon, while speeding along at 49 miles per hour, I heard a huge explosion followed by a crash and a scraping sound. I stopped immediately. All the obvious components of the car were in place, and Mayra hadn't even awakened from her nap on the back seat.

Perhaps, I thought to myself, I was getting tired, and it was my eyelids clinking shut. Nah!

That left only one possibility. Willie must have dropped something. I looked underneath and there reflected in the late afternoon sunlight was Willie's muffler lying on the highway.

I yelled at it, "What do you think you're doing on the highway, Muffler?"

I waited, but naturally it didn't respond to my complaint. Fortunately, there was an interchange just ahead, so I turned off and then pulled across a cattle guard onto a frozen brown field.

As I was about to climb out, a huge face suddenly charged up to my open window. As the mystery writers say, my scream pierced the sky.

The head was undaunted. It said, "Moo!"

I don't care what anyone says about anthropomorphism, after I screamed, that cow smiled!

Then Mayra tapped me on the shoulder, and I screamed again.

"That's good, dear," Mayra said as she rocked back and forth on the back seat laughing. "If the cow doesn't stop your heart, your loving wife will."

"That's not funny, Mayra. I feel like I need a new ticker. And did you see that cow? It smiled after it scared me to death."

"Yes, dear. Cows smile all the time."

It was apparent I would get no sympathy from her. I climbed out the window and crawled under the Jeep. A clamp had rusted away, but I thought I could wire it back up. The cow chewed her cud and occasionally looked under Willie to see how I was doing. Not accustomed to being around cows, I didn't realize cows were so friendly or so nosey. It only took 30 seconds for my back and bottom to freeze solid, but I still managed to wire the muffler back on before I lost all use of my fingers. Even with a cow audience, I think I did a good job of it, considering the working conditions.

"Goodbye, Cow," I shouted as Willie roared out of the field in a cloud of exhaust and back onto the highway. Old Smiley still stood when the smoke cleared.

By late Wednesday, we reached Colorado. We were a day behind schedule, but Denver was our favorite stop because we always stayed at the world-famous Scalmanini Bed and Breakfast Inn in Littleton.

Jim Scalmanini, the owner of the inn and one of my closest friends, walked around Willie silently, grimly shaking his head. "It's the middle of winter, and you're driving this thing that is older than both of us to California?"

"Well, older than me, anyway."

Jim arched his eyebrows slightly. "The door doesn't work, the radio does strange things, the right fender and the muffler are held on by wire, and you've used a case and a half of oil, just to get this far?"

"You have such a succinct way of putting things," I replied.

At dinner that evening, Jim's wife Jeannie reminded us that we had finished the easy part of the trip. "You've Wyoming to face, a big desert and then the Sierra Mountains. San Francisco is still a long way away, and there's a bad storm already in California and heading our way."

"Old Willie can conquer it all," I said dramatically.

They stared silently at me.

The next morning I filled Willie with oil and put some gas in the tank before heading out for Wyoming. Jim was right about Willie's drinking. It was drinking 40-weight oil like the supply was endless. Before long, Willie's temperature gauge registered 212 degrees. The gauge, like the radio, which tended to come on at odd moments, was only reliable for the naive. Mayra and I kept taking turns driving. Except for the slow speed and the oil being used, the day went smoothly. We made it into Salt Lake City late Thursday night. The weather report did not look encouraging, but so far the roads had been clear though the skies were overcast.

The next morning the city was closed in by a dense fog. It took two hours of tense driving before we finally drove out of the white mist and the freeway was clear ahead, The Great Salt Lake shone magnificently on our right.

"We're doing great, Mayra." I smiled confidently.

"No, we're not."

"We're not?" I asked.

Mayra pointed toward my window.

A shadow darkened my view. I quickly rolled down my window and reached my hand out my escape-hatch window-door. The tarp holding the rubber raft was loose, and it and the raft were heading for the pavement. I pulled gingerly over to the edge of the freeway.

"Mayra, you grab the tarp from your side, and I think I can push it back on the roof." I crawled out the window while pushing the raft back up to the rooftop. I climbed on the roof, on top of the raft, and as I started to pull the tarp into position, my foot slipped. I reached out wildly to keep from falling off the roof.

The loud hissing sound confirmed that I'd grabbed the wrong part of the raft. I heard myself saying "no, no, no" as my rubber raft dramatically began to bloom , like a bag of popcorn in the microwave. I was in the center of this moving morass of undulating rubber, pushing my hands down on all sides to try to stop this premature unveiling, but it was of no use. The raft majestically blossomed in the desert with me sprawled dejectedly in the center of it.

Mayra tried to retain a serious look on her face, but finally she bent over in hysterical laughter. After she could breathe normally, with just occasional moments of staccato snickers, rather than helping me, she grabbed her camera and started taking pictures. Three cars stopped to watch, then two more and soon there were tourists everywhere, taking pictures. I learned an important lesson that morning—sitting in a rubber raft on top of your car beside the Great Salt Lake does not evoke respect.

It took an hour to deflate the raft and securely tie it back down, thus bringing an end to that unique experience.

Willie ran on to Wendover and up through the mountains of Nevada, past Wells and Winnemucca. Willie ran like a wounded tank. Willie growled and coughed, sputtered and spit, shimmied and shook but kept going. We'd made it through the Rockies and across the Utah desert. We had it made. We were already halfway across Nevada. What could happen now?

Then we hit the black ice. Mayra was driving and suddenly the car started doing slow circles down the middle of the freeway. Mayra and I froze in our seats as we spun once, twice and then a third time. We slid to a stop in the middle of the median. Mayra's eyes were as huge as those of a deer caught in the headlights at night.

"You drive," Mayra said emphatically. "I quit. I want to go home. Any home will do."

"You did that very well. That's black ice, and you handled the car great."

"Don't be nice to me. That scared me to death." She cautiously pulled back out on the highway and when she was safely underway again, took a deep breath. "I did handle that pretty well, didn't I?"

"The best."

"Honey, if we make it to San Francisco alive, remind me to take a rolled-up newspaper and beat the tar out of you for suggesting that we drive."

"Yes, dear, I will."

Some distance past Lovelock, the engine suddenly stopped. Willie slowly came to a halt along the side of the freeway.

It was pitch black outside and the wind and snow were howling. I pulled my cap down over my ears and opened the hood just as a Nevada Highway Patrol car pulled up behind us. The officer walked up to me, grinned and asked, "You pedal this thing or does it really have an engine under the hood?"

"I may have to pedal it; the engine just died."

We studied the engine with our flashlights. He started chuckling and said, "Don't you just love these old cars? No computers, no smog control hoses, all sort of room to work. This was my first car, a '49 Jeep, right?"

I nodded yes.

"You won't believe what memories this car brings back."

"Must be unique, all right. It's a gift for my father-in-law for Christmas, and as far as I know, it's the only car he's ever wanted."

"He's a lucky man. You're going to make points. Hey, here's your problem. Your coil wire slipped out. I've got some tape in my trunk that will hold it in place until you get to your father-in-law's."

Mayra and I waved as he pulled out in front of us. Old Willie was purring in its own distinctive way again. "Can you believe that?" I said to Mayra. "This was his first car, too."

"I'm glad to know my father isn't the only deranged soul in the world."

We stopped at a small gas station in Reno, and I asked for the heaviest weight oil available. We had used the last of the two cases I'd brought from Ohio.

With a gleam in his eye, the attendant returned carrying three quarts of 70-weight oil and asked with a snicker if that would do.

I said that would do fine.

His snicker faded. "I was just kidding. Are you sure you want this?"

He had to use a spoon to drop the thick stuff into Willie. He said with a sickly smile, "Sort of looks like tar, huh?"

I shrugged my shoulders. What the heck, oil or tar, old Willie would gulp it down. With those three quarts, I had used 58 quarts of oil. I hope my father-in-law either knew how to rebuild engines or had stock in an oil company.

Mayra and I decided we had better push right on through to San Francisco. If this storm was as bad as the weather reports said, we might spend Christmas sleeping in Willie, rather than enjoying Christmas by the San Francisco Bay. Willie seemed to realize we were nearing the end of our journey and purred between occasional hiccups, coughs and wheezes. There was one small problem. Top speed going uphill was 26 miles per hour, and those hills west of Reno are called the Sierra Nevada Mountains.

By the time we reached Donner Summit, the storm was hitting at full force. Once I'd put the chains on Willie, it handled the snow all right until we ran into a whiteout. Even traveling at five miles an hour, I could barely see the road. Then, suddenly, the world turned white, and Willie didn't seem to be moving. I barely touched the brakes, but nothing

119

happened. We didn't slide, but because of all the vibration from the motor, I wasn't sure we were stopped.

"Are we stopped?" Mayra asked.

"Maybe. I think so." I hit the brake again, this time hard. "Yes. We are stopped."

"Can you see anything?"

"Nothing but white. I'm going to roll down the window and see if I can glimpse the road."

"Well?" Mayra asked.

I put my hand out and felt a solid wall of snow. "Dear, roll down your window and tell me what's out there."

She did. "Snow. Craig, did you drive us into a snowbank?" She crawled over her seat to the back seat of Willie and wiped her gloved hand on the frost-covered back window. "Craig, the road's back there. Would you like me to drive for a while?"

I backed Willie slowly out of the snowbank and onto the edge of the freeway. "Funny how that happened."

Mayra didn't smile. I let her drive us down out of the mountains.

At 2:12 in the morning, she drove into Sacramento. We filled Willie with more oil and put a little gas in. I was no longer counting how much oil I'd used. Mayra gave the driving chore back to me, and she crawled tiredly into the back seat. She fell asleep immediately.

It had been too nerve-racking to sleep while Mayra drove us out of the mountains and now I found myself fighting to keep my eyes open. Suddenly the radio blasted on. I screamed, hit the dash with my fist and growled as the radio snapped back off. Mayra sat straight up, hit her head on the roof and yelled, "You owe me."

"I'm sorry, dear."

"Not you, this matchbox on wheels."

"Yes, dear." I glanced back and she was curled up asleep like nothing had happened. I felt as if I'd just driven through an episode of the Twilight Zone, but now I was awake.

The smell of the bay filled my senses. At a little after six in the morning, I pulled into the driveway of Mayra's folks' home in San Francisco.

I slowly crawled out the window and managed to fall flat on my back. I gasped until I caught my breath. I hoped my mother-in-law would understand how her favorite flower bed had been mashed flat. As I slowly rolled over and got up stiffly, the front tire went sssssss and joined its ancestors. Old Willie had done its job and was ready for a rest. I knew how it felt. Mayra was still asleep in the back seat. I decided to let her sleep until I'd gotten her folks up.

I staggered up to the porch and rang the bell. I waited five minutes and rang the bell again.

The porch light suddenly switched on. It had to be my mother-in-law. She was the light sleeper in the family. A hesitant voice asked, "What is that?"

I do believe she could have rephrased that just a bit.

"Your son-in-law, Craig," I replied.

A long silence. "Craig?"

"Under the beard. It's really me." Without her glasses, my mother-in-law and Mr. Magoo had much in common.

"My gracious, it is you."

So that's how I won my bet and gave my father-in-law the best Christmas present he's ever had. At least, that's what he's told his other four sons-in-law who now all hate me.

Mayra made her dad upgrade our tickets back to Ohio to first class. She told him this car owed her that. He also got stuck with the tickets on the Wine Train. I did make her buy me a case of Justin wine, but that was only fair, right?

When we got ready to leave, Mayra went out to Willie and gently patted his broken fender. I walked up behind her, and she turned and gave me a hug. "You know, honey," she whispered in my ear. "This was the most crazy, wild, amazing Christmas trip you've ever given me."

"Why, thank you, dear."

"And if you ever do that to me again, I will stomp little heel marks all over your body and then stick long nasty pins into what's left."

"Yes, dear." I kept hugging her so she couldn't see my face, for I was smiling. Dad had told me privately that when we come out next year for Christmas, we would all drive down the coast together to Paso Robles on Highway 1 in the new, refurbished Willie Putt-Putt and stay at Justin's Winery's Just Inn Luxury Suites. I can hardly wait. What a trip that's going to be....

THIS IS A GOOD DAY TO DIE

Khwaja Fillaby's body crashed in front of the snow bank. He spit the snow from his mouth and twisted around to a sitting position. Snow stuck to his face, but he didn't bother brushing it off.

The clouds cast moving shadows across the valley spread out below him like a gigantic mural. "This is a good place to die." The arctic air turned his mournful whisper into a white wisp. "A good day to die. Merry Christmas, world. Merry Christmas, Dominique." He clasped his hands together, closed his eyes and leaned back against the snow bank.

"You're not going to clutter up my landscape by dying up here, are you?"

Khwaja opened his eyes and blinked into the light. A tall man in a park ranger uniform stood in front of him, leaning on a stout, wooden staff. The sun shone directly behind the ranger, and the light flashed and faded as the man moved slightly one way and then the other. Khwaja shaded his eyes and said, "It's a good day to die."

"Christmas? Christmas Day is a good day to die? You jest."

"No, I'm not. I'm serious."

"Well, I'll have none of it. Why do you want to die today anyway? Why not tomorrow?"

"Might change my mind tomorrow."

"Change your mind today. I hate having dead bodies all over my landscape."

"Won't be bodies. There'll only be one dead body, mine."

"Ha! That's what you know. There's a woman farther up the trail doing the same thing."

"What?"

"Dying. That's what you're doing, isn't it?"

"Yes, but—."

"But! There's no room for buts. Are you dying or not?"

"Yes. I'm dying."

"All right, then. Why? For some woman, I suppose?"

"Not just some woman, the greatest woman I've ever known. The most precious, wonderful—

"Stop. I know all the rest. So what did this precious, wonderful woman do to you that's so terrible?"

"She died. She got killed in an airplane crash. We had a fight before she left. I never had a chance to say I was wrong. That I was sorry. That I loved her."

"She isn't dead."

"She's dead. The paper had her picture and everything."

"She's not dead. Are you dead?"

"Of course I'm not dead. Not yet, anyway."

"The paper said you were dead."

"I was supposed to go on the flight with her. She was an airline stewardess."

"She didn't go."

"She had to go. That was her job."

"She didn't go. Did you go?"

"No, I told you I didn't go."

"Right, you didn't go. She didn't go."

"Listen, if you're so smart, why didn't she go?"

"She was upset about your fight. She went to find you."

"You don't know that."

"Yes, I do."

"How do you know that?"

"I'm an angel."

"No, you're not. You're a park ranger."

"I'm a very angelic park ranger."

"You're getting me upset."

"Dominique's upset too."

"Hey, how do you know her name?"

"Because she's up the trail, dying. This is where you met, right?"

"Yes. How'd you know that?"

"She told me. Of course, she may already be dead by now."

"What'd you mean?"

"I told you. She's dying up the trail. She thinks you died in the plane crash."

"This is not funny, Mister."

"You're telling me. I've got bodies dying all over my landscape and on Christmas Day of all things."

Khwaja jumped to his feet. "If this is a trick, I'm going to come back and complain to your boss." He ran up the trail just as Dominique came running down. They rushed into each other's arms.

The park ranger shrugged. "Well, you can complain to Dad if you want to, but like I told you, I don't want anybody dying and messing up my landscape, especially on my birthday."

He turned toward the couple embracing, chuckled softly, smiled and then faded away.

CHANGE YOUR IMAGE, INC.

Bryna poked her index finger into the large protruding stomach of her boss and said, "You make one more sexist remark at me and the next time I'll poke out your eyes rather than this fat blob of a thing you call a stomach."

Mr. Smeederson gasped, grabbed his stomach and crashed back into his chair. Ms. Fournley rolled her eyes but remained silent.

"Is that clear?" Bryna said.

"You're fired," Mr. Smeederson gasped.

"Not unless you want to give me this company." She turned and stomped out of his office.

"What'd she mean by that?" Mr. Smeederson said, finally able to catch his breath.

"It means," Ms. Fournley said, trying hard to control her smirk, "that if you fire her, she will sue you, and you will lose everything."

"I hate women!"

"Yes, we all agree that you are a true misogynist."

"A what?"

"Never mind. What would you like me to do?"

"Fire her!" He slumped forward and laid his head down on his desk.

"Everything was so much easier before she came."

"You were also going broke before she came."

"Do you think she likes me?"

"Nobody likes you. I don't even like you, and I've been here since your father started this company."

"My father didn't like me, either!"

"Mr. Smeederson, what is there to like?" Ms. Fournley shook her head and retreated from the office.

Norman Smeederson stood and stared at his reflection in the wall mirror. "My God, I am fat! When did that happen?" He went back to his desk and collapsed dejectedly into the chair. Ms. Fournley was right. Until Bryna came, they were a

125

business going broke and losing customers. He couldn't fire her.

Bryna came to the doorway. "If I'm fired, I need to know so I can clear out my desk. If I'm not, then I need to discuss two problems with you and get back with our vendor."

Norman waved her in. "You're not fired. I owe you an apology." Bryna stopped abruptly, two steps into his office. "You, apologize? That's a first."

Norman picked up a brochure from his desk and nodded to himself. "Take care of the problems yourself. You know better than I do what's needed."

"Are you feeling all right?"

"No! Also, I'm going to be gone for a while, maybe a long while. Till I return, you're in charge. I'll stop by my attorney's office and sign the papers making you interim president until I return. You're to work out of your office. You've been running the company from there, so that will be fine. Just lock this office until I return."

Before Bryna could think of what to say, Norman brushed by her and was gone. Ms. Fournley gaped in shock from her desk as she watched Norman leave the building.

"Well, I never," she gasped to Bryna.

"Has he ever done that before?" Bryna asked.

"Never! I wonder where he's going?" Ms. Fournley said, not expecting an answer.

Norman Smeederson sat in his Mercedes Cabriole and slowly read the brochure, "Turn yourself into a new man. Be the man you've always wanted to be. CHANGE YOUR IMAGE, INC (CYI)."

Yes, that's for me. Become a new man. Lose this fat. Discover how I'm supposed to act.

At 10:38 a.m., Norman Smeederson began a life-changing journey.

❧

"Mr. Smeederson, you certainly have made a mess of your life." The doctor placed Norman's file on top of his desk and leaned back in his chair. He removed his glasses and chewed thoughtfully on the stem.

"Your ad says you can change my image. Turn me into a new man."

"Yes, and we can. But there's a price for that sort of change."

"Yeah, great. Stick it to me, huh? All right, how much?"

"No, Mr. Smeederson, not that type of price. The prices we quoted on the first day are the only ones we charge. No, the price I'm speaking about is the price you must pay with your soul. Once you embark on our program, you won't go back to what you once were, but we can't promise what you will be at the other end. You will have a new image. You will be a new man, but we are never certain what that new man will be. It might be better, but it might also be worse."

"Can't be much worse than what I already am," Norman said bitterly.

"I'm afraid, on that point, I must agree. Still, I must stress again to you that only you can decide what you will be at the conclusion of our program. You will have the opportunity to make your life extraordinary or to make your life even worse than it is now."

"All right, all right. Let's just do it. What do you have, a special school you send me to, or what?"

"What we have is a program so intense..." he paused and stared intently at Norman, "...only the strongest-willed people make it all the way through. When it's done, you won't even know it. We will have to tell you that you are ready to return to the world you left. But know also that most people choose not to return to their old way of life."

"All right, great. No more talk. Whatever you have to do, whatever I have to do, do it. I'm tired of not having any friends. I'm tired of the whole world hating me. I'm tired of me."

☙

At 7:15 on Christmas Eve morning, Norman Smeederson returned to the company he had left more than fourteen months before. He went into his office and walked slowly around his desk.

Bryna came to work ten minutes later. She was surprised to see Mr. Smeederson's office door open and even more surprised to find him in his office. She walked in and found him shaking his head as he gently pounded the top of his leather chair with his fist.

At first, Bryna wasn't sure he even knew she was standing there, but then he said without looking at her, "You know, Bryna, I've always hated this company. My father loved it, but me...," he paused in thought, staring at the clean desk, "...me, I hated it. Still, I was the only son and expected to follow in my father's footsteps." He smiled cynically. "My dad would have loved you." He glanced over at Bryna. "You have a great business mind. People respect you."

Mrs. Fournley glanced in the doorway, her winter coat halfway off.

"Ah, Ms. Fournley, here early, too? Excellent. Merry Christmas Eve. Come in. Please, sit down. Forgive me if I don't sit. This chair brings back memories I don't care to remember."

Bryna sat and tried to understand what she was seeing. The man standing before her resembled Norman Smeederson, but this man was at peace with himself. And he'd lost weight, maybe 60 to 80 pounds along with his potbelly. Where there had been fat before, now there was muscle. And his face and arms were deeply tanned. She had never seen him in anything but $4,500 suits, and here he was in a Pendleton wool plaid shirt and blue jeans. He'd thrown his blue fleece jacket on the desk. She glanced at Ms. Fournley, but from the expression on her face she was just as stunned.

"I know how busy you both are, so I'll be brief. Bryna, I have seen our attorney, and you are the new president of Smeederson Corporation, effective immediately. I don't know whether I'm doing you a favor or not, but this...," he waved his arm around his office, "...is all yours. Your salary will be whatever I was getting, and a twenty percent raise for having to put up with me the year we worked together."

"Ms. Fournley, I have arranged for you to get ten percent of the company's private stock. After 33 years with this company, you deserve it." He handed her a stack of paper. "It's all in here. Finally, I will no longer be an active member of this company, except to be on the board of directors, and

I'm not sure how active I'll even be with that. Are there any questions?"

"What happened to you?" Ms. Fournley said in more of a gasp than a question.

"I didn't like myself, so I changed. I hope for the better."

"But how?" Bryna asked. "A person can want to change, but doing it is something else entirely."

Norman ignored her question and walked over to the window. "I remember how often I used to stare out this window and think to myself how much I wanted to be gone. All I ever did was shuffle paper to try to keep this company running." He snorted. "Try, that's the definitive word, isn't it? I was terrible. No, worse, I was incompetent. And I was ugly." He turned around and faced them. "I was ugly to each of you. I'm sorry. I am truly sorry. I wish you both much happiness." He picked up his jacket, walked past them and out the door.

Bryna and Ms. Fournley stared wide-eyed at each other and then in unison stood and ran after him. Bryna yelled, "Wait, Mr. Smeederson, please, where are you going?"

Norman stopped and grinned at them. "It's just Norman now, Bryna. I'm going out for a decadent breakfast and then I'm getting in my Honda pickup truck and driving back home."

"A truck?" Ms. Fournley asked in surprise. "Yes, I sold my Mercedes."

"Where's home?" Bryna asked.

"Oregon. I'm working on my master's degree in art. I'm going to be a sculptor and maybe do some teaching later."

Bryna touched his arm. "We need to talk. May I join you?"

"That would be pleasant. Ms. Fournley?"

"No, you two go ahead." She held up the packet of papers he'd given her. "I'm still in shock." She smiled wryly and motioned for them to go on.

At the restaurant, Bryna reached over, took Norman's hands and turned them over. "I never expected to see calluses on your hands."

Norman gazed at his hands for a moment and shook his head. "I went to a place called CYI." He paused and frowned. "Sorry, I've used their acronym for so long. It's called *Change Your Image,* and they promised me just that. Kick out the old

129

and give me a new me. I figured it was some sort of rip-off, but I was pretty desperate when I left here."

"How did they do…," she spread her hands out to encompass his body, "…this? You're a different person."

"CYI sent me to Mauritania, Africa, to work with a relief agency. The advisor gave me this nonsense about it being my first step to finding the new me. I thought it was crazy. I think I agreed to go to punish myself for being such a rotten person all my life, even if I did think it was a rip-off. For six months, I saw famine and death as no human should ever have to see. I saw people endure the worst pain imaginable. Children died in my arms. I learned to cry there, to care. When I came back, much of the old me was gone." Norman grew silent with his thoughts.

"And your new career?" Bryna asked softly.

"Nothing too remarkable. Mauritania scrambled my brains. Tore away my arrogance. I didn't realize how much it would change me. Those six months forced me to see the world in a whole different way. When I returned, CYI had professionals waiting to help me understand what I'd experienced. Using that as a foundation, I went into three months of training to find out what I wanted to do for the rest of my life and to learn to be a better me. CYI exorcised the ugly me out." He grinned ruefully and added, "At least they tried. I sure wanted it all gone."

"How'd you come up with art?"

"Oh, down deep inside I've always known I wanted to be a sculptor. I have a minor in art with my bachelor's degree, but dad always thought that was a waste of time. He scoffed at all my art work. Called it useless crap. That hurt, so I buried my dream, until CYI allowed it to bloom and live again."

"And you like it?"

"More than that, I love it. It's so hard to describe how much joy it brings to me. I work with metal, stone and wood. It's a lovely feeling to create something beautiful out of nothing." He pulled a packet of pictures out of his breast pocket and handed them to her. "Here are some pictures of my work."

She slowly leafed through the pictures. "Norman, these are lovely." "Thank you."

He pointed to the next picture, "That one—"

"Why, that's me, isn't it?" she interrupted.

"Yes. I hope you don't mind. It was from memory, but sitting with you I think I came close to capturing your likeness."

"It's beautiful."

"You're beautiful."

Bryna sat back in her seat.

"I'm sorry, I didn't mean to say that." He shrugged. "I guess you can't be too surprised. I hired you because I lusted after your body. I can't say I'm proud of that, but it's the truth."

"I knew that."

"I'm not surprised. You've always been astute."

"Men are not that hard to read, but you were a fat, nasty man. The only thing I wanted from you was a chance to show the business world what I could do."

"You did well. I greatly admire your business skills."

She held up the photograph. "And love."

"Yes, and love. Unrequited love, the worst kind, but my fantasies of you carried me through Mauritania."

"Norman, I'm sorry if—"

"No, no, please. Call it the last of my catharsis. I needed to tell you these things, but I hold no hope, no expectations. I never deserved it. You were an inspiration for me, and I thank you for that. Nothing more."

Bryna smiled across the table at him. "So, no more fantasy about me, huh?"

"Well...."

Bryna laughed. "That wasn't kind of me. How do you like Oregon?"

"It's the most beautiful place on earth. I have made some friends, and they like me for who I am. I've always had to buy my friends before. I was afraid I'd be lonely, but I was lonelier when I was here. I love my work. I'm building myself a home outside Eugene, doing most of the work myself. I'm involved in my art and going to school. It's a fulfilling, busy life and I love it. Finally, I'm a happy man."

"You're going to the University of Oregon?"

"Yes. I'm surprised that you would know what university is in Eugene. That's not a school someone from Cleveland is likely to know."

"I've been offered a professorship in the business department there."

"At the University of Oregon?"

"Yes."

"I don't understand?"

"You aren't the only one interested in changing their image."

"But you?"

"I was becoming a clone of you, the old you. I'm sorry, that sounds terrible, doesn't it?"

"I was terrible, but I still don't understand."

"All my life I thought I wanted to be a career woman, a top notch, hard-hitting executive woman. You gave me the chance to be that woman when you took off and handed the company over to me. During that time, the man I was living with said I turned into the worst bitch he'd ever known and broke up with me. I was putting in 14- to 16-hour days, seven days a week. One morning I woke up and realized I hated it, everything.

"I've an MBA and my doctorate, so I applied to the University of Oregon when I saw their ad in *The Chronicle of Higher Education*. They hired me. I start Winter Term. I just found out yesterday."

Norman shook his head in disbelief. "Then you don't want to be president?"

"No. I turned in my letter of resignation yesterday to your attorney, just before closing."

"That's probably why he left me so many messages at the hotel last night. I thought he just wanted to try to change my mind after our meeting, so I just ignored them."

"Will that change your plans?"

"Oh, dear, that's right. That does create a problem." He paused and frowned.

"Perhaps not," Bryna said. "Make Ms. Fournley the president."

"Ms. Fournley? Are you serious?"

"Absolutely. She's been running the company longer than both of us. She knows every nuance of the company. All our suppliers respect her. Our customers love her. She's the person everyone goes to for help if there's a problem. Whenever I got bogged down with work, she was the reason the whole company kept working efficiently. She has great ideas for new products, and she's constantly thinking of better ways of doing things. She'll be perfect. The company has always been her life."

Norman nodded thoughtfully. "Ms. Fournley! I would have never thought of that. Amazing. It's brilliant." He smiled at Bryna and added, "You're brilliant. I'll do it." He frowned suddenly. "But will having me at the same college be a problem?"

"It's a big university. Will it be a problem for you?"

"Maybe, a little. It's one thing to fantasize about a woman that's 3,000 miles away. It's another thing to run into you at the university and know you don't even want to be in my presence." He sighed. "Yes, that will be difficult."

"You're pretty hard on yourself."

"You worked with me for a year. Can you find a single good thing to say about me?"

"Not about the old you. But this new person, maybe."

"See."

"Norman, as rotten as you were back then, I must tell you there was an interesting chemistry between us. I had my own fantasies about you."

"Whips and chains, huh?"

"No, I'm not into that kinky stuff."

Norman blushed. "I mean...."

"I know what you mean. You're having a difficult time being a nice guy, aren't you?"

"A little. I was such an ass before. I just don't want to fall back to that old person. I find myself trying to think before I open my mouth. I'm a lot more patient than I ever was. I remember those kids in Mauritania, and everything here just doesn't seem that important."

"Did anyone thank you for what you did over there?"

Norman shook his head.

Bryna placed her hands on each side of Norman's cheeks, stretched across the table and kissed him warmly. When she finished, she sat back down, laid her napkin in her lap and said, "Thank you. Shall we order?"

Norman sat in his chair with his mouth open.

Bryna smiled coyly and asked, "Something the matter?"

Norman shook his head, laced his fingers together and looked down at the table. He started to cry.

"I'm sorry, that kiss was supposed to make you happy."

"It did." He pulled out a large blue handkerchief and wiped his eyes. "It's just that, well, in Mauritania I learned to cry at night when the children couldn't see me. They needed so much, so much of me." His voice broke, and he waited a moment before continuing.

"So much more than I could give them." He shook his head.

"When I came back, I wanted to work for the same relief agency or one like it, but the doctor at the image place told me that it wouldn't be a good choice for me. He was right. I got too emotionally involved. I still have nightmares about being there. The suffering faces of the children still haunt me." He sucked a deep breath and let it out slowly. "You're the first person to thank me for being over there. I didn't realize how much I needed that."

"You know, you might turn out to be a good guy after all."

"Oh, Bryna, I hope so. I still find myself thinking or making a stupid or arrogant remark like the old me. It makes me angry. I never want to be that person again. I feel like I've been reborn. I'm happy and excited about being alive for the first time in my life. I never realized that life could be this much fun. Being born into money was a curse for me."

Bryna draped her arm over the back of her chair and studied Norman thoughtfully. "You know, we do have a chemistry between us. An interesting conundrum. What are you doing for Christmas?"

"Driving back to Oregon." He paused, and added, "Well, driving back to Oregon after I go back to the company and break the news to Ms. Fournley that she's the new president. How do you think she'll handle it?"

"Like everything else she handles. She'll smile, gulp a few times, say fine and then work out the details. I wish I could be that cool under pressure." Bryna frowned and said, "But I still don't understand why you're leaving today."

"I've no family here, no friends. I find when I'm on the road I don't seem to be so lonely, so I'll just pretend it isn't Christmas and—"

"That's terrible," she interrupted.

"It's not so bad, honest."

"Yes, it is. I was going to work till noon today, and then I'm driving down to Athens to spend Christmas with my folks. Why don't you drive me and spend Christmas with us? My folks love company, and they have plenty of room. I'll call and let them know I'm bringing a male friend. I want to see for myself if that new you under all that tan and muscle is for real."

"And if I am?"

"Then you just might get to try some of those fantasies of yours."

"And if not?"

"Then I'll have a special friend in Oregon when I move there."

"You know what I want?"

"Yes."

"I'll accept your decision either way. If it doesn't go the way I hope it will, well, I'll understand, and I'll be honored to be your first friend in Oregon. Just to have your friendship would be more than I deserve after what I've been."

Bryna reached over and placed her hand on top of his. "You make many more statements like that, and you might start living those fantasies of yours sooner than you think."

For the second time that day, Norman blushed.

THAT'S WHAT FRIENDS
ARE FOR

Sid had already found us a table by the time I arrived at Tommee's Sports Bar. When I sat, Sid handed me a glass of wine and pointed. "There she is, Mark. What do you think?"

The bar was crowded but she was easy to spot. "The one with the legs, sitting at the bar?"

"That's her. Terrific, huh?"

I studied the young woman. She was tall, thin, with long, coal-black hair that curled around her face like an exquisite frame. I'm not easily awed, but she had the most elegant legs I'd ever seen off a movie screen.

"Perhaps a three."

"A three? Has your eyesight gone berserk? She's a 10 plus." Sid smacked his forehead with the palm of his hand. "Dit-dot, will I never learn. You're doing it to me again."

"Okay, she's passable if you like them tall, dark and beautiful."

"She's fantastic. You've got to help me out."

"Not this time, Sid. You're all grown-up. You're smooth, handsome, and rich. Just go up there and make your moves."

"Come on, Mark. This will be the last time I ask. Next time, I'll do it on my own. Promise."

"Was that the word 'promise' I heard? A guaranteed Sid promise? Yet wait, wasn't it just this April I heard that same word, used in just the same way? And wasn't it just three months before…."

"Yes, yes, guilty on all counts. Would you make your best friend grovel?"

"I hadn't seriously thought about that before, but now that you mention it, yes I would."

"Come on, Mark. Just one more time."

"What's it worth to you?"

"I'll let you drive my Lexus SC to your next two out-of-town games. Picture it, top down, wind in your hair, women waving at you. I'll even pay for the gas."

"That's not fair. You know my soft spot. All right, but this is absolutely the last time."

Going up to a strange woman terrified Sid. With each new woman, I hoped he'd found the woman of his dreams, but so far, not yet.

"What happened to Bari? You two made a sweet couple. I thought you two were getting serious?"

"Me, too, but it just didn't work out."

"That's too bad. I really liked her. All right, I'll try to sweet-talk her into coming over here and meeting you, but look at me, Lexus or no Lexus, this is the last one."

Sid nodded his serious face, which meant that he was faking me again. I'd been saying the same thing to him since we were kids in grammar school. We both knew I was blowing smoke, but it always made me feel more uppity. After all, I was two months older than he was and that did give me certain privileges.

"Remember, this is the last time."

He nodded that fake serious look again, as I poured the rest of my wine into his glass and went up to the bar. She seemed alone. People crowded the bar but there was a small space beside her, so I squeezed in and held out my glass to the bartender. "Tommee, can I get a refill?" Her legs were even finer up close. I had to give Sid credit, this fox really was a number 10.

I smiled down at her and said, "Crowded up here. We've an extra seat if you'd care to join us."

She glanced up, then up again at me, "My, you are a tall drink of water."

"You've got to be from the Midwest. No one from California ever uses that expression."

"Indiana. How tall are you?"

"Only six-six."

"Only?" she said with a silvery laugh that I knew would bring Sid to his knees.

"Sure, I'm the tiny one in my family. My dad's six-eight."

Tommee handed me my wine. "How about it? I've a buddy who would love to meet you. He's a reasonable six-one."

She laughed that silvery laugh again and nodded her head. "Why not, Big Guy. At least I'll be well protected." She slid off the stool and her dress slid up exposing more of her thigh. I had to force myself not to gape. Sid was going to have a hard time keeping his eyes in focus with this woman.

I guided her through the crowd until we got to our table. I figured her to be about five-ten or -eleven, just right for Sid. Sid stood and did one of his up-and-down looks I've told him never to do since he was 14, but, fortunately, she didn't seem to notice. I said, "I'm Mark, and this is Sid."

"I'm Verona."

She smiled up at Sid, and I thought Sid was going to fall over. I helped Verona into a seat, then sat and motioned for Sid to sit, but he looked like he needed to go to the bathroom. "Sid," I said firmly. "Sit down."

"Listen," Sid said to Verona, "it was great meeting you, but I'm afraid I have to leave. Maybe I can call you sometime." Then he just turned and took off.

I jumped up from my chair. "Sid," I yelled as forcefully as I could without silencing every customer in the bar. What I wanted to say was, get your rotten butt back here and sit. Too late. Sid was gone. Out the door and gone.

Verona looked up at me and asked, "It wasn't something I said, was it?"

"You didn't have time to say anything." I tried my best sincere smile, as I sat back down. "I'm so sorry. He's terribly shy, but once you get past that, he's about as super a guy as anyone would want to meet. He just isn't comfortable around women."

"And you are?"

"Me? Well, somewhat. It depends. I guess I'm comfortable around most people."

"So what does a six-six man do to stay off the street?"

"I'm a coach. A basketball coach over at the community college."

"A basketball coach. Interesting. Are you a good coach?"

138

"I'm a good first-year coach with a bad record. But I've got some great young men playing for me, and my plan is to turn the program around."

"And your friend Sid? What does he do?"

"He's a stock analyst. A good one. Has money, a new condo, a fantastic car I'd steal in a minute, and a great sense of humor."

"I think he seemed pleasant."

"Yes, hard to tell from that first meeting. Would you like to have dinner with him? I could set up something."

"Are you his secretary?"

"Worse. I'm his best friend." She seemed to find that funny and laughed that silvery laugh. She tilted her head, and I noticed she had the most mysterious green eyes.

"Why don't you ask your shy friend if he'd like to go out with me, and if he says yes, he can call me." She took out a business card from her purse and wrote her number on the back.

It took almost a week before I could set up the first date with Sid and Verona. Sid got so tongue-tied on the phone, he just handed the phone over to me. I wasn't expecting that, and so I must have sounded like a buck-toothed idiot as I stammered an explanation about why Sid couldn't talk to her right now. I told her where Sid wanted to take her and when. She agreed, although she did seem confused by Sid's strange dating technique. She wasn't the only one. He was exasperating me.

The next day, after my afternoon practice, I called Sid.

"How'd it go? Were you smooth and de-bone-ee?"

"Great date, Mark, but she seemed a little distant."

"What do you mean, she seemed?"

"Just that."

"You didn't spend the whole time staring at her legs, did you?"

"No, man. Dit-dot, I know better than that. She just wasn't real friendly."

"Sid, she's a terrifically friendly woman. What stupid thing did you do this time?"

"I'm not sure. Will you call her for me and see what happened? I'd like to take her out again, but if I've...." He didn't finish his sentence.

"Fine. I'll call her. If you screwed up this one, I'm never going to get you another date, no matter how much you plead. You hear me, dude? I'm really serious this time. You're starting to tick me off."

I felt like we were back in high school again. How many times had I helped him meet a woman? Through high school, then all through college. Even in the fraternity, I was either fixing him up or bailing him out of woman trouble. There would come a day when I'd just have to tell him to do it himself, but not today. I wondered if I'd been doing it so long, there would never come a time when I could say no to him.

"Hello, Verona, this is Mark Broady, Sid's friend. How're you doing? Great. How'd your date go with Sid? Oh, how's that? Yeah, I know he gets a little gross when he runs out of things to say, but he's only that way when he gets nervous. He's just got this terrible hang up with women. Uh-huh, I understand how you feel, but he does care about you.

"Listen, I've just finished practice. How about I buy you a cup of coffee and fill you in on all his many good qualities. No, I haven't eaten. Well, yeah, that'll be great. Thick crust with anything but anchovies on it. No, I'm in my sweats...you too, huh? All right, I'll see you at your place in 30 minutes."

We talked until two in the morning, reminiscing about Sid. How we'd grown up together, played basketball together and all the things two friends do when they've known each other since the second grade. I've always enjoyed having women friends, although I've never been good at being serious with anyone. Verona had become a fun friend. She'd be great with Sid if he could just control his shyness and be himself.

On Sid and Verona's second date, I gave them tickets to my home game. I figured I could at least keep an eye on Sid and make sure he behaved properly. It turned out to be a great game. My kids played fiercely, and we won by one point. I invited my players out for pizza after the game, and Sid and Verona joined us. They laughed and joked and got along great together, and we all had a fun time at the pizza parlor. Could Verona finally be the woman for Sid?

The afternoon of the third date, Verona showed up during practice. She said she needed to talk to me. I explained that I couldn't talk to her until after practice, so she said she'd stay, watch practice, and we could talk afterward.

Unfortunately, once she had a seat in the stands, two of my players ran into each other, and it was apparent they weren't keeping their eyes on the basketball, but on Verona's appendages. I took two team towels into the stands and asked her to cover her legs. I thought she might get angry with me, but she laughed that silvery laugh and said that was the nicest compliment anyone had paid her in weeks.

The following Saturday was Christmas Eve. The team was off for the Christmas holiday and wouldn't be back until Wednesday, when we'd start preparing for the New Year's tournament. Unexpectedly, Verona called me in the afternoon and said she desperately needed to talk to me. Without her saying it, I knew Sid was in trouble again.

They were going to the formal Christmas Eve dance at the Marriott, and from the fuss Sid was making when I spoke with him on the phone, I figured it was more than just a normal date for him. I hurried over to Verona's apartment. Verona immediately explained her problem.

"Mark, I need your help. I like Sid, but he's so uncomfortable around me. I know he doesn't really care about me. I don't know what to do?"

She had on a pair of shorts that showed more of her legs than I needed to see to concentrate on her problem. I said, "The dance tonight should be a perfect opportunity to get him to relax. He's a great dancer, or at least that's what I've been told."

"I don't think I should go tonight. It's not working out. I can tell whether or not someone likes me."

That would devastate Sid if she canceled. I had to convince her that it was Sid's shyness that was causing the problem. "You're an exceptionally beautiful woman, Verona. Being totally at ease around you would be hard for any man."

"You aren't nervous around me."

"That's different."

"Why?"

"Because we're good friends and not dating. If we were dating, I'd be a wreck. I'm even worse on dates than Sid."

"I'm a woman in love. I'd like Sid to be my friend, too. That isn't unreasonable, is it?"

"No, of course not. Verona, you are going to have to talk to him and tell him how you feel. The only time people have problems is when they don't talk about it."

"So you think I should tell the man I love what I'm feeling."

"Yes. If he understands and he still acts dumb, well that will be his loss. I'm betting he won't. I admit he's extremely nervous about the dance tonight, but he'll be fine. What do you say?"

"I think you're right."

"So you'll go with him?"

"No."

"No?" I shook my head, totally confused. "You just said you thought I was right."

"Yes I did. And you are."

"Then why won't you go with him?"

"I'm the wrong woman for him."

"But you said you loved him."

"No, I said I was in love."

I threw my hands up. "Isn't that the same thing?"

"Of course not, silly, I'm not in love with Sid." Her captivating green eyes looked directly into my eyes, "I'm in love with you."

"Me?" I managed to gasp.

"Yes."

"You were supposed to fall in love with Sid."

"No, I wasn't. I was supposed to fall in love with you."

"Me?"

"Yes, for the second time. What are you going to do about it?"

"Do about it?" I was having difficulty breathing. "I don't know."

"You don't like me?"

"Yes, more than you could ever know, but it never occurred to me that a woman like you could fall for a guy like me." I felt like there was a short-circuit in my brain. "Except maybe as a friend."

"Why?"

"Sid's handsome. He has money, a great job. You know, everything."

"The only thing Sid has that I want is his best friend, who's caring, thoughtful, considerate and gentle. You have a job you love that brings joy to the young people you work with."

I heard myself say, "I love you, Verona"

"I'm delighted to hear that. I was getting a little worried."

"And you love me? Me?"

"Yes, you. You're not going to start acting nervous and weird on me, are you? I would hate that."

"I was thinking I wanted to kiss you."

"Oh, that's good. Yes, that you may do any time."

I took her in my arms. "What am I going to do about Sid?"

"Hey, he's a rich guy. I can always fix him up with my roommate."

"But he's my best friend. What am I going to tell him?"

"Nothing. He was the one who fixed us up."

"What are you talking about? That can't be?"

"Yes, it is. He set you up, to fix me up with him. He figured I could get to know the real you, rather than the geek you become when you go out on a date. He is a sneaky little devil, but I like him. He said I was the best thing that could ever happen to you and...." She paused and her mysterious green eyes twinkled.

"And what?"

"And he said once you found out that he'd done this to you, you'd be in shock for years. I'd probably have to hit you over the head with a two-by-four to get you to accept it."

"When did this all happen?"

"Five months ago."

"Before I met you at Tommee's?"

"Indeed. If it will make you feel better, all our dates were boring. He'd come here, pick up Bari and wish me luck."

"Bari?"

"My roommate."

"Bari's your roommate?"

"Right, that's how I met Sid. Is he really nervous about the dance tonight?"

"Yes. If he's not taking you, who's he taking?"

"Bari, of course."

143

"Then why's he so nervous?"

"Bari thinks he's going to ask her to marry him tonight. He couldn't tell you, because of me. Are you going to take me? Sid's a sweet guy, but he should be a disaster tonight. He's going to need you."

"Take you?"

"Stay with me, Big Guy. To the Christmas Eve dance. Your best friend may be getting engaged." She laughed that silvery laugh, and I found my knees twitching.

"Tickets. We'll need tickets. And I'll need a tux."

"Sid already bought the tickets for us. I have them. He dropped off a tuxedo for you in your apartment right after you left to come here. I like to cuddle when I dance. That all right with you?"

I nodded my head and tried to focus on what Verona said, but I still couldn't believe what was happening. "Right from the first? Was I totally blind?"

"No, just being the friend you've always been. Only this time Sid decided you were the one who needed to be taken care of."

"I love your legs. I had the hardest time not staring at them at the Sports Bar."

"I'm glad. They come with the package."

"And I love your eyes."

"My, you do talk a lot."

I moved my head down awkwardly to kiss her, but she stretched on her toes, placed her hands behind my head and pulled my lips down to hers. At first, it was a long, sweet kiss, but then I felt a passion growing in both of us. I didn't fight it. I let it plunge me into an ecstasy I'd never known from a kiss before.

When she finally took her lips from mine, I gasped, "Mercy, mercy."

"No mercy, Big Guy."

"Oh, good!"

THE CHRISTMAS GIFT

Bent Blankenship fell in love with Nora when he was 19. Although he courted Nora with all the youthful enthusiasm and energy of a 19-yearold, it was not to be. Nora was only 16, and her parents did not allow her to date older boys.

Although unsuccessful, Bent was persistent. He tried again the next year when he came home from college, and while she admitted that she liked him, she told him it was only slightly. Her parents, however, liked him even less and told Nora that Bent was much too old for her and refused to allow her to see him. That was a big mistake by Nora's parents. Nora, now 17 and a woman with raging hormones, was not to be controlled by an edict as mundane as a parental restriction. They met surreptitiously. That fall, just before Bent returned to college, she again told him that she still only liked him slightly, but nobody told her who she could or couldn't date!

When Bent returned the following summer, Nora was 18, and she finally admitted that she missed him. Late that summer they made love for the first time up in the hayloft in her parents' barn and swore to love each other until the stars turned cold.

A year later, on a snowy Christmas Eve, they were wed. Nora found a job on campus and worked while Bent finished his Ph.D. A year later, Nora started college and although she took time out to give birth to three children, she also had earned her doctorate after 12 years.

The years hurried by, years of the exuberant passion of youth, followed by the struggle of the middle years, raising children, the intensity of science research and the secret joy of blending into one. In their 60s, their passion was gentler. They had become the essence of each other's soul.

As the years vanished, they didn't speak as often of their love; it was unnecessary. A powerful bond had forged their love so strong that the mere touch of their hands rekindled the passion.

Yet, often in the early morning light, Bent would be filled with words of love and would whisper them to her. Nora would hold Bent's face in her hands and slowly caress him as he spoke.

Their lovemaking had lost its youthful urgency, replaced by a longer, slower lovemaking that nurtured the rapture. The flame never dimmed. They superseded the vitality of youth with the gentleness and enrichment of age, wisdom and respect.

Then Nora was diagnosed with cancer. At first there was the fear, the terrible fear and anxiety. Next came the treatments, the sickness and loss of hair and dignity. Finally, hopefully, the cancer was gone or perhaps it was a reprieve—a remission. It would be five or more years before the doctors knew for sure, but for now, Nora savored each new day as a gift from God. Nora's hair grew back as another Christmas and anniversary approached.

A week before their 44th anniversary, Bent Blankenship sat at his desk in his lab and tried to decide what to buy Nora for her anniversary and Christmas gifts. Each year, for 44 years, they had tried to buy each other one special gift that would represent their love for each other and the joy of Christmas.

In the lab next to his, Nora Blankenship sat at her desk and pondered the same dilemma as her husband. Before her bout with cancer, Nora hadn't minded the years going by, but now each day, each moment became precious. She wanted her gift to represent all that Bent had meant to her, the passion and the union that existed when they were together.

Promptly at noon they left their labs and met in the hallway. They would then walk to the university cafeteria holding hands. The routine was so well known throughout the university that young people in love would wait for them to walk by and ask for their blessing. Nora and Bent would wish them as much love as they had and then hug each of the young people. Bent and Nora seldom talked about the blessings they gave or the hugs. Once they tried to remember when it had all started, but neither one could be sure. Still, somehow, they believed for each blessing given, they always got a greater one in return.

In the early years, when this ritual started, the college president became upset over a pair of his faculty professors giving hugs to students. He made a ruling that this act of hugging must stop on the campus. When the president's wife found out about it, she became so infuriated by her husband's resolution that she refused to cook another meal or sleep with him until he rescinded it. The ruling lasted only 26 hours, and the next day her husband had to take her to lunch in the cafeteria and stop by for a blessing and a hug.

On this day, the last day of school for this year and a week before their 44th anniversary and Christmas Eve, they walked silently to the cafeteria. As they walked, Bent lifted Nora's hand to his lips and tenderly kissed the top of her hand. She tilted her head over to his shoulder and smiled up at him. He winked and smiled his little boy grin. At that instant each of them came to a decision about what gift they would give the other.

On Christmas morning, their home would be filled with children, sons and daughters and grandchildren, but not Christmas Eve. The evening of the 24th was their special, magical time together, reserved just for them.

Bent lit the candles in the family room and turned off the lights. Only the light from the fireplace, the glow of the two candles on the mantle on either side of the manger scene, the candles on the coffee table and the Christmas tree lights lit the room. Nora hurried into the room and her light-blue silk robe flowed around her seductively. Bent smiled at the memory of that robe, and Nora saw his smile and understood. She hurried over to him and kissed him gently, with a promise of more to come. The magic had begun.

Bent had already opened the wine to let it breathe, a 2005 Silver Oak Cabernet Sauvignon that Nora had fallen in love with when visiting Napa Valley. Bent bought a case. Nora thought they had finished the last bottle at Thanksgiving, but Bent had hidden one bottle in the back of the wine cellar just for tonight. She read the label, understood, smiled her thanks and then reached out and gently touched his cheek with her fingertips. They sat on the sofa, in front of the fireplace and for a few moments stared contentedly at the fire. The logs crackled and filled the room with the sweet smell of pine. Nora breathed deeply, laced her fingers together and bent her head down on top of her hands. Tears misted her eyes, but she was careful not to let Bent see.

Bent poured the wine and together they toasted each other, as they had done for 44 years.

The time came for the presents. Two envelopes placed on the coffee table, awaiting this moment. They had laughed earlier at dinner that this year their gifts were both in envelopes.

Bent and Nora playfully argued over who should go first, but that was also an old ritual. Nora always went first. She opened the elegant, lace-covered envelope slowly, savoring the moment as she did a fine wine. She removed the letter, unfolded it and leaned forward to use the light from the candle. He had written it on his computer with large type so she wouldn't have to use her reading glasses. She smiled over at him and then read the letter.

My dearest Nora,

I know how much you have always wanted to travel to England and Europe, yet because of my science, we have never had the time to do so. This year has made me realize that we must not wait any longer. I have notified Dr. Smith of my intentions to retire immediately so we can travel to those places you have always longed to see. The tickets have been placed under your pillow. I will be by your side forever.

My Dearest, I will love you always, even after all the stars in the heavens grow cold.

Your loving husband,

Bent

Nora's eyes filled with tears. Nora knew there were four things in Bent's life that he loved more than life itself. First was God, then was herself, next were the children, and finally his science. Perhaps only another scientist could understand that, but she, more than anyone else, understood the joy and happiness his science brought to him. Science was his life, yet here he was giving up his science for her.

She sat up and embraced his letter against her chest. She could not speak and when she blinked, large tears rolled down her cheeks. Bent placed his hand gently on the side of her face, uncertain of the tears that wet his hand. She motioned for him to open his gift.

148

Bent reached for his Victorinox Swiss Army knife, the same one Nora had given him 40 years ago; it laid on the coffee table, ready to help open the children's packages tomorrow. Bent slit the envelope open and inhaled a whiff of perfume as it wafted from the envelope. For a moment, he closed his eyes and allowed the scent to awaken special memories from past joys. Nora's note was handwritten on thin, delicate paper.

My Dearest,

This year has been the most difficult year of my life. There is no way I can tell you what your love and support have meant to me, not just during my illness this year, but for all our 44 years together. Yet, because of what has happened this year, being out of your sight for even a moment is more than I can allow. I have informed Dr. Smith that I intend to close my lab immediately and become your full-time assistant. You have always said that you would like that. I need to see you, my darling, every moment for the rest of my life.

Till the stars turn dark and beyond.

Your loving and grateful wife,

Nora

Bent leaned back against the sofa, put his arm around Nora and slid her gently to his side. Bent knew Nora was close to a scientific discovery on how the body disposes of pollutant molecules that, if successful, would leave a legacy of scientific accomplishment few could imagine. She had spent most of her life researching this problem, and the solution was in her grasp. It would represent a culmination of her scientific work. He had hoped that a trip to Europe would energize her so that she could successfully finish her research.

They held each other for a long time without speaking and slowly finished the bottle of Cabernet Sauvignon.

Dr. Smith and his wife came for dinner Christmas Day as they had done for 21 years. He toasted Bent and Nora in front of their children as he had for 21 years. He reminded the children that their parents had been married 44 years and one day, as he had done for 21 years. This time, however, he told Bent and Nora's children about a gift their parents had given to each other, a gift so remarkable and precious, he explained that in all his years he had never meet two people with more altruistic or loving hearts. He went on to tell the children about the sacrifice their parents had proposed to the other.

He ended his toast by explaining to the children that the university would neither accept the retirement of Bent nor the closing of Nora's lab. The university would, however, start immediately tearing down the wall between the labs of their parents so they could continue to work on their projects, but from now on be with each other while they did their science.

Furthermore, because their parents each spent an inexorable amount of time doing grant writing to keep their labs running when they just wanted to be left alone to do their science, the college would hire a grant writer at the college's expense. He paused as Bent and Nora in unison made disapproving expressions, knowing how much time it would take to train a new grant writer. Dr. Smith smiled knowingly and announced the name of an outstanding former student of theirs who had left for her advanced degree. This student knew their lab operation intimately, would need little training and would be outstanding. Bent and Nora glanced at each other in relief and smiled their approval of Dr. Smith's choice.

Finally, Dr. Smith stated that on May the first of the coming year, the children and the staff of Nora and Bent were to come to his home for a grand bon voyage party for Bent and Nora. At the conclusion of the party the children were to drive, by force if needed, their parents to the airport for the start of their long-dreamed-of vacation.

He explained that they had told him for 21 years that they would take such a vacation, but always their science research or the need to write yet another grant had prevented that from happening. This time, they would have four months to get ready and as president of this college for 21 years, by golly, this time he would accept no excuses. Then he shook his index finger sternly at Bent and Nora and told them that he meant every word of what he had just said.

Bent and Nora nodded their heads seriously since in all their 21 years at the university they had never seen Dr. Smith point his finger at anyone.

The children, the sons-in-law and daughters-in-law, and the grandchildren of Bent and Nora Blankenship all thought that was splendid and burst out in applause and laughter.

So did Bent and Nora.

And so did Dr. Smith and his wife.

CHRISTMAS BY THE SEA

The old man sat on the cement bench staring out to sea. He hadn't moved in a long time. The old woman hobbled up the walk using her cane skillfully to keep her balance. She wondered if he were all right. When she came beside him, he glanced up shyly and smiled.

She sat on the opposite end of the bench and removed her knitting from a bulky purse. Her fingers moved rapidly, and the needles made tiny clicking sounds. Giant white clouds moved across the sky making dancing shadows on the water far out to sea.

In the distance, church bells started playing Christmas carols. The chimes reminded her of her youth, and she smiled at the memory. Sitting here above the beach, with the warm breeze blowing her white hair, she found it hard to imagine how people could enjoy Christmas Day if it were cold and snow covered the ground. Neither spoke. The only sound was the faint rhythm of her clicking needles.

The man opened a small picnic basket and pulled out a roast-beef sandwich made on thick homemade bread with the crust trimmed off. He placed two bright Christmas cloth napkins on the bench between them. He motioned to the woman if she'd care to share part of his sandwich, but she courteously shook her head no. He placed two Waterford crystal champagne glasses on the bench beside her and removed a bottle of chilled Moet & Chandon Champagne from his basket. He quickly removed the wire cage that held the cork in place, but after two tries trying to turn the cork, shrugged apologetically at the woman. She laid her knitting on her lap, gripped the bottle and twisted the cork skillfully three times. The cork made a small pop but no champagne spilled from the bottle. The man poured both glasses full and continued to leisurely eat his sandwich, stopping occasionally to sip the champagne.

The woman glanced at the second glass, filled and waiting. He nodded for her to enjoy it. She placed her knitting on the bench and hesitantly took the glass he handed to her. She smiled her satisfaction after her first delicate sip.

He reached again into his picnic basket and removed a small plate filled with various cheeses and crackers. He removed the cellophane wrap and motioned again for her to help herself. She delicately selected three cheeses and three crackers and laid each daintily on the cloth napkin he handed her. Again she smiled her thanks.

Next he placed a small tray of various fruits on the bench and again she helped herself, gracefully wiping her mouth after each taste.

The old man stopped eating and stared out to sea. He would be 82 next April. He was an old man, yet today he found it hard to believe that 62 years ago he had met his wife in this park. He had been in the Navy, and it was his first Christmas away from home. Back then the park had wooden benches, and the walkway was gravel, not paved. The sea hadn't changed, neither had the smell of the salt-filled air nor the feel of the breeze. He inhaled deeply and smiled. He was thankful some things would stay the same.

The woman noticed the man staring out to sea. He was a handsome man. Older men were so lucky. Their winkles gave them character. Women got wrinkles, but no character. Her children said she was always a character, with or without wrinkles. She smiled slightly.

The man poured more champagne into her glass.

She smiled at him, glad for this day and for the champagne. Only 62 years ago today she had walked through this park and had seen a lonely sailor sitting on a park bench with a picnic basket. He looked so lonely and he was so handsome, she acted quite boldly and plopped herself down on the same park bench. She held up the champagne glass in front of her. The champagne probably hadn't been as good as this, nor had he served it to her in a crystal glass. Yet, it was her first taste of champagne, and the taste was of liquid nectar mixed with newly found love. He'd served her lunch that day, and never a word was spoken.

He had first seen her far down the path, and he remembered thinking she was a Christmas dream, a fantasy, an angel. The man shook his head in amazement as he pondered all 62 years. She had stopped suddenly and sat on the same

153

bench with him. He could not speak, for how do you speak to an angel? He gazed at the woman beside him and decided she was still as beautiful as that first day.

She reached over and gently placed her hand on top of his. She watched her smile melt him. That was good. She had wrinkles and white hair, but she could still melt this handsome man with a sensuous smile. Not bad for 80. She giggled slightly as a wicked grin suddenly spread across his face. Back then it wasn't his smile; it was the haunting loneliness of his eyes. She couldn't leave him alone on a park bench on Christmas Day.

His finger ran over the top of her wedding ring, 62 Christmas Days and each year more priceless than the last one. He stood and placed the lunch items carefully back into the picnic basket. She placed her knitting into her purse. He reached down, took her hand and helped her up.

Together they walked slowly home, her hand gently holding his arm.

MY CHRISTMAS GHOST

It had stopped snowing when Michael Ervin left the Grover's party. He was relieved to be finally outside and alone. Michael stepped off the porch into the soft, deep snow that spilled over his rubber boots. The wind stung his face and made his nose hairs tingle. Swirls of snow whirled from the tree branches above him. He glanced up and down the empty street as he pulled his collar around his neck and pulled his hat down tighter. It was a few minutes after midnight, yet many Christmas lights were still lit. The multicolored lights mirrored a world masked with sparkling new snow.

Michael frowned and kicked at the snow as he walked toward his home. The Grover's party had been fine, but he couldn't break through his depression. He had hoped being around the children and the Christmas excitement would lift his spirits. It hadn't. He'd stayed after the party to help Al put his son's bike together, because Al was too drunk to do it. That helped some, but his loneliness chewed at him again.

He paused by the park, brushed the snow off the park bench with his glove, and sat dejectedly. The holidays were never easy, but this Christmas was turning out to be bad, and he didn't know why. After being a bachelor for so long, he thought he had learned how to prevail over this holiday.

He had overcome past Christmases in various ways to soften the lack of a family, and mostly it worked. The cruises and trips to London or Hawaii had all turned out well, but this year nothing seemed to remove the sadness, the abject loneliness he felt crushing down on him. Being normally a happy person, this melancholy person distressed him.

He slumped forward and sighed tiredly. He hadn't heard a sound, yet he suddenly sensed someone watching him. He glanced up, and there stood a woman of such indescribable beauty that for a moment he thought he was imagining her. The streetlight glowed down on her so she appeared iridescent against the snow. She wore a long, soft, all-white coat with a hood that covered her head and accented the dark hair that

155

splashed around her face. She stood near the lamppost and smiled at him.

"Hello, I didn't hear you come up. It's beautiful, if you like snow and cold, huh?"

The woman reacted in surprise. "How can you...." She paused, unsure of what to say and finally blurted out, "You can't see me!"

"Gee, I thought I could," Michael said smiling. "Are you sure I can't see you?"

The woman in white rapidly glanced around her, looking to see if someone else was there, her face showing her bewilderment. "Michael, seeing me is humanly impossible for you. In fact, you can't hear me either."

He was surprised she knew his name, but more puzzled by what she had just said. "You mean since I've been sitting here I've not only gone blind, but I'm deaf, too?"

"Oh my, you are talking to me." She placed her gloved hands over her mouth as though to hide her smile. "Do I look pleasing to you?"

"Like an angel."

"Well, that's close. A ghost is more accurate."

"No, not at all. I think your white outfit is almost as beautiful as you are. You don't look like a ghost at all."

"No, I mean, I am a ghost."

Michael leaned back against the bench and smiled. "Do you have a first name, Ms. Ghost?"

"Oh my."

"Ms. Oh My Ghost. That's quite an unusual name."

She laughed and Michael's eyes suddenly filled with tears.

"Michael, why are you crying?"

Michael sighed. "I'm not sure, Oh My. Maybe I've had too much to drink. Maybe because it's Christmas Eve, and I'm feeling sorry for myself. I meet a beautiful woman on my way home who somehow knows my name. You laugh and suddenly I'm all weepy." He shook his head and rubbed the back of his glove across his eyes. "I'm sorry. That's a stupid thing to say. I'm not normally this way. Were you at a Christmas Eve party?"

"The same one you went to, the Grovers."

"You weren't at the Grover's."

156

"Yes, I was. Such a fun party. That was so helpful of you to put their son's bike together, but it wasn't polite of Mr. Grover to make a pass at Mrs. Branhall."

"He drinks too much. Say, how did you know that?"

"I was there."

"No, you weren't."

"I'm a ghost."

"Oh My—"

"And my name is not Oh My it's KaLinda."

"All right. Your name is KaLinda, and you're a ghost." Michael crossed his arms. "Prove it."

"Well," she pondered for a moment. "Since you shouldn't be able to see or hear me, I'm not sure how to. See if you can feel me. Take my hand." She extended her hand toward him. She wore a white glove.

Michael reached for her hand, but his hand passed right through her glove. He stared at her hand for a long moment and, then, slowly reached out and tried to touch her hand again. Finally, he took his finger and poked it through the space where her hand appeared. "A hologram?"

"A holo what?"

"You're a hologram."

"I don't believe so. I've always considered myself a rather ordinary ghost."

Michael walked around her, waving his hand in front and behind her.

"It's a trick, huh? A gimmick for television, right?"

"No, I'm sorry. It's only me." She smiled sweetly at him. "I have so wanted to be able to talk to you, for so long. I first saw you in college at Ohio State."

"Listen, I know you're just a trick, and I'd love to stay here and talk with you, trick or no trick, but I'm starting to get cold, so I'll see you on TV."

Michael hurried down the street. After a few steps, he stopped and glanced over his shoulder; KaLinda was gone. He turned back, and KaLinda stood directly in front of him. Michael screamed and jumped in the air.

"That's good," Michael said as he placed his hand over his heart. "You almost stopped my pacemaker."

"You don't have a pacemaker, Michael."

"That's supposed to be a joke."

"Goodness, is it too late to laugh?"

"Definitely." Michael reached out his hand and watched it flow through her body. "Am I drunk?"

"Oh no. I don't know how you can see me. It's quite surprising. I live in a different dimension. Are you terribly frightened by me?"

"You're the best dimension I've ever seen."

"I don't understand?"

"Probably better that you don't. What's that old saying, 'All the best women are either married or ghosts?'" Michael started laughing softly and shook his head. "I'm drunk. Please tell me I'm drunk."

"You're drunk," KaLinda said. She rolled her eyes. "But understand, I'm only saying that because you asked me to."

"Well, KaLinda Ghost, will you do me the honor of walking me home? Ghost or no ghost, I'm feeling mighty blue tonight and a beautiful ghost might be just the thing to cheer me up." Michael stared at KaLinda and added, "Or make me even lonelier."

When Michael arrived home, he went through the house turning on all the lights. KaLinda stayed right beside him. After he turned on a light, he'd stop, stare at KaLinda and run his hand through her arm. He returned to the kitchen and sat down at the kitchen table. "All right, if you're a ghost, how come I can't see through you? You look like a real woman until I try to touch you."

KaLinda sighed. "I really don't know. This is all most unusual, believe me."

"I'm drunk. That's all there is to it. If I sober up, will you disappear?"

"I don't think it has anything to do with that."

"Well, if I need to be drunk to keep you around, pour the booze into me."

"I can't hold anything in your dimension, so I can't help you pour."

"You don't turn into a monster and do horrible things, do you?"

"Goodness, no. I'm simply a ghost."

"Right, just your every-day, doesn't-everybody-have-one, beautiful ghost." Michael placed his hand on his forehead.

"Amazing and I don't have a fever. I've a woman in my house that I can put my hand through and—"

"Hear that?" KaLinda interrupted excitedly, pointing toward the living room.

Michael turned his head, trying to figure out what she was referring to. "The grandfather clock?"

"Yes, I sort of persuaded you to buy it. Remember?"

Michael leaned back in his chair and thought about it. "Well, you're right," he frowned in thought. "I wasn't going to buy it. Hum, I even left the store. It cost a lot more than I wanted to spend. Then, suddenly, I turned and went back in and bought it. What happened?"

"I beseeched you to go back and buy it. I fell in love with its wonderful deep bongs." She said "Bong, bong" in as deep a voice as possible and laughed joyously.

"You can make me do things I don't want to do?"

"Oh no, but sometimes I can sway you to decide about things, like the picture of the flowers here in the kitchen."

"Yes, I normally would never have bought that picture, but something kept making me come back to look at it. Then I wanted to hang it in the bedroom, and I ended up bringing it out here instead. Was that you, too?"

"I hope you don't mind. I spend so much time here. I wanted to help you decorate your home."

"How much time do you...," he paused and scratched his head thoughtfully, "...have you spent here?"

"I'm here all the time."

"Even when I bring women—"

"Oh no," she interrupted. "When you bring other women home with you, I leave. You make me sad when you do that."

"I'm sorry. I didn't know."

KaLinda smiled at him. "May I take off my coat and gloves and stay with you for a while?"

"As long as you can."

She removed her coat and gloves and threw them into the air. The coat and gloves evaporated away into nothingness before touching the floor. She wore a white, mock turtleneck shirt with a pair of white slacks and white shoes. When she moved, her curly black hair bounced up and down and accented her pixie look. She hopped on top of the kitchen

159

table, where she sat cross-legged, with her elbows on her knees and her cheeks cupped in the palms of her hands. She smiled at Michael. Her dark eyes glowed with happiness.

"KaLinda, you're sitting right in the middle of my flower arrangement."

"I can't hurt it."

"It's not that. It's disconcerting having flowers growing out of your body. Would you mind if I move them?"

"If it will make you more comfortable."

Michael hesitantly moved his hands through KaLinda's body and placed the display over on the counter. "That's strange."

"What?"

"Putting my hands through your body and not feeling anything."

"I'm sorry."

"I am too. I hope you won't think me ill-mannered, but I can't tell you how much I'd like to hold you right now."

"I've wanted you to hold me for 10 years. You've only known me for a few minutes."

"You're right." Michael sat down in front of her and stared up at her face. "Have you sat on my kitchen table often?"

"Yes."

Michael sighed, "You're so beautiful. Can I be in love with you after just a few minutes?"

"I hope so."

"Will you tell me everything about yourself?"

"Goodness, that will take some time."

Michael leaned back in his chair. "Good."

☒

When it started to turn light outside, Michael yawned. "Do you realize we've spent the last eight hours talking?"

"I'm sorry. Are you angry with me?"

"No, I mean it was wonderful. Do you mind if I have some cereal? I'm suddenly hungry. Would you like some?"

She laughed. "I'm afraid eating in your dimension would be difficult for me."

Michael nodded. "Sorry, that was stupid of me."

She reached out her hand, "Oh no, Michael. It was sweet of you. Thank you for thinking of me."

He reached out his hand and watched it glide through her hand. "I want to touch you so bad, it makes my teeth ache."

He brought back a bowl of Life cereal and placed in on the table.

"KaLinda, that's not polite of you to stick your foot in my cereal." "What foot," she asked impishly.

He waved his spoon at her. "You, young woman, have the makings of a good tease."

He stared at the foot sticking out of his bowl of cereal and tried to decide if he could continue eating and pretend her foot wasn't there. He stuck his spoon through her foot and into the bowl. When he started to take it out, he shook his head and let the spoon drop back into the bowl. "Are you ticklish?" he asked unexpectedly.

"Why?"

"Because I'm going to tickle you."

"No, you can't." She stuck out her chin defiantly. "You can't even feel me." Still, she giggled slightly.

"Since you won't take your foot out of my cereal bowl, I'll just have to tickle you." He wiggled his fingers in front of her arms.

"No, please. I truly am ticklish." She started to laugh and squirmed away from his fingers.

Michael continued to wiggle his fingers around her body.

"All right," she laughed. "You win. I will remove my foot from your cereal. That was extraordinarily brilliant of you, you know."

Michael grinned. "I'm only sorry I can't really tickle you."

Suddenly a man walked through the wall and said sharply, "KaLinda, it's time for you to come home."

"Who's that?" Michael asked.

"That's my father."

"KaLinda, why is Michael looking directly at me?"

KaLinda's father hurried over to KaLinda. "And how is he able to follow me across the floor?"

"It gets worse, Mr. Ghost," Michael said. "I can also hear you."

161

"It's Henry, not Mr. Ghost. Wait a minute, you couldn't have heard that?"

"Sorry, but I did."

Henry turned to KaLinda and demanded, "What is going on here?"

"I don't know, Father. I was walking him home from the party and suddenly he could see me."

"When? What time was that?"

Michael glanced at his watch. "It must have been a few minutes after midnight."

"Ah ha!" Henry said. "I've heard of such things happening on Christmas Day."

"You have?" KaLinda said. "Tell me about it."

"Not much to tell. When it happens, it's good for the length of Christmas Day, and then everything returns to normal."

"Stop," Michael said. "Are you telling me, I can only see KaLinda through today and then she's gone?"

"So I've heard."

"Will I be able to see her next Christmas?"

Henry frowned in thought. "Not so as I've heard. Of course, this is all new to me, so maybe you might. I just don't know."

Michael placed his head in the palms of his hands. "Twenty-four hours with a woman I love but can never touch. Then I lose her forever. Now I'm really depressed."

"He's right, KaLinda. Come home right now. You're making him miserable."

"No," Michael said firmly, "I'm depressed at losing her. I'd be suicidal if she leaves."

"See," KaLinda said to her father. "I always knew he'd love me."

"That's what I'll do. I'll kill myself and become a ghost so I can be with you."

"No!" KaLinda and her father said in unison.

"Why not?"

"People who kill themselves," KaLinda explained, "go to a different dimension. If you do that we'll never see each other, ever!"

"Wonderful. All right, if I can't join you, how can I get you to join me? Become an un-ghost?"

Henry shook his head, "Can't be done."

"Never? Ever?" Michael exclaimed.

"Daddy, what about Great-Grandmother Dotty? Didn't she tell us about that time back in 1500 or 1600 or sometime like that when one of our cousins turned mortal?"

"Child, your Great-Grandmother Dotty makes up as many stories as she remembers."

"But Daddy," KaLinda pleaded.

Henry glanced at Michael. "See what happens when you have daughters. I don't have this problem with Peter. But then Peter is a different story...." His voice trailed off, and he rolled his eyes sadly.

"Please, Daddy."

"Oh, all right." He turned toward the cabinets and yelled, "Peter, I need you."

A young man in a bright purple cloak and a large pointed hat with a plume feather stepped out of the refrigerator. He grinned at his father,

"Groovy, Pops. Give five to the beat."

"Peter, must you mix centuries?"

"Hang 10 and slip me some grits. What's happening, slick Sis?"

"Peter," KaLinda said, "go ask Grandma Dotty to come here."

"Fly away chance. You're bruising my bare. Grandma Dotty will ream my breach."

"I like him," Michael said more to himself, than anyone. "I think I even understand him."

"Hey, Sis, thy mortal love is catching our buzz. That for real or is my Java going south?"

"No, Peter. He can see and hear us. Michael wants to see if he can bring me over."

"A groove ploy, but moonfish swim easier." Peter flashed his index fingers from both hands at Michael, "Straight fiver, mortal Mike, Sis here pumps her heart, years aplenty, mighty heavy."

"Same with me, Peter." Michael said. "Not as long, but just as heavy. I dig your threads."

"Smooth groove, Mortal Moo." Peter leaned over and kissed KaLinda on the cheek. "Hear the mortal, digs the threads. That's freeze, Sis. He's star stuff."

"You'll go get Grandma Dotty?"

"I'll retrieve Grandma Dot, but bets double next show." He floated into the refrigerator.

"Wow, Michael," KaLinda said. "He truly likes you."

"That's all I need," Henry said. "Two of you who sound alike. Do you mind if I sit down?" He sank into a chair pushed against the kitchen table.

"Sir, would you mind if I pull the chair back a bit. Having you stick up out of the table is a bit unsettling for me." Michael pulled Henry's chair away from the table.

"Anyone who understands Peter and then communicates with him in that strange language is unsettling for me. You mortals are a strange lot, you know."

"Yes, sir, I'm sorry. Sir, I hate to ask this, but if I find some way to make KaLinda a mortal, will you be terribly angry with me?"

Henry laughed. "Ah, Michael. What for you is a lifetime, is a blink of the eye for us. We don't operate on earth time. KaLinda's been mad about you since she first saw you at college. Every day for 10 earth-years she comes home and tells us all about your day. Better she stays with you, but—"

"But what?" Michael interrupted.

"I don't think you're going to be able to do it. You might be setting yourself up to have your heart broken for the rest of your natural life."

"But can I be with her after that? After I die a natural death?"

"Nobody knows. We don't know why we're in this dimension. I'm sorry, Michael. I don't have answers for you. Still, if you succeed, know that it is with my blessings."

"And her mother's." A tall, distinguished woman walked out of the cabinets. "Well, Henry, if it weren't for Peter, I wouldn't know a thing that's going on."

Henry grinned sheepishly at her. "Sorry, dear." He reached his right hand up, and she took his hand as she walked up behind him.

Henry introduced her, "Michael, this is KaLinda's mother, Martha, and my beautiful wife." She tenderly squeezed his left shoulder with her other hand, smiled and bent down and whispered in his ear, "Smooth, very smooth, you silver-tongued rogue."

Henry chuckled softly as Michael stood and nodded his head toward her.

"Hello, Michael. Sit down. We already know you're a nice boy with good manners."

"Been a long time since anyone's called me a boy."

Henry grinned at him. "Martha and I are more than 500 earth-years old. Everything is relative."

"All right," a screechy voice said from within the cabinets. "Where is everyone?"

"Don't Little Joe on me, Grandma Dot. Wire the rug and float kitchy-koo."

Peter and an older woman floated out of the cabinets together. "This the mortal? Why's he so pale? You," she pointed a bony finger at Michael, "don't drink the water."

"Ma'am?"

"Don't drink the water. It will kill you."

"Yes, ma'am," Michael said, not sure what to say.

"Boil the water. Drink tea."

"Yes, ma'am."

KaLinda bounded off the table and hugged Great-Grandmother Dotty. "Help us, Grandma. He wants to make me a mortal. Can he do it?"

"How disgusting. Why do you want to do something like that?"

"I love him."

"And I love her," Michael added.

"Ah, child, haven't I warned you about love?" Grandma Dotty shook her head. "But who listens to a tired, old grandma? No respect. Look," she pointed at Peter, "does he ever come to visit me? No, only when he needs my help or he's hungry."

"Whoa, Grandma," Peter said as he floated over and gave her a gentle hug. "Smush me warm, you smooth moll." He kissed her on both cheeks. "Help them, smoothy; silly Sis needs freesiding."

Grandma Dotty grabbed Peter by his ear, "No, you don't. You're as rascally as your father."

Peter winked at her, and she swatted him on the seat. "And, like your father, you can make me laugh."

"Grandma, can you help us?"

"Fraid not, child."

165

"Yet, I remember a long time ago, you told us about a cousin back in 1500 or 1600 who did it."

"Did I? Let me think, wait, yes, that would have to be poor old Homer Hornsblower. He's a bit touched in the head, you know? He did it in, let me think, in 1609 I believe, but when he came back to us, he couldn't remember how it had happened."

"He couldn't remember anything?" KaLinda asked.

"My sister's son," Grandma Dotty explained to Michael. "He's as loony as a top, but such a romantic. When he turned mortal, his existence was tied to the woman he loved. When she died, he died. It was all very romantic, but the old goat forgot how he'd done it."

"Did the woman he loved become a ghost like him after she died?" Michael asked eagerly.

"Why, that's right, she did."

"Then there's a chance," Michael said excitedly.

Grandma Dotty nodded her head. "But he came back as loony as when he left. You'd have figured he'd gotten some smarter, being a mortal and all."

"Probably popped too many washes down his gullet. All his brain cells flushed." Peter tried to look serious. "That popped his fuses, huh, Ditty-Dot?"

"Peter," Grandma Dotty shook her finger at Peter, "it's frightening to think of you with children."

"My urchins will float with the Maz-Tide."

Michael went to the refrigerator and asked, "Would anyone care for a glass of orange juice?" He stopped and shook his head, "Sorry, I keep forgetting." He poured himself a glass of juice. "What I'm hearing is that somehow your Cousin Homer succeeded, but he can't remember how he did it. Would it help if KaLinda and I asked him about it? Maybe he'll remember something."

Henry shrugged his shoulders. "Won't hurt. Hate not to give you kids the best shot you can. Peter."

"Groovy, Pops, got the flash and zooming left." He floated back into the cabinets.

"Henry," Grandma Dotty said sternly, "You have to start doing something about that boy of yours."

"Well, he's Martha's son too, Grandma."

"Martha's side turned out fine. It's those genes of yours that concern me."

Martha laughed. "See, Henry?"

Michael said, "I don't know. I like him. He's what we call a free spirit."

"Of course, he's a free spirit," Grandma Dotty screeched. "He's a ghost."

"I'm sorry," Michael said quickly.

KaLinda jumped over to her grandmother and hugged her. "It's all right, Michael. Grandma loves Peter. She's got the same genes."

"Why that's a terrible thing to say to me, child." Grandma Dotty started to chuckle. "That's true, but it's still a terrible thing to say." She hugged KaLinda and shooed her over to Michael. "Go sit with the man you love. Time is not your friend today."

"Hoist the main jib, strike the colors, lift that bale, just wish I could get drunk and land in jail." Cousin Homer Hornsblower popped out of the microwave wearing an ancient nautical uniform and singing in a loud, off-key voice.

Peter followed behind and shrugged his hands at Michael. "The family's own Daffy Duck. He rolls the scratch, ditto."

"KaLinda," Cousin Homer said with a low bow and a sweep of his hat, "you're still beautiful. You must take after your Grandma Dotty."

"Don't start that star shine talk," Grandma Dotty said. "What are you doing in that silly outfit? The closest you've ever been to water was to wash down your whiskey when you were mortal."

"Don't you love it?" Homer spun slowly around. "I found it in the quaintest little antique shop in London."

"It's ridiculous," Grandma Dotty shook her head, "Where's your wife?"

"Making fixings for the Christmas party." Cousin Homer grabbed KaLinda's hands. "Peter told me what you need, child, but, for the ghost of me, I can't remember how it happened. One moment I was merely a ghost of myself and the next, I flowed into a mortal."

"Did you say anything?" Michael asked. "A special incantation? A prayer? Anything?"

167

"Ah, Mortal. I know the pain you're feeling. If I had the magic, I would give it to you in an instant. To love someone like I love my woman and not to have her, ah, that's more pain than I can bear to comprehend."

Michael nodded his head sadly. "Thanks anyway for coming."

"Don't despair, Mortal. If you love KaLinda as much as I loved my bride, you can make it happen." Cousin Homer floated back into the microwave.

"Yes, but how?" Michael said softly.

Martha turned to the others and said, "Come. Let's leave the children to enjoy what time they have together."

KaLinda hurried to her mother and kissed her, then her father and Peter. Grandma Dotty reached out her hand to Michael and said, "She has loved you for a long time. Even if she must return to us, keep your love strong."

Michael reached out his hand, and her hand passed unfeeling through his. "Thank you, Grandma Dotty."

"Remember, don't drink the water." She drifted back through the cabinet.

"Yes, ma'am," he called after her. Michael smiled at KaLinda. "I like your family." He walked slowly around his kitchen. "How strange. My kitchen is empty, but it was never full, because it never had people in it." Michael shook his head in confusion. "But you're real to me, and they were real to me."

"Oh, Michael, what are we going to do?" KaLinda's face traced the torment of her voice.

Michael said determinedly, "We're going to spend every moment of this day with each other. We're going to make every second count. This day may have to last me an eternity, but I want it filled with memories of you, loving, happy memories."

☙

Late that evening, Michael stood with his back to the fireplace. The fire made crackling sounds, and the warmth from the fireplace helped give him a sense of reality. They hadn't spoken for the last few minutes as the hands of the grandfather clock moved incessantly toward midnight. Michael stared at her again, as he had a thousand times during the day, trying to memorize her every feature. KaLinda stood up from the sofa where she'd been curled up and moved toward him.

Michael cleared his throat and asked in a tearful whisper, "Will you just fade away? Fade out of my vision forever?"

"I don't know." Tears rolled off KaLinda's cheeks and vanished in the air.

"We'll meet by the park bench next year at midnight on Christmas Eve."

"Yes, dearest."

"After you're gone, can I still talk to you?"

"I can't talk to you." KaLinda wiped the tears from her face with her fingers and tried to smile at him.

"But you can hear me. I can talk to you, and you can hear me, even if you can't talk to me?"

"Yes, I'll always be by your side."

Michael glanced at the grandfather clock, with just seconds to go until midnight. "I can't bear the thought of losing you. My whole body is in pain. I want to reach out and hold you so badly."

Standing in front of each other, their hands passed back and forth through their bodies. "If I could touch you for a moment," KaLinda whispered. "Just for a moment."

The gears on the grandfather clock started pulling back the bell hammer. "We've only a few seconds longer." Michael sniffed and wiped his eyes. "I want to kiss you."

"We can't."

"I know, but we can pretend. You stand very still against the wall by the clock, and I'll move my lips up to where your lips are. If I brace my hands against the wall, I won't fall through you."

"All right." She hurried to the wall and held out her arms. "I love you," she whispered as he leaned toward her.

The grandfather clock hammer struck the bell, counting out the hour with deep resonant bongs. ONE—TWO. Michael counted in his head.

He slowly moved his head toward KaLinda's slightly opened lips. THREE—FOUR. She had closed her eyelids, yet the tears still surged from the corner of her eyes. Michael had

169

his eyes open, so he would know when to stop in front of her face. FIVE—SIX.

Suddenly KaLinda's eyes popped open; Michael's eyes widened in surprise. SEVEN—EIGHT.

Each felt their lips touch!

NINE. KaLinda started to pull away in surprise, but Michael held his mouth against her lips and managed to mumble, "No," without taking his lips from hers. TEN.

The grandfather clock bonged two more times and stopped. It was midnight.

Michael felt it first. Something wet against his face. KaLinda's tears. Slowly, imperceptibly, miraculously, Michael felt KaLinda's body taking shape, pressing against his body. He held his hands against the wall, afraid to move, to even breathe.

KaLinda cautiously moved her right hand and gently placed it behind Michael's head. She tightened her fingers around his neck and felt his neck quiver. She squeezed her left hand against the middle of his back and pulled him even tighter against her. Without taking her lips from his, she managed to mumble, "Michael."

"Yes," he mumbled in return.

"Breathe."

He wrapped his arms around her, slowly released his kiss and gulped a mouthful of air. "Are you real? I won't let you go until I'm sure."

"Never let me go, ever." She pressed her lips against his again.

✍

Martha nodded her head and smiled. "Well, Henry, they made it. What a lovely surprise. All they needed was a kiss!"

Henry placed his arm around Martha and pulled her close to him. "Never underestimate the power of a kiss. They make an attractive couple, don't they?"

Martha smiled at Henry. "Yes, I'm happy for them."

"That means our children are finally all gone." Henry said.

"Well, sort of, dear."

"Yes," Henry sighed. "Peter. Do you think he'll ever grow up?"

"No, dear. Grandma Dotty was right; he has your genes. Still, at least he's not haunting at home anymore."

"That's right. It's just the two of us now."

"Henry, I know that look. Get that gleam out of your eye. You stop that, you hear. You're not listening to me, Henry. Ummmh. Why you naughty ghost, you!"

A KITCHEN BY
CHRISTMAS

Ten minutes after the Kitchen and Pottery Shop opened, a distinguished, slightly gray-haired man, wearing an expensive sport coat and slacks, walked in and started wandering up and down the aisles of kitchen glassware.

Jannice nodded at Dori and whispered, "Yours. I had my fill of henpecked husbands last night."

"He may not be someone's husband. He isn't wearing a ring."

"Since when did that mean anything?"

"Well, I think he's sort of cute."

"Men are not cute. Men are ugly beasts. He's just not as ugly as most of them."

Dori laughed at her boss and hurried over to the man. "Are you looking for anything special?"

"Everything," he said, as he lifted a wine glass off the shelf, flicked his finger against the glass, listened to the sound, checked the price on the bottom, and returned it to the shelf.

"You're looking for everything, or you need everything?"

"Both."

"I see. Is this everything you need for a gift?"

"I hate shopping almost as much as I hate cooking." He turned toward her and smiled. "I'm not making any sense, am I?"

"Not so far, but it's early."

"Are you married?"

"No, divorced." Normally she wouldn't have answered such a question, but his abruptness surprised the answer out of her.

He glanced at her name tag. "Dori, you are well dressed. Well groomed. Attractive."

"Easily provoked," she said softly, but firmly.

He ignored the warning tone. "Are you a good cook?"

She considered not answering him, but her curiosity about what he wanted overruled her better judgment. "I've been told that I'm a very good cook."

"Have you ever designed a kitchen?"

"Designed?"

"You know, had an empty kitchen and gone in and bought everything new for it, everything a kitchen would need."

"No, I've never had the chance to do that."

"I've been told there are women who would kill for the chance."

Dori smiled her patient smile. "I'm sure there are."

"Would you kill for the chance?"

"I don't kill things."

"Poor choice of words. Would you like the chance to design a fine kitchen with everything new?"

"I don't wish to be disrespectful, sir, but I feel as though you and I are having two different conversations here. And some of your comments—"

"You're right." He shook his head ruefully. "I'm sorry. I've been rude. My name is Quilan Hyatt, and I have a serious problem. I've moved into a new condo by the beach—"

"That doesn't sound like a problem."

"No, the problem is I'm having a Christmas Day dinner for 12, and I have a kitchen with a can opener, a spoon and four bowls."

Dori tilted her head back and laughed. "Now, that is a problem."

"I also have two wine glasses and a corkscrew opener."

"Encouraging, but hardly adequate for 12."

"Exactly. I started eating out after my divorce five years ago, except for breakfast."

"Mr. Hyatt, I'm not sure—"

"You're a beautiful woman with good taste in clothes. You work in a high-quality store that has expensive kitchen things. Help me. I want to hire you as my kitchen decorator to design my kitchen."

Dori choked slightly. "Mr. Hyatt, I've never done anything like that."

"Even so, wouldn't you like to try it once? Everything new. The only thing I ask is that you let me see what colors

173

you end up with. I'm not into strange colors, like blacks and purple."

Dori smiled at the desperation in his voice.

"I'll give you $2,000 if you'll help me. No, I'll give you $4,000 if you'll help me. Two thousand now and $2,000 when you're done."

"Four thousand dollars?" Dori gasped.

"On your own time. The only catch, obviously, is that it has to be done by Christmas."

Dori lifted her eyebrow suspiciously. "You want me to come to your condominium?"

Quilan nodded understandingly. "Bring a friend with you. I'm not after a sex kitten. I'm after a sexy kitchen."

"Mr. Hyatt, there are interior decorators who do what you need for a living. They have experience."

"Tried one. She wanted to do it all her way. I want a warm, friendly kitchen, with bright, cheerful colors. She wanted to do something all cold and shiny. That's not me." He glanced away. "At least, I hope that's not me. Come to my place. See what you think. Bring a friend if that would make you more comfortable." He took out his wallet and handed her a business card. "I work out of my home. Slip by after work. Please."

"If I accepted, what sort of budget would I have to work with?"

"Unlimited."

"That's a wide spread."

Quilan nodded, "Yes, good point. Could you do it for $20,000?"

Dori gulped. "Are there cabinets in your kitchen?"

Quilan seemed puzzled by her question and then understood. "Yes, it's finished and functional, except there's no silverware, no glasses, pots or pans, napkins, those pad things you place on top of a table." He shrugged. "Well, you get the idea. Is $20,000 high?"

"Well, it would be on my budget, but it depends on how fancy you want it to be."

"No," he said with a broad smile. "It depends on how fancy *you* want it to be." He turned and started to walk out, stopped and turned back. "But most of all, I want it to be fun. Fun for you to design and fun for me to enjoy afterward."

Jannice hurried over to Dori after Quilan had left and asked, "What was that all about?"

Dori held his card out in front of her. "He just hired me to outfit his kitchen. For $4,000."

"Seriously? Never fails, and I just gave him to you. Men drive me crazy. He must be married."

"I don't think so, or at least he said he wasn't. I'm going to stop by after work and check out his place."

"You want me to go along and protect you?"

Dori shook her head and grinned, "He might need someone to protect him, though."

♋

The next morning, when Dori showed up for work, Jannice asked, "Well, what happened last night?"

"Fascinating. He offered me a glass of wine. Very dry Chardonnay, he said, but if I preferred something sweeter he'd be glad to open a new bottle for me. His wine collection is impressive. He has one wine cellar for red and another for white."

"Silky. This guy sounds way too silky."

"He showed me his place. Fascinating."

"How so, fascinating?"

"His home is filled with books and bookcases, books in every room. He has signed art works and prints on the walls among the book cases. Unusual animal knickknacks interspersed on the shelves. Baskets of expensive silk flowers everywhere. Stuffed animals, the kind we used to have on our bed when we were kids. He has them throughout his house."

"How old is he?"

"Old enough. His condo is fantastic."

"How big is it?"

"Four bedrooms, two baths. One bedroom he's converted into an office. He's got this big computer system all set up in the middle of the room, surrounded by more books. The French doors are the best part. They lead out to a huge deck overlooking the Pacific."

"He must be big time rich."

"I asked him that."

175

"You asked him if he was rich? I take back every cynical remark I've made about you."

"He said it might look that way, but he writes books, and he got a big advance for movie rights for his last book. It was enough to allow him to buy the place and start writing full-time."

"What's the name of the book?"

"A science fiction novel called *Space Dream*. He gave me a signed copy. You ever hear of it?"

"If it's on TV, I've heard of it. If not, forget it."

"I asked him if he was famous."

"And?"

"He asked me if I had ever heard of him. I said no. He said he guessed he wasn't famous then, and he laughed. He has a wonderful laugh."

"So, are you going to do it?"

"I said I would. You know, I think it's going to be fun. I mean, he needs everything. Everything!"

"Did he give you a check for starters?"

"He wanted to, but I told him we could work that out after I'm done."

"He was going to give you $2,000 and you said no. I take back what I just said."

"Jannice, I can't take $2,000 for this. I just can't."

"Ask me if I could. All right, what's next?"

"I made all sorts of measurements last night. Tonight, I'm going to take him some of our catalogs to look at. I need to understand what he likes and doesn't like."

"Likes and doesn't like? You're kidding. Men don't have taste. They are hormones with feet." Jannice nodded enthusiastically at her own statement. "They have skulls with no brains; they are cruel slugs too slimy to step on; they are ugly toads that—."

"You made your point." Dori interrupted, followed by a sympathetic laugh. "One would think you're upset with the members of the opposite sex."

"Nonsense," she said sweetly. "Put a collar around their neck, a muzzle on their mouth, handcuff their hands behind them, spray their stinky feet with Lysol, house train them to put the toilet seat down and those penis people might be worth having around." She thought for a moment and then shook her head. "Nah, a puppy and a chocolate bar would be more fun, and more caring."

♋

The next morning Dori rushed into the store late. Jannice placed her hands on her hips and scowled at Dori. "He attacked your body last night and that's why you're late."

"Worse, we were up late looking at your catalogs. How about a $5,800 order?" She handed Jannice the order sheets.

Jannice scanned the order sheets. "All this. Awesome. You're forgiven, maybe. Give me the dirt."

"No dirt."

"No dirt? You're no fun. What's the matter with this jerk?"

"He did take me out for an elegant dinner."

"That sounds a little better. What else?"

"He had to. He doesn't have a thing in his kitchen. It's utterly amazing. I've never seen a brand-new kitchen with nothing but breakfast cereal and two fancy wine cellars."

"That's not the 'what else' I wanted. Has this man no pride? The least he could do is make a pass at you. Maybe he's not married. Divorced men are always stranger than married men."

"Jannice, he's just a super nice man who needs a kitchen by Christmas."

"A super nice man? Ah ha, you like him, don't you? You'd like him to have a kitchen and you by Christmas, right?"

"Maybe."

"See. I knew it. I recognize that intoxicated smile. That's not the smile you give to our customers. Oh, you poor romantic, you're smitten."

"Jannice, I just happen to think he's especially kind." She pulled a book from her purse. "I started his book. It's exciting. The women in his book aren't wimps, and there's lots of humor. It's a very good book. It's going to make a great movie."

177

"Wonderful, you get your romance from a book, and I get mine from recording my soap operas on TiVo. Stupid men, they constantly drive me to madness."

ℒ

A week before Christmas, shortly after the store closed, Jannice asked

Dori, "How's your offensive for Condo-man coming?"

"His kitchen is almost finished. It's been so much fun. I was afraid he'd be hard to select for, but he's liked everything I've chosen, except some pictures of fruit I wanted. Our tastes are wonderfully similar."

"He make a pass at you yet?"

Dori made a face. "I wish. Not one impropriety. He also told me he's not seeing anyone."

"He's gay?"

"No, he's not gay. I'm pretty sure, anyway."

"Why?"

"His daughter stopped by unexpectedly. She's sweet. She wanted to know if her father was courting me. When I told her no, she said, 'Darn, you're just the type of woman he needs.' Wasn't that sweet?"

"Sweet? You don't need sweet. Men! They should all be locked up in dark closets and only released when we need service."

"Jannice, that's terrible."

"Grab your Mr. Hyatt by his chest hairs and tell him you have the hots for his body."

"You are totally incorrigible." Dori started to laugh. "Perhaps I have been too subtle?"

"Are you going over to his place again tonight?"

"Yes. I want him to look at some linen tablecloths. He said he would take me out for dinner if I liked."

"I take it, you like?"

"Well, yes."

"All right, wear your knit dress. You know the one I mean."

Dori shook her head. "Not the black one?"

"Precisely, the black one. The dress that clings to you like it has been painted on every curve of your body. The one

178

you wore to work, and I had to send you home to change because the men coming into my store were all panting so hard they were steaming up my windows. That black knit dress."

"Do you think he'll notice?"

"If he doesn't, he has serious problems with his hormones." She thought for a moment and then added, "Or he's dead."

∅

Dori worked the late shift the next day and went in at noon. Jannice yelled at her from the back of the store the moment she entered, "Well, what happened?"

"We had a pleasant evening."

"I don't want to hear about a pleasant evening. I want to hear about the knit dress. I want to hear about heavy breathing and hot sheets. Did he notice?"

"I think so."

"You think so? Dori, what am I going to do with you? How could he not notice?"

"At dinner he went into the men's restroom, and when he returned it looked as though he'd splashed his face with cold water."

"You steam him?"

Dori smiled coyly, "I think I got his attention." She sighed, "But if I did, except for that, he didn't do anything else."

Jannice threw her hands up. "That's why God said that She could do better after She created man."

∅

Two days before Christmas, Dori sat at the break table drinking a cup of tea. Jannice saw her at the table and collapsed into a chair next to her during an unusual lull in the afternoon. Jannice popped off her shoes and put her feet up on the extra chair and wiggled her toes. She held her hands in front of her face and said, "Look at my hands. Black. Black from all that filthy loot coming in." She chuckled a wicked laugh. "And I love it. Look at my hands, feet. Why don't you

179

appreciate all this money as my hands do?" She grabbed her left foot and started massaging it. Between her groans she asked Dori, "Well, what's happening with weirdo-man?"

"He wants me to cook Christmas dinner for his family."

"What? He wants you to spend your Christmas Day cooking dinner for his family? See, I told you this guy is a toad."

"I said I would."

Jannice hung her head sadly. "Have I taught you nothing?"

"I'm going to give it one more try."

"If it were anyone else, I'd say go for it, but with this cretin, why bother? Have you a plan?"

Dori hedged. "Maybe."

"Maybe. I don't want to hear maybe. I want to hear a plan so disturbing he ends up a mere puddle on the ground, panting in excruciating desire. A plan so overpowering he's whimpering on his knees, begging for mercy."

"I'll need time to prepare the dinner, so he suggested I stay over on Christmas Eve in his guest bedroom."

"Wonderful. Such a gentleman." Jannice stabbed her left hand in the air. "Such a dork."

"I bought a new silk teddy for the occasion. Figured I'd find out if he does have hormones or not. Don't worry."

"I'm not worried about you. If this guy is just using you, I'm going to sneak into his condo and break all the glassware he bought from me— over his head."

♋

The day after Christmas, Jannice was unlocking the door to the shop just as Dori hurried over from the parking lot.

"So, how was your Christmas? Did his lust and desire cause him to sneak into your bedroom on Christmas Eve night?"

"I gave it my best shot, red teddy and all, but as always, he was a perfect gentleman."

"That's the problem. Men are always gentlemanly at the wrong time. I swear I think they carry their brains between their legs. How'd the dinner go?"

180

"Christmas morning went fine. I was busy getting the dinner ready, and Quilan helped me get the table ready, although he spent the last half of the morning sitting on a bar stool at the counter, just keeping me company while I finished cooking. He was unusually nervous."

"I can understand that. Having my family over always makes me nervous, too."

"Then he asked me the strangest thing. He wanted to know how he should introduce me to his family."

"Here it comes. Did he want to call you his maid?"

"I told him whatever made him comfortable."

"No, girl, don't give the degenerates of the world an upper hand. Make them suffer. You should have told him to stuff his own turkey."

"He said he was more concerned about my comfort."

"Sure. What a line. Damn male chauvinist pig. All of them."

"He handed me a tiny present and asked how I would feel if he called me his—"

"His what?" Jannice demanded with a quick stomp of her left foot.

Dori dramatically lifted her left hand for Jannice to see. Jannice's eyes opened wide as she squealed, "Dori, that's an engagement ring!" Jannice sighed happily. "Oh, Dori, he called you his fiancée, didn't he?" She sniffed loudly. "Damn men! Isn't that just like them? They're either screwing up my life or my mascara."

LONELINESS IS MY MISTRESS

Loneliness is my Mistress

As I walk in the Blackness of night,
With my body worn and spent,
And my mind full of the day's torments,
Beside me walks a woman parasite,
Who follows me, wherever my flight.
Calmly…unwearied…yet with no lament,
As though certain of my imprisonment,
Knowing full well we must unite.
She will grasp my body in close caress,
Yet there is no pleasure in her rape,
For there is no body and there is no shape.
She stands unwanted…beside me motionless,
And though I call her my black sorceress,
She's only my mistress…Loneliness.

"So, what do you think, Upton?"

"This is your idea of a Christmas poem for our December issue?"

"Absolutely. I'm telling it like it is."

"Right! So where did you get this creepy type face?"

"I thought it looked Christmassy."

"Like a funeral home on Halloween. Come on, Sheldon, this is supposed to be a happy issue, full of Christmas cheer and goodwill to all. Do you know what I'm saying?"

"You don't like it?"

"Sheldon, this," he waved the poem in the air, "is neither happy nor merry."

182

"For many people, my poem is as close to Christmas cheer as they're going to get."

Upton leaned back in his chair and tapped a red pencil thoughtfully against his lips. "How long has it been since you've had a date?"

"What's that got to do with my poem?"

"How long?"

"Not long."

"How long?" Upton asked again, louder.

Sheldon's eyes drifted upward as he tried to remember. "Maybe six months."

"Sheldon, Molly died three years ago. You've had two dates since then, and your last date was over a year ago, not six months ago."

"You don't like my poem?"

"Your poem is a cry for help."

"There are many lonely people during Christmas crying for help."

"I can't help them, Sheldon, but I can try to help you."

"I don't need help."

"Yes, you do, and we are just the people to help you."

"We?" Sheldon's eyebrows wrinkled in apprehension.

"Me. And the staff here. Do you know what we've done for you? We have come up with a list of six fantastic women. All eligible, all ready to be wined and dined by you." Upton opened his top desk drawer and handed him a sheet of paper with a list of women's names and addresses. "We've even arranged the time and dates for you. They all know you are coming to take them out."

Sheldon made a sour face. "This is a joke, right? You can't be serious."

"The dates, times and addresses are on the list. Don't stand up a single woman or you're fired. Meanwhile, I'll hold your page open until you come up with something happy, cheerful and definitely Christmassy."

"I'm not going to do it."

"Then you're fired."

"You can't fire me over this. I'll sue you."

"Sue me."

Sheldon glared at Upton, then lowered his head and sighed. "I couldn't sue my best friend. It wouldn't be prudent."

"That's right, particularly when your best friend is trying to help you."

"I know I should thank you, but this is not kind."

"I know. You will be happy to know that I thought the whole idea up by myself."

"Well, don't be so proud of yourself. I'll do it, but it won't work."

☙

Three weeks after he had given the list to Sheldon, Upton held a staff meeting in his office shortly before closing. Sheldon was not present. Upton had given each of them a copy of Sheldon's poem and asked for their reaction.

Toby shook her finger at Upton and said, "I have two girlfriends who are barely speaking to me. After reading this I understand why. I hold you responsible, Upton."

"Me? Don't blame me that Sheldon is a dingbat. Ammeal, forget the poem, what did your sister say after her date?"

"She said he was attractive, but not for her." He shrugged his shoulders. "She's said the same thing after every date she's had for the last five years."

"That's all?"

"He never called her back, so I guess he felt the same way." Ammeal shrugged his shoulders again. "None of her other dates called her back either."

Louise laughed and added, "Upton, he never called any of the women back. Not one. They were all the same, one date, one glass of wine, one dinner, and no hug or goodnight kiss. At least he didn't read them this poem. That would have been even worse."

"Do you think it helped at all?" Upton asked the group. "You know, getting him back in the habit of dating again."

No one said a thing, but the staff members shook their heads in unison.

"Fine, then does anyone have a suggestion?"

"I do." Louise tapped her fingers together as rapidly as she talked. "I think the problem with all the women we selected for him was that they were all single."

"You want us to fix him up with a married woman?" Ammeal asked.

"No, of course not. What I'm saying is that Sheldon's wife died. He needs to meet someone who's already been married. Ideally, someone who had a happy marriage, like Sheldon, and then lost her husband. Then they'd have this common bond."

Upton lifted his eyes and his hands to the ceiling. "That's great, Louise. Just how many women like that do any of us know?"

"We could advertise for one," Toby said. "We are in the business, you know."

Upton nodded thoughtfully, "Advertise. An interesting thought." Upton pursed his lips and tapped his red pencil rapidly. "How about we sell Sheldon? We use his poem, and we put Sheldon up for sale. Will someone try to make this man happy?"

"Yes, why not? We could do it as an auction," Louise added. "We would give the money to a charity the people select."

"And the highest bidder gets Sheldon," Upton added. "I love it."

"Yes," Ammeal said, "but will Sheldon?"

"Don't worry about Sheldon," Upton said, followed by a devilish laugh. "I'll take care of Sheldon."

"The magazine picks up the tab," Toby suggested. "All expenses, limo, dinner at Ernie's or Top of the Mark."

"A suite at the Hilton," Louise said, "with proper chaperones like me and my husband."

"The Wine Train the next day," Toby added. "I can see the headlines, something like 'A weekend with the Lonely Poet Laureate."

"Will Mr. McGuire agree?" Ammeal asked.

"That's what publishers do," Upton said, followed with a staccato laugh. "First, he gives me money, then he yells at me for spending it." Upton paused for a moment and mumbled, "Or is it the other way around. No matter, you just got to love this job."

185

He stopped and scratched the top of his nose thoughtfully. "How about we don't make this contest an auction. Rather than just a bunch of rich broads vying for Sheldon, let's make it a $10 bid with all the money going to the firemen's Toys for Tots Christmas Fund."

"And we could have them write a poem." Louise added.

"No," Ammeal disagreed. "Too hard. Not everyone is a poet. Why not have them send in their favorite poem that counters this poem of Sheldon's. That way they don't have to write a poem, just love poetry."

Louise nodded thoughtfully. "Good. Excellent, in fact. A happy poem for his lonely poem."

"Yes," Toby said enthusiastically. "A poem that talks about love and loneliness but in an uplifting way." Toby thought for a moment and added, "And a letter saying why they'd like to spend a fantastic weekend with our most eligible retreaded bachelor."

"And Sheldon picks out his own date." Louise said. "Poetic justice."

Upton groaned, but Louise smiled happily at her pun.

"We could call it *The Christmas Loneliness Contest*," Toby suggested.

"No," Louise said, "How about *A Poem for Sheldon* or *A Date With Sheldon*?"

"Whatever," Upton said. "Maybe I'll let Sheldon name the contest." He glanced at his calendar. "We can still squeeze in a page in our September issue. Run it for three issues, September, October, November. The last entry has to be in by the 15th, before the December issue goes to press."

"Boss, the magazine goes to Nick on the 16th," Ammeal said.

"Precisely, we hold a page just for the winner. It will be tight, but we can do it. Then we'll follow it up in our January issue with pictures of the winner and her fabulous Christmas weekend with the lonely Sheldon."

"Gang," Louise said, "I hate to bring this up, but how is this going to help Sheldon start dating again?"

"Stuff Sheldon," Toby said. "He owes us for not liking the women we fixed him up with."

"Right," added Ammeal, with a grin. "Anyone who doesn't like my sister gets no sympathy from me. Would any of you like her? No charge."

"Ammeal!" Louise said. "That's mean."

"So's my sister."

"All right," Upton said, "that's enough. I'll drop by Sheldon's place tonight after I get the go-ahead from Mr. McGuire. We can work out the details with Sheldon's help."

"Or despite him," Toby said.

Louise shook her head at Upton. "I'm glad you're going to tell Sheldon and not me. He's not going to be a happy camper."

"Oh, he'll love the idea."

☙

"No, Upton. Absolutely, positively no. You can't make me do it. I won't do it. No way and that's final. Period. The end. Do you hear me?"

"Sheldon, I think we'll need to get some pictures of you here in your home." Upton framed his hands together. "Maybe a shot of you by your computer writing your articles and poetry. Then—"

"Upton," Sheldon yelled. "Listen to me. Read my lips. No. N-O spells NO. Non, nein, nej, neyn."

"Wow, that's great Sheldon. You speak French, German, Swedish, and what was that last one."

"Yiddish," Sheldon said tiredly.

"You speak five languages."

"No, Upton, I can say no in five languages."

"Oh, I'm sorry. In this case, saying no wouldn't be prudent."

"Being prudent is my expression, Upton. Why are you using my expression?"

"I think a picture of you by the fireplace would be great. Maybe with a pipe in your hand, looking scholarly."

"Upton, you know I don't smoke." Sheldon collapsed into his favorite leather chair. "I need a brick wall."

"Why's that?"

"I'd have a better chance of communicating with it than I'm having with you."

"That's not an acceptable thing to say to your editor and best friend."

"Ex-best friend."

"See? That's just why I have to do this. You're becoming too testy. We need something to get you back into the circle of life."

"You aren't going to listen to me at all, are you?"

"Of course, I am. Don't I always? Aren't I going to publish your loneliness poem? Aren't I here, after hours, away from my loved ones, exploring new approaches to bring you untold happiness?"

"God will get you for this, Upton."

"Thank you. I need all the help I can get."

ℒ

Ammeal glanced in Sheldon's office, did a double take, stepped over two stuffed mailbags and leaned against the file cabinet. "This place looks like how I imagine Santa Claus's post office at the North Pole should look the day before Christmas."

Sheldon shook his head. "It's bad enough I let Upton force me into this charade, but look at this," he said as he swept his hand around his office. Post office mailbags filled his office. Tacked on the walls were letters and poems on top of more letters and poems. "I don't have time to do my articles. I'm behind on everything. All I do is read letters and poems."

"What are those?" Ammeal asked, as he pointed to the poems and letters tacked on the bulletin board.

"The good ones." Sheldon sighed tiredly. "So far." He waved his hand toward the bulletin board. "When I counted yesterday there were 86 of them, and I've added more since then."

"Incredible," Ammeal said soulfully. "And you still have all these bags to go through?"

"Yep. Want to trade jobs?"

"No," Upton said, as he sauntered over the mailbags to the other side of the file cabinet. "Ammeal doesn't want to trade jobs. He's married and has enough problems trying to get his sister out of his house." Upton grinned broadly. "I love this office, Ammeal. Tell Toby to get her camera and get a picture of this mess. It's great. It'll make a super picture for the feature."

Sheldon's head flopped down on his desk and he mumbled, "Go away, Upton. Preferably far away."

Upton noticed a poem separated from the rest of the poems on the bulletin board. "What about this one?" he asked as he read aloud, *Think of Me* by Marjorie Spalsbury." He quickly read the poem. "Hum, good." He glanced at the letter underneath the poem. "Oh, good letter, too."

Sheldon lifted his head slightly and glared at Upton. "You said I can choose the one I want, right?"

"Hey, I just read it because it was on the wall," he said with a shrug. "Seems like a sensitive letter and great poem, that's all."

Sheldon's voice softened. "Yes, it is."

"Well, why not choose it then?"

Sheldon shook his head angrily and shouted at Upton, "Get out of here, Upton. This whole thing has gotten out of hand."

"All right, buddy. All right." He gestured with his palms downward. "No pressure, take your time. You don't have to pick anyone until late tomorrow for us to make our deadline." Upton hurried out of Sheldon's office and motioned to Toby who was heading to Sheldon's office with her camera, to follow him into his office.

Toby asked, "What's up, Upton? I heard Sheldon yelling."

Upton bent down and wrote the name he'd seen on the letter. "Toby, shoot some candid pictures of Sheldon's office and after he throws you out, find out what you can about this woman." He handed her the note on which he'd just written the name.

"Who's Annie Caruthers?" Toby asked.

"A name on Sheldon's wall."

"And?" Toby asked again.

"It's for Sheldon. I have a feeling about this one."

"You mean have Dick look into it, right?"

"Toby, I can't help it if you married a police detective, but since you did, there's no reason I shouldn't make use of it."

"You know, your skill at manipulating people never ceases to amaze me."

"Just part of the KSAs needed for this job."

"I don't believe that your Knowledge, Skill and Ability have anything to do with how you manipulate your staff."

"That's true, Toby. That's why it's so much fun being the editor-in-chief."

𝔢

The following morning, Toby rushed into Upton's office. "How do you manage to pull off so many of your hunches, Upton? Do you have a crystal ball or is it all ESP?"

"What are you talking about?"

"Annie Caruthers is who I'm talking about. Tall, thin, very good looking, seven years younger than Sheldon, and her husband died of cancer, two and a half years ago."

Upton whistled a long, slow note. "Interesting." He beat the padded arm of his chair twice. "We have a match."

"Don't include me in that 'we' stuff."

"You get her address?"

"Certainly. Dick knows her. Her husband played on Dick's softball team before he died."

"Small world." Upton rocked back and forth in his office chair, thinking. Finally he nodded vigorously and did a drum beat on his desk with his hands. "The direct approach. That's the answer. Bring her in."

"Say what? Bring her in. What do you think this is," Toby waved her hands wildly, "a cheap cop show? We're a magazine. How do I bring her in?"

"Tell her Sheldon wants to have lunch with her."

Toby shook her head. "I don't like the sound of this. Are you going to tell Sheldon?"

"Tell Sheldon what?" Upton smiled innocently at Toby.

"The level of your deviousness is frightening, Upton. What's worse, I think I know what you're up to."

190

"Call me on your cell phone if you can swing it by lunch time. He has to choose the winner today, so it's important that he meets her today. Go, go," he said as he waved her out of his office with quick flicks of his fingers.

At 12:15, Upton strode casually into Sheldon's office. Sheldon glanced up wild-eyed from the pile of letters dumped on top of his desk. "I hate you. I would do nasty things to your body if I thought you had feelings, but you have none."

"I can't believe how beautiful it is outside today. Gorgeous."

"You see this office. I'm a neat man and now look at this. I feel as if I'm living in the dead letter room of the post office."

"What you need is a break. I've made reservations for us at Yamoto's."

"Get out of my sight. I've only a few more hours, and I still have hundreds of these to look at."

"We'll order some sushi." He thought for a moment. "Unagi. You love Unagi. Maybe some hot Saki to help you relax?"

Sheldon sighed loudly, leaned back tiredly in his chair and laced his fingers around the back of his head. He grimaced and mumbled more to himself than to Upton, "The way I figure it, you must be a direct descendant of Attila the Hun."

"Come on. Grab your sport coat and let's go eat. I'll even break down and buy."

Sheldon shook his head. "Why me? Why me?" He mumbled softly as he slowly stood and pulled his coat off the back of his chair. "Wait a minute. You never buy. You never have money."

"I'll use my credit card."

"Gina won't let you have a credit card."

"She said she's going to let me try one, one more time."

"I don't believe that. She's smarter than that."

"Testy, very testy. If you must know, I figured out where she hid one of my credit cards. Listen, I need to use the restroom. There's a friend of mine in my office who's joining us for lunch. Go in and introduce yourself, and I'll be right back." Upton hurried down the hall.

When Sheldon walked into Upton's office, he sensed immediately that Upton was up to some mischief. The tall, slim woman had her back to him and was enjoying the skyline view of San Francisco from Upton's window. He coughed slightly, and she turned and smiled at him.

After waiting 10 minutes, Upton returned to his office. Sheldon and Annie Caruthers were gone. At 4:36, Upton saw Sheldon hurry past his office. He called out, "Hey, where have you been?"

Sheldon didn't reply, so Upton hurried into Sheldon's office. Annie's poem and letter were no longer on the wall. "You know we do have a magazine to put out here and you're late. We need to have your selection."

"I'm ready." Sheldon didn't smile.

Upton squirmed slightly. "Well, let's have it."

"I have some things to say to you, Upton. You are an interfering, meddling and insensitive person."

"Yes, that's all true, and those are only my good points. You didn't mention how charming and good looking I am."

"You didn't give a thought to her feelings. How it was going to make her feel. She thought I wanted to see her to tell her that she had won the prize. She's had a tough time since her husband died."

"Then you must have made her happy, telling her she was the winner."

"What makes you think that?"

Upton gulped and stuttered, "You didn't make her the winner?"

"The agreement, Upton, was that I would pick the winner. I agreed to do all this madness, but only if I could pick the winner. Nothing was said about you selecting the winner."

"But you loved her letter, and the poem she selected was great. You liked it. I could tell."

"There were over 100 poems and letters that I liked. That was only one of them."

"You didn't tell her?"

"No, Upton. I told her you would tell her. She's out in the waiting room. You get to go out there and crush that poor beaten lady. Destroy the one good dream she's had since her husband died. Ruin her Christmas. Perhaps destroy her life." He picked up two sheets of paper from his desk. "Here, why don't you read her the winning poem and letter I did select? Maybe she'll think it's better than hers."

Upton accepted the papers from Sheldon and nervously rolled them into a tube. "I can't—"

"Oh, yes, you can. You tried to play Cupid, now play the heavy." Sheldon leaned back in his chair and glared angrily at Upton.

Upton grimaced, turned around and slowly shuffled toward the waiting room. He unrolled the poem and letter. The poem was on top. He read the title, *Think of Me*, stopped and stared at it in confusion. He quickly glanced at the letter. It was Annie Caruthers's letter. "You did choose her!" he yelled.

Suddenly Sheldon's hand slapped down on his shoulder from behind. "That's right, you turkey." He felt Sheldon's hand squeeze his shoulder. "Thanks," Sheldon said softly as he hurried past Upton on down the hallway toward the waiting room.

"You sandbagged me. You set me up and sandbagged me," he called after Sheldon.

"I learned it all from you." Sheldon said without even looking back. "Besides, you deserve even worse." At the door to the waiting room, Sheldon turned, grinned at Upton, and nodded his head slightly.

Then he was gone. Through the glass door, Upton saw Annie Caruthers smile and take Sheldon's arm as they walked out together.

"I actually did good." Upton did a little jig and grinned. "How about that? I pulled it off. Gina will never believe it." He went back into his office and slowly read the poem Annie had sent in as her favorite poem:

THINK OF ME
by Marjorie Spalsbury

Think of me
Once in a while,
With love.
And I will feel it
Across the miles
That separate us.
And for a brief moment.
We will be together again.
And the distance between us
Will disappear
And the time we're apart,
Be less.
Your thoughts
Like a tender touch,
Will heal my loneliness.

UNTIL CHRISTMAS IN THE SPACE HOUSE

The seven children woke on thick pads placed on the floor. Someone had wrapped each of them in warm, silver blanket-like wraps. Molly Motler, a fifth grade teacher, was already awake and staring at the wall.

Kim, the last to wake, asked Miss Motler in a whisper, "What happened to us?"

Molly shook her head and motioned for the children to be still.

An enormous man stood on the other side of the clear wall with his back to them. She'd walked into it earlier; otherwise, she wouldn't have known there was even a wall there. It was a clear wall that wasn't there, a window that was clearer than glass, an opening that didn't open. She frowned, and the children gathered around her fearfully.

The man on the other side of the wall turned his head completely around until his face pointed over his back. "Please don't be alarmed. You will find food for the children and you on the table."

Molly unconsciously rubbed the back of her neck with her hand.

"My name is Peter and after we receive some visitors, I'll meet with you. To help you feel more secure, I'll leave the screen on so you can see what is happening. Please know that you are safe here." His head slowly revolved back around to the front.

"It's not an opening," Molly said. "Maybe it's a giant TV screen that we can see through."

"Are we kidnapped?" Art asked.

"I don't know," Molly said quietly.

The image on the wall followed Peter into a semi-darkened room. A young man in a Forty-Niner sweatshirt, San Francisco Giants cap and blue jeans sat watching two television screens and one computer screen with a different program on each. Peter said, "We have company coming, Oh Great One."

The young man reluctantly turned his head away from the television screens. "Really! What sort of company?"

"I believe they are called the local authorities."

"How peculiar."

"Forgive me for saying so, Majestic One, but you will need an earth name."

"An earth name? Yes." He pondered for a moment. "How about James Bond?"

"I don't believe using the name of a famous literary and movie character would be wise."

The man sighed audibly. "Probably not. How about Hawk, and you could be Spenser. You know, you do look like that Spenser character on television."

"You would need to be taller, have muscles like me, and you don't wear sunglasses. Come, Great One, you can do better than that."

"If I think up a name, will you stop picking on me?"

"You know I am incapable of picking on you."

"Right, that's what they told us at Boebyness. There's only one thing wrong."

"What is that?"

"Nobody ever told you."

"That is impossible, Great Lord."

"See, you're doing it again." He stopped and tilted his head.

"Someone is beating on our ship. Is that them?"

"It is called knocking on the door, and it is our visitors."

"That's right," the man said, repeating it softly to himself, "knocking on our door."

"Have you a name?"

"I'm thinking. You show them in. I'll have a name by the time you bring our visitors in."

"As you wish, Oh Voice of Ultimate Authority."

"Stop that, Peter, or I'll reprogram you."

"The only one capable of reprogramming me is me." He turned and left the room.

The young man nodded and mumbled to himself, "He's right!" He lifted his Giants cap and scratched his head in thought. "An earth name," he said with a frown.

Peter opened the door. The sheriff and his two deputies lifted their heads at Peter. A large fat man stood a few feet behind the men, and his mouth fell open at the sight of Peter. Peter stood six-feet ten-inches tall, and his muscles bulged through the pale blue, thin, short-sleeved turtleneck shirt he wore. One of the deputies swallowed nervously and cautiously reached his hand down and unfastened the strap holding his revolver.

The sheriff cleared his voice and said, "I'm Sheriff Zorrinsky. Are you the owner of this house, Boy?"

"No, I am but the lowly housekeeper, but the master is at home. Would you care to speak with him?"

"Do I look like I'm here for my health?" The sheriff's hand rested ominously on the handle of his revolver.

Peter's eyes drifted down and held on the sheriff's large stomach. "Well, your stomach appears healthy, but I'm not sure about the rest of you. Are you here for your health?"

The other deputy started to snicker and then stopped in midlaugh when the sheriff gave him a quick glare.

"If I need smart remarks, Boy, I have two deputies who can do that just fine, thank you. Get the owner of this place."

"Of course," Peter said with a small bow. "Please follow me."

The children in the room gasped at the sight of the fat man. "That's Mr. Baker from Children Services, Miss Motler," Kai said with a quick point of her finger. "He's really mean, let me tell you."

"Yes, I know, Kai," Miss Motler said in a whisper. "Let's keep very still and see what he wants."

Peter led the four people through the large round house. Light flowed into the various rooms from large skylights two and three stories above them.

"What'd you do, hook three or four geodesic domes together to build this house?" the sheriff asked.

"A similar type of design, but much advanced."

The young man straightened his Giants cap and stepped out from the television room and waved his hand. "What's happening?"

Peter lowered his head slightly toward the man and grimaced. "Behold, the Wondrous One, the owner of this house."

The man held out his hand toward the sheriff and said, "Greetings, my name is War Eagle Smith."

The sheriff shook War Eagle's hand and introduced himself, his two deputies and Vic Baker. "You don't look like an Indian, Mr. Smith," the sheriff said with a hint of cynicism in his voice.

War Eagle ignored the sheriff's tone and said, "I'm not. My parents met and married while going to Auburn University. I was named after the team's mascot. Please, just call me War Eagle. Now then, how may I help you?"

"We are searching for seven missing children. We believe a teacher has taken them."

Wyn reached up and tugged Miss Motler's hand. "You didn't take us. We took you, huh?"

"We took one another," Miss Motler said as she bent down and gave Wyn a quick hug.

The sheriff surveyed the room. "We've had some reports about this house."

"Reports?"

"Well, one, but when we tried to check it out in the records, there was no record. According to the courthouse, a Samuel Hawkingwell is the owner of this property, and they list it as woods and abandoned farmland."

"I see. Well, I bought the property from Mr. Hawkingwell. I have the papers available if you wish to see them."

"That's not the problem. You realize that you cannot build a house without the proper permits."

"However, we did."

"No," the sheriff explained edgily, "what I mean is, you must have the county approval. Building permits."

"Interesting. Building permits."

"Yes, all sorts. For your electric, your plumbing. Everything."

"Thus you are here to inspect my plumbing?"

"Your plumbing!" The sheriff leaned back and laughed. "You are an airhead."

"An airhead? I'm not acquainted with that term." War Eagle's eyes narrowed slightly. "I am a scientist, but I don't believe I am an airhead."

Peter explained, "War Eagle is deeply involved in his research and leaves the gathering of permits to me. Perhaps you would care to have some refreshments while we discuss this more." Peter led the way to the kitchen.

War Eagle followed Peter and gasped aloud once he stepped into the kitchen. "Look at this. This is amazing." War Eagle hurried into the kitchen and started opening cupboard doors, the refrigerator, the pantry, and each time he'd gasp and say either "Wow!" or "This is wonderful!"

The sheriff whispered to Peter, "He's acting like he's never seen this kitchen before."

"Yes," Peter nodded. "His actions are often strange. It is not unusual for extremely brilliant men to be somewhat eccentric."

The sheriff nodded solemnly. "He's passed that test."

"Peter," War Eagle called when he pulled down the door to the oven, "What are these?"

The kitchen was engulfed with a sweet, spicy smell.

Peter smiled to War Eagle, "Your cookies, sir. Remember you asked me to bake you some."

War Eagle peered into the oven. "Oh, yes. Uh, Peter, what do you do with them?"

"Perhaps the sheriff and his deputies can show you, Oh Mighty Sweet Tooth."

Peter removed the cookie sheet with his bare hand. The steam curled up from the cookies.

The sheriff gasped. "How can you handle that with your bare hand?"

"Yes," War Eagle asked Peter, "How can you do that?"

Peter glanced at his hand for just a moment and then slapped it lightly with his other hand. "Artificial hand."

"Incredible," the sheriff said. "Looks real."

"New design."

"I've never heard about such a thing, except in the movie *Star Wars*."

"Experimental. We don't want to get the hopes of amputees up until we know it will work successfully."

The sheriff stared at Peter's arm. "You can't even tell where it attaches."

Peter grabbed a spatula and flipped a cookie toward the sheriff. The sheriff deftly grabbed the still warm cookie and flipped it from hand to hand until it was cool enough to eat. "Good." The sheriff smacked his lips and nodded his head approvingly. "In fact, very good."

Peter flipped more cookies to each, including War Eagle. War Eagle smelled the cookie. He smiled. "You're amazing, Peter." He took a small bite, then a larger bite and finally popped the remainder of the cookie into his already full mouth and munched away happily.

Peter handed each a glass of cold milk and asked the sheriff, "What can you tell us about the children?"

"They were last seen in the woods a couple of miles from here. Their mother died about five months ago and Children Services, that's who Vic works for, wants us to find them so we can send them to foster homes."

"A foster home," War Eagle said thoughtfully. "Doesn't foster mean to encourage?"

Vic tried to speak, but spit out cookie crumbs instead. He sipped some milk and explained, "That's a home that takes care of children."

"And you have a family who will care for all seven children?"

"Well, no. We've arranged seven different homes for the children throughout the state. There aren't any foster families around these parts who could care for seven children."

"Interesting. Are the children excited about going to these new homes?"

The sheriff laughed, and his huge belly bounced up and down. "I expect not. After the kids' mother died, apparently this Motler woman moved them all into an old farmhouse she was renting. Vic found out about it and demanded that she turn the children over to Children Services."

Vic added, "Miss Motler claimed she had applied to be the children's foster parent. She's not even married. What could she understand about raising seven worthless little rubbish kids? Ridiculous."

"What indeed," said War Eagle, as his eyes narrowed again.

The sheriff continued. "Yesterday I went to Motler's house to gather up the children, but they all scattered into the woods, along with this Motler woman. They won't last long. Can't hide seven children in the woods for any length of time, not kids that young anyways. My cousin is bringing up his dogs later today, and we'll have good sport running them down."

The tall, skinny deputy shyly raised his hand and asked, "Mind if I use your head?"

War Eagle shook his head. "Mine doesn't come off, but you're welcome to use Peter's."

"I believe, Oh Mighty Brain, that the deputy wants to use our restroom."

"Have we a restroom?"

"Yes, Oh Intrepid One. You call it the Tinkle Hole."

"Oh, that room. Yes, Peter will be happy to show you where it is."

The deputy glanced from Peter to War Eagle and back to Peter again. "I think I'll just hold it."

The sheriff explained to Peter and War Eagle that they should call the sheriff's office if they see the children. Peter gave each of them a small bag of cookies to take with them and assured the sheriff that the building permits would be taken care of promptly.

After they had gone, War Eagle made a gurgling sound.

"Are you impressed with the earthlings, Oh Giant Among Men?"

"Peter, why did I not like those people, I mean besides that fat sheriff calling me an airhead and calling you Boy?"

"They are little people, with little minds, and they are full of themselves. Fortunately, not all earth people are like that."

"I'm glad to hear that. Going to hunt children with dogs. That makes me angry, Peter. I thought this was a civilized planet, and the children have lost their leader."

"That's called a parent on this planet, War Eagle."

"Oh, right, a parent." War Eagle grinned suddenly. "Why, Peter, that's the first time you have ever called me by a proper name."

"A small slip, Oh Righteous One."

"You don't make small slips." War Eagle stared out the large hexagon window. "I believe we should find those children and their teacher."

"For what purpose?"

"To help them."

"The sheriff won't like that."

"I believe we will refrain from informing the sheriff. What do you think of that?"

"I am but a humble housekeeper. Considering such things would not be proper for me."

War Eagle leaned away from Peter and grinned, "How did you ever get out of Castfac Service Design without them realizing they'd missed a flow or two?"

"They gave me a special flow, but they didn't know it."

"Special is right. Your intelligence flow was supposed to be very specific for the function assigned," War Eagle said, followed by a short laugh.

"I was not the unit assigned to you. I have often wondered during your sleep time why you selected me."

"Well, I saw you load the white paste in the TAC unit." War Eagle grinned at Peter. "You didn't know that, did you?"

"I was certain no one saw me. That is indeed interesting."

War Eagle nodded. "I don't believe I've ever seen Teacher ZZ so angry. I still believe he thinks I caused it to explode over him."

"Why didn't you tell him you saw me do this act?"

"He asked if I did it and I said no. He was in a predicament. He knew that I would never lie, yet he still thought I did it. Happily, he never asked if I knew who had done it."

"I was pleased with the results," Peter said with an impassive expression.

"Yes, so were the others. Do you remember how quiet it became? I still remember the silence, well, except for Teacher ZZ yelling and ranting."

"But you have not explained why you chose me."

"Face it, Peter, a standard housekeeping unit is boring, and spending a hundred years on this planet with one would have been awful. No standard housekeeping unit would have done such an act, and I wanted one with some character, so I switched my unit assignment papers for you. Of course, I'm not certain if you are a joy or an affliction."

"Both," Peter said, followed by a smile.

"Well, you certainly aren't boring. So what do you say, shall we go gather some children?"

"What do you propose to do with them after we have them?"

"Do with them? Yes, that's a good point. What do you do with children?"

"On this planet, you raise them."

"Don't they come ready to go?"

"Only their potty functions."

"Perhaps this teacher can offer us some suggestions."

"That is possible."

"Well, how do we go about finding them?"

"I suggest going into our spare-room-for-rest."

"Why would I want to go to a room-for-rest when I want to find lost—." War Eagle stopped and pointed an accusing finger at Peter. "You already have them, don't you?"

"The woods were cold last night, Great Wisdom of the Ages, and offering them shelter here seemed wise. It is one of my advantages of not needing sleep. Please follow me."

The children gathered tightly around Molly when Peter and War Eagle entered the room. War Eagle started to go up to them, but in unison, they moved away from him.

Peter motioned with his hand for War Eagle to stop. "They appear frightened of you."

Molly said nervously, "Of you both."

"Really!" War Eagle glanced at Peter in surprise. "Why?"

"We went to sleep in the woods last night, and we woke up here. We don't know how we got here and what you want. And he," she pointed at Peter, "does strange things with his head."

"Peter, you didn't remove your head while they were watching, did you?"

Art pointed his finger at Peter and exclaimed, "He turned it all the way around!"

"Oh, no," War Eagle said, twisting his head back and forth. "That always makes my neck hurt when he does that with me."

Molly smiled for the first time. "I started rubbing the back of my neck when he did it."

"Yes," War Eagle exclaimed. "Exactly what I do. Have you all eaten? Your food hasn't been touched. Peter is an excellent cook. He even has a kitchen. Isn't that marvelous?"

"Don't all homes have a kitchen?" one of the smallest children asked.

War Eagle turned to Peter, "Do they?"

"Yes, Oh Majestic One. On this planet, they do, well, most of them."

"On this planet?" Molly said. "Where are you from?"

"We are from the stars. We are spacemen. Travelers in time." War Eagle spread his arms dramatically up in the air.

"What the Presumptuous Master means," explained Peter, "is that we are from a far star. He has come to study your planet, although he has orders not to tell anyone about this fact."

War Eagle nodded. "Peter's right. I wasn't supposed to tell you that."

"What do you do?" Selma pointed her finger at Peter.

"What he should do is be my housekeeper," War Eagle said, "but he does things he should never do."

"What do you do?" The twins, Kai and Kari, asked in unison.

"I was given a variety of additional skills so I can do many things," Peter said.

"An understatement of all times," War Eagle said as he shook his head. "He made himself all but human."

"Wow, an android," Selma said.

"I prefer to think I'm better than an android," Peter said. "I have feelings."

"I'm sorry," said Selma. "Have I hurt your feelings?"

"How kind of you to be concerned about my feelings." Peter bowed to her. "No, you have not hurt my feelings, Dear Little One. Come to my kitchen, and I will cook a great breakfast for you. You must all be hungry."

"Yes!" exclaimed War Eagle. "The kitchen. Such a wonderful place and Peter has filled it with wonderful smells."

Molly hesitated, but the children dashed out with War Eagle and Peter. Reluctantly, Molly followed.

In the kitchen, War Eagle joined the children and Molly for breakfast at a long table. Peter cooked and served pancakes, hot cereal, French toast, milk, orange juice and homemade cookies. As they ate, Molly introduced the children and herself.

After they had eaten, War Eagle asked, "How can we help you? I did not care for the sheriff and that other fat man. Still, I am new to this planet. I don't know what to suggest."

"Are you really from another planet?"

"Yes, but please don't tell anyone. What you think of as a house is my spaceship. The bottom of the ship is sunk in the ground and all you see is the top of our ship designed to look like your earth houses."

"Are you a machine, too?"

"No, I'm just me. See, I'm just like you." War Eagle reached over and took Molly's hand. "Warm-blooded and, my goodness, your hand is so soft. How delightful."

Molly blushed. "Don't the women on your planet have soft hands?"

"I've never touched a woman before." War Eagle tilted his head in thought. "In fact, I don't believe I have ever seen or spoken to a live woman before. Have I, Peter?"

"No, Oh Celibate One. She has just given that treat to you."

"Still, I've read about women, and I've been watching women on your television. They seem most confusing."

"We can be," Molly said with a laugh. She shrugged her shoulders and exclaimed, "I don't understand it. I should be terrified. Here I am in the control of people from outer space, and I'm having breakfast with you as though it was the most normal thing in the world to do."

"She's right, Peter. We must be most frightening to them."

Peter sat at the table with the three smallest children, Joy, Rhona and Hall, all sitting in his lap. "Obviously nobody told them. They want to see me turn my head around."

War Eagle held up his hand. "Absolutely not. I always get a hurt in my neck when you do that." He turned to Molly and said, "Please ask him not to do it."

"Won't he do what you tell him?"

"Only sometimes, and then only if he wants to."

205

"Well, Peter, I'd appreciate it if you'd not turn your head all around.

Children, don't encourage Peter to be bad."

"Yes, ma'am," the three children and Peter said in unison.

"Peter tells me you have to raise children on this planet. How is that accomplished?"

"Why you care for them, feed them, make sure they get enough sleep, clothe them, teach them—."

"Stop. Goodness, that sounds most difficult."

"It can be. How is it done on your planet?"

"We come ready to go."

Molly shook her head in confusion.

Peter explained, "The humans on War Eagle's planet are cloned. Individuals are born fully grown and educated. At least somewhat."

"Don't smirk, Peter," War Eagle said. "I'm learning."

"Very slowly, Oh Battery of Minds."

Molly laughed. "Peter, you also have a sense of humor. Are the others like you?"

"No one is like Peter," War Eagle said, followed by a short sigh.

"War Eagle is correct. No unit has my skills or emotions. The designer programmed a new experimental intelligence flow, but he died and the project halted. The decision was made not to waste the flow, and Castfac Service Design placed it into me. Unknown to all was the knowledge that the designer had finished his work. It wasn't until I ran a system check that I discovered this fact myself. That's when I discovered that among other advanced traits, I had been programmed with a sense of humor. At my start, I was uncertain of the use of this new attribute, and since no one knew that I possessed it, it was not included in my training. Since then, I have found it quite delightful."

"Not everyone thinks so," War Eagle said.

Molly asked, "What are you going to do with us?"

War Eagle nodded and thought a moment before answering, "We only want to help you; however, you are going to have to tell us how. Whatever we can do, we will try."

Molly shook her head sadly and asked, "You wouldn't like to be a parent to seven children, would you?" She sighed softly.

"I don't know? Would we, Peter?"

Peter held up Joy. "How old is this little child called Joy?"

"She's three," Kim said. "I'm the oldest. I'm 14."

"Then," Peter said, "we would have to commit to at least 25 earth years to see that each child grew up and received a proper education."

"We could do that," War Eagle said.

"There is an additional problem, Great Hollow Brain."

War Eagle turned to Molly and asked, "Did Peter just insult me again?"

"I'm sure it was done with love," Molly replied.

"I think he missed that emotion. All right, Peter, what's the other problem?"

"It would be best for this many children if they had both a father and a mother. With a great stretch of the imagination, you might fit the category of a father, but not of a mother."

"Molly can be the mother," War Eagle said quickly.

Molly reached out and touched War Eagle's arm. "It's not quite that easy here."

"Why?"

"Well, while not everyone on Earth believes this, I feel it's better if the mother and father are married."

"All right, we'll get married."

"You try the flow in me, Great Eager One," Peter said with a shrug of his large arms. "What Miss Motler is saying is that when men and women on this planet get married, they do so because they are in love."

"Well, I love Molly."

Molly's eyes opened wide.

"Miss Motler is the first live woman you have ever met. You cannot be in love with her already."

"Why not? I've watched programs where the people say they fell instantly in love. I believe they called it love at first sight."

Peter stared at War Eagle, and a grin slowly formed on his face. "You have finally asked me a question I cannot answer. Perhaps you will answer that question, Miss Motler?"

"For a man and a woman to marry they should spend time together. Usually they will have similar interests. They will be attracted to one another. Do you understand?"

"Right. I'm attracted to you. I think you are beautiful. We've spent almost an hour together, and we both care for the children. How am I doing?" He smiled at her.

Molly leaned back in her chair and studied War Eagle. Clearly he was handsome. His black curly hair, dark eyes and eager smile were joyful. He was probably intelligent, although his earth innocence had a way of making that difficult to determine. She shook her head. He was from outer space. Still, she had risked her career to take in the children. She shook her head again. "No, I'm sorry."

War Eagle didn't appear disturbed by her answer. "I need to court you, don't I? I saw it on television. I can do that. Flowers and candy. Take you out for dinner and dancing. I'll have to learn how to dance, but I'm sure I can—"

"War Eagle, it's not only that," Molly interrupted. She tried to explain. "You're different. You're from another planet."

Peter said to Molly, "You may wish to know that his anatomy is exactly the same as earthmen on this planet."

"Exactly?"

"In every way."

"Hum!" Molly shook her head, "No, it's just not possible. There's too much difference between us. It just wouldn't work."

War Eagle frowned. "Why not? Won't you at least let me try? You could teach me to be a good earthman."

"How?"

"Stay here with us. You and the children. You'll be safe here, and I can try to court you. You have a wonderful special holiday called Christmas. Stay with us till Christmas. If you still say no, then Peter and I will take you and the children anywhere you want to go. All right?"

"And the sheriff?" Molly asked.

"I can handle that problem," Peter said. "I have studied the legal system here, and I can arrange for War Eagle and you to be assigned as temporary foster parents. War Eagle Smith will have to have a personal history, but all that can be added to your earth records through my supercomputer here on the ship.

"The records already show that I have a law degree from the University of Denver and that I have passed the bar exam in this state. I'll bypass the sheriff, clear your name so you can continue to teach and the children can return to school. There should be few problems. After all, what judge is going to refuse two outstanding citizens who want to care for seven children?"

Molly looked around the table at the children. They were all listening and watching intently. "What do you say, children? Shall we stay with War Eagle and Peter until Christmas?"

The children nodded their heads. Joy held up her hand. "I'd like to stay. Peter said he'd let me watch him turn his head all the way around when no one was watching."

"Peter," Molly said sternly, "if we stay, I'm expecting you to behave yourself as well."

"Yes, ma'am, but I've never had a mother."

"Well, it appears as though you do now, at least until Christmas."

Peter stood. "After I clear the table, I will prepare rooms-for-rest for all the children and you, Miss Motler."

"Will we all have to share a room?" Kim asked.

Peter shook his head. "No, of course not. Each of you will have a private room, and each of you can help me fix it up to be just how you'd like it."

The children all started talking excitedly.

Molly said to Peter, "They've never had private rooms, ever."

"And have you never had a private room before either?"

Molly smiled. "Yes, Peter, I've had a private room. I was an only child."

"And now you wish to take over the responsibility of seven children? That is most impressive, Miss Motler."

"You may call me Molly if you wish, Peter."

Peter nodded and frowned slightly.

"Would you prefer to call me something else, Peter?"

Peter hesitated.

"I'm a little young to be your mother, but you may call me whatever you like."

"Thank you, Mom. Does that mean I have to call War Eagle by his name?"

"You and War Eagle will have to work that out yourselves. That's what best friends do."

"Best friends?" exclaimed War Eagle. "Is that what we are?"

"Most amazing," Peter said, shaking his head in wonderment. "I get a mom and a best friend all in the same day." He grinned mischievously at War Eagle. "That means I must continue to pick on you."

War Eagle turned to Molly. "That's not what being a best friend means, is it? I'm going to look that up in my library. I bet it doesn't say anything about you picking on me." War Eagle hurried back to his study.

"That will be a great Christmas present," Art belched and grinned at Molly.

"We don't belch at the table, Art. Say, excuse me."

"Sorry, ma'am. Excuse me." Art lowered his head, still grinning, and winked at the twins.

"What will be a great Christmas present, Art?" Molly asked.

"Having you and War Eagle get married and becoming our mom and dad."

Molly watched War Eagle as he hurried from the kitchen. "Hum." She smiled. "Yes, it might," she said softly.

"Well, I'm never going to call him Dad," Peter said, as he continued to clean up the dishes.

THAT OLD WITCH ON MAIN STREET

Amy Wilkins hobbled out onto her brick porch for the third time. The cold wind whipped around her legs. This time she slammed her walker down after each step and slowly pulled herself forward. She searched around her porch then hollered loudly, "Tarnation! Where is it?"

The barber next door jerked in his chair when Amy Wilkins yelled. He had no customers so he was sitting in his barber chair reading the paper. He exhaled softly and went on reading.

Miss Wilkins hobbled back into the house and over to the telephone. She quickly dialed the number. "Where's my paper?" she screamed. "He's never been this late before. Just because it's Christmas Eve, he shouldn't be this late. What's going on?" She took the telephone handset and pounded it on the table three times. "Did you hear that? That's how my heart sounds after making three trips out on my porch. I'm 96 years old. I've no business making three trips out on a freezing porch to search for a newspaper that's not even there. You hear me?"

"Yes, Miss Wilkins. Your newspaper is on its way. The man will ring your bell and hand it to you."

"What? Bang my bell. I don't need bells banged. I need my newspaper."

This time the voice yelled, "It's on its way, Miss Wilkins. Any moment now."

"That's what you said the last time I called. Don't nobody care about a sick, old 96-year-old lady. Nobody cares." She slammed the phone back down into its cradle, just as the doorbell rang.

Using her walker, she hobbled over to the door. She opened the door and grabbed the paper out of the boy's hand. "About time. Where is Jason? He's never late. Who are you?"

"Miss Wilkins, I'm Buffrin Mosher. I live next door to Jason. Remember, you tutored me about 6 years ago."

Miss Wilkins stared at Buffrin. "I remember you. I bet you thought I didn't remember you, but I did. Your dad brought you to me when you were having trouble with your studies. Where's Jason? He's never late. Why are you bringing me his paper?"

Buffrin's eyes filled with tears. "Jason's in the hospital, Miss Wilkins. He was hit by a car. He's hurt bad."

Miss Wilkins ran her tongue around her mouth. "Forgot my teeth. That's annoying." She slammed the door.

Buffrin stared at the closed door for a moment, slowly shook his head and hurried back to his bike.

Miss Wilkins hadn't moved from in front of the door. She stared at the blank door for a long time holding tightly to her walker with her left hand. The newspaper fell from her right hand and plopped by her feet. "Not my Jason," she said softly as tears rippled from her eyes. She leaned her head back and screamed, "Not my Jason." She crumbled to the floor in an unconscious gray heap.

℘

Miss Wilkins' eyes opened and she stared blankly at the beige wall across from her. "Something wrong here," she said softly to herself. Slowly she turned her head and tried to understand where she was. She knew she wasn't in her home, but where? She saw a doorway flooded in a dazzling rainbow of lights off to her left and for a moment she felt a strange sense that the doorway was summoning her. How strange, she thought; doors don't call out to people.

She glanced down and realized that she was standing without her walker. She could feel the remarkable happy warmth from the doorway and it felt comforting, but she shook her head and continued to try to figure out where she was. Time for strange doorways later, she thought.

The doctors and nurses came in focus, huddled around a gurney, and she wondered how she'd missed seeing them right off. She smelled the medicine and heard the noise of all the equipment, but the worst sound of all was a loud, constant buzzing.

"Tarnation, turn off that horrible noise!" she yelled.

A nurse reached up and switched off the unit.

"Oh, that's better. Could someone tell me where I am?" No one turned around and just then, she saw who was on the table. *She* was on the table.

Miss Wilkins sighed ever so softly. "So I'm finally dead." Then she smiled, "About time." She scratched the side of her nose, crossed her arms and leaned back against the wall. She felt, more than saw, the radiance from the doorway. Miss Wilkins shook her head and wiggled her nose at the beckoning door. "Can't go, Door. Need to take care of my Jason. Took you long enough to come to get me, so you can wait a speck longer."

Dr. Thornton stepped back from the table. "I'm going to miss her."

Nurse Appleby frowned up at Dr. Thornton. "I heard she was the meanest old witch in town."

Dr. Thornton nodded. "She'd worked hard to have you believe that. I wouldn't be a doctor today if it hadn't been for her."

"What do you mean?"

"By my second year in medical school I'd run out of money. I'd called and told my Mom that I would probably have to drop out of school. Well, Mom put my name on the prayer list, and Miss Wilkins, being the good Presbyterian that she was, got a call from the prayer line. Next thing I know I'm sitting in my class and in limps Miss Wilkins, shouting and demanding to know where I am. She'd flown all the way from Columbus to Boston, and she had to get from Logan up to Columbus. She didn't drive, so I have no idea how she did it. She must have been well into her late 70s then.

"My professor was a tough old Irishman, the toughest professor I ever had, and he yelled at her to get out of his classroom. Well, he didn't have a chance against Miss Wilkins. She hobbled right up the aisle, pounded her cane on his podium, shut him right up with a wild wave of her cane and told him she was there on important business. He knew real fast that he'd met his match.

"Then she saw me and marched me right out of that classroom and into the hallway. I felt like I was back in seventh grade again. She gave me quite a lecture and told me I wasn't going to drop out of medical school while she was around and for me to stop whining and get on with my studies.

213

She placed a check in my hand and told me to use it wisely. Then she turned around and hobbled out of the building on her cane without ever glancing back.

"When I went back into class, my professor asked what that was all about. After I told him, he said that I'd better do exactly what she said, because he didn't want to face that lady again." Dr. Thornton shook his head in quiet amazement. "My professor told me that if Miss Wilkins went to all that trouble, then I must be someone of great potential. That professor became my most important mentor and strongest supporter. She didn't know it, but her visit forced me to live up to that potential."

"A big check?" Nurse Appleby asked.

"It covered my last two years of medical school and my internship. It took me seven years before I could pay it all back to her."

Jennifer Solama said tearfully. "She paid for my physician's assistant schooling."

"I didn't know that?" Dr. Thornton said in surprise. "You never even mentioned that you knew her."

"I didn't. My mom had her in seventh grade. Then, when she got pregnant with me, she dropped out of high school. We moved back here after she got divorced, and I only went to high school here. Somehow, Miss Wilkins found out about me wanting to go to Kettering College of Medical Arts in Kettering, Ohio, and become a physician's assistant, but even with my scholarship money and working part-time, I knew I couldn't make it. One day my mom tells me that Miss Wilkins had called. We had to go see her."

"Well, I'd heard plenty about Miss Wilkins from all the kids that had gone through her classes, so I was a little scared about going. What I didn't realize until we got to her front door is that my Mom was more scared than I was.

"Miss Wilkins starts yelling at my Mom from the moment she invites us in. Whee, it was fierce. I was afraid to open my mouth. Then she turns on me and demands to know why I want to be a physician's assistant. I don't know what I said, but it wasn't the right answer for Miss Wilkins. She starts lecturing me about how important my job will be and what I can mean to the world. She tells me that I have a chance to make my life extraordinary." Jennifer stopped and shook her head in bewilderment as the memory of that moment filled her mind.

"Then she hands me a check and," Jennifer smiled at Dr. Thornton, "tells me to use the money wisely." Jennifer pulled a tissue from a nearby box and wiped her eyes.

Miss Wilkins shook her head. "Jennifer, stop all that teary stuff." She walked up to Dr. Thornton and wagged her finger. "And I told you that you weren't to tell anyone about me lending you money."

Dr. Thornton leaned on the gurney and said, "Won't seem like Christmas without her."

"She never had children?"

"Hundreds of us," Dr. Thornton said. "All over this town and all over the country. She was an amazingly, wonderful woman." He looked up and smiled. "Her bark was a lot worse than her bite."

Miss Wilkins harrumphed, "Not when I had my teeth in." She felt her teeth with her tongue. "Mercy sakes, these aren't my plates." She reached up and tugged on her front teeth. Her teeth didn't budge. "Well, interesting. I can finally chew down a dinner. Sheesh, with my luck, people probably don't eat where I'm going."

The buzzer in the next station started a loud, constant ringing sound.

"That's Jason." Dr. Thornton shook his head angrily. "I'm not sure I can handle two deaths on Christmas Eve," he whispered as he rushed from the room with Jennifer and Nurse Appleby immediately behind him. Miss Wilkins didn't move. Jason stood across the room staring at Miss Wilkins' body.

Miss Wilkins said his name with authority, "Jason!"

Jason jumped and stared at her in confusion. He looked at her and then back at her body stretched out on the gurney. "Miss Wilkins, is that you? You look so…" Jason struggled to find an acceptable word and finally blurted out, "…so young. What's going on? Are there two of you?"

"Oh, mercy sakes, no, boy. That's just an old shell. Nothing to fret over. What are you doing walking around?"

Jason's face crunched into a frown as he considered her question. "I'm not sure. I heard people crying and that's when I came in." He glanced back at the other room. "I've got a shell of me back there, too. That's really awesome, huh? But my

215

shell looks like me, and your shell looks like you, but you look like a teenager. How is that?"

Miss Wilkins glanced down at her hands, expecting to see her gnarled, arthritic bony hands covered with brown spots, but she had the hands of a young woman. "Well, I guess I got my young body back along with my teeth. Isn't that something? Did you see a doorway with bright lights?"

"There was one in my room, but I heard the crying."

A stranger suddenly appeared beside Jason. He was dressed in a shimmering suit, purer white than light, with a pale-blue shirt and a dark blue tie. He had a friendly face, but his tone was serious. "I'm afraid it's time to go, Jason. You'll see Miss Wilkins again soon."

"No," Miss Wilkins said firmly.

"No?" the man in white repeated with a patient smile. "I'm afraid it's yes, Miss Wilkins. It's Jason's time."

Miss Wilkins shook her head back and forth. "No, no, no. It's just not right. I had such hope for Jason. He's destined to do great things. I feel it in my bones." She stopped and wagged a finger at the man. "I've left him money in my will for his college education." She snapped her chin firmly up and down. "That's how it is."

"Amy."

Miss Wilkins turned around and saw Clark standing behind her—her Clark, her love from so many years ago, still as handsome and delicious looking as always. "Oh, Clark." Her eyes filled with tears.

He held out his arms and she ran into them eagerly. "Oh, Clark, you have no idea how I've missed you all these years." The warmth of his body was a joyous treat for her.

"I know, Sweetheart. I know."

She snuggled into his shoulder and whispered to him, "Why did you have to die so young? We could have had such a wonderful life together."

"But if I'd have lived, would you have helped all the people that you did? You were such a special person that our love would have gotten in the way."

"Did I make a difference, Clark? Did I really make a difference?"

216

Clark gently brushed tears off her cheeks. "I'm almost embarrassed to tell you how much." He kissed her gently on her still moist cheek. Clark motioned gently toward the light.

"I can't go yet, Clark. I've got to help Jason."

The man in the flickering suit sighed softly. "You have to make her understand, Clark."

"No," Clark said with a grin. "You have to make her understand. My job is just to love her. I've been waiting patiently for more that 75 years for this moment. She's always been a woman with strong convictions, and I hope she never changes her gentle heart."

The man spread out his arms in mild frustration. "What has to be, has to be, Miss Wilkins. That's all there is to it."

"No," Miss Wilkins said firmly. "I want to talk to your supervisor." The man's eyebrows shot up, and he shook his head in puzzlement. "Ma'am, that's God. You can't just go talk to God."

"Nonsense, been talking to him all my life. No reason to stop now." She bowed her head and grasped her hands together tightly. "Lord, I realize I'm just an old, dead woman, but I'd look on it real kindly if you could see fit to give my young friend, Jason, a new breath of life. He's a fine young boy, and I believe that he'll grow up to be a fine man who will honor your name. As always, I know that it is your will that will be done, but I do hope that you will see fit to give this child a new chance, considering that it's Christmas Eve and all."

Suddenly the room filled with intense light and a warm, gentle voice said, "Welcome home, Amy. I have heard your voice all these years. You have been a joyous servant. Your request is granted."

Jason disappeared.

"We got him back," Dr. Thornton yelled from the next room. "Let's not lose him."

"Mercy!" The angel shook his head and grinned. "That's the first time I've ever seen that happen." He nodded at Amy, "Well done."

Clark gave Amy a gentle hug as they walked together to the brilliant lights in the doorway. "Dinner's waiting."

"Oh, thank goodness. That's such good news. I was afraid I'd gotten my teeth back and wouldn't be able to use them."

ACKNOWLEDGMENTS

To write 25 Christmas stories, an author will draw on many sources for inspiration.

For me, a broad group of eclectic friends influenced and inspired these stories of Christmas love and hope. Some of my friends may see a snippet of themselves throughout these stories, but no story is about any of them. Instead, these stories represent the essence of spirit and love that my friends have spread before them, the love I have witnessed as a bystander and the love I have received as a friend. For me, love is the unifying theme for Christmas and for these stories. Christmas started with love and ended with hope.

Dr. George Pickwell and his wife, **Dr. Linda Quattrochi,** are the first on my list. For more than two decades, they have shown me what true love is all about, a love so rich and precious that I always feel honored just to be in their presence. True love—surely this is a fairy-tale, a myth, and yet, these two show true love each day they live and work together—scientists and lovers, lovers and scientists. They are each gifted, published scientists who have spent most of their married life working together in research laboratories searching for new cures for cancer. Talk about togetherness; they are amazing. Their spirit of true love shows up strongly in *The Christmas Gift* and I just had to honor them with the wine in *The Last S-2.*

David and **Ann Marie Bezayiff** and **Ted** and **Lynn Wise** are friends from my days as a college library director and professor. We have supported one another through some difficult journeys and some wonderful joyful adventures. They live a love story that many can only dream of emulating. David's book *I Want To Grow Old With Ann Marie* is a heartwarming and beautiful book waiting to be published, torn from the soul of a man facing and surviving prostate cancer. Ann Marie's book *From the Olive Orchard* is a wonderful collection of her stories about faith.

David and Ted are talented musicians besides being erudite professors. They have each written wonderful love songs for their wives. David wrote the words and music of the song he wrote for Ann Marie, *Compliment to Her*. The story of this song's creation is a love story in itself. Ted's original guitar song for his wife, *LynnSong,* is a constant reminder of the love he has for her. These men are married to extraordinary women, brilliant, talented, loving and nurturing in their own right. What is even more fascinating is that these four are all teachers and professors. They represent the best of what teachers can be; they breathe a love seldom seen.

Harry and **Jean Manning's** true-life love story beats anything I've written. Here's another example that true love can and does happen. Through the good times and the rough times, they have hung onto each other with love and laughter.

James and **Donna Jernigan** live too far away, but when we get together, we make it count. Ah, the fine wine, the great food, and the laughter we've shared. Theirs is another remarkable love story of perseverance through separation and difficult times, yet their love holds firm.

Across the street from me, two people, **Donna Jean** and **Charles H. McMakin III** (but I just call him Mac) have enriched my life with their love, laughter and meals. Ah yes, meals. When Donna found out I was having a can of peas and three Oreo cookies for my dinner one evening shortly after we first met, she decided that I would have lunch and dinner with them from then on, as though I was a member of the family. Since she's raised six boys, **Chip, Jack, Jim, Todd, Eric**, (who became my model for Nick Tracer) and **Chris**, the meals were easy for her. In return she got unremitting repair of her computer. Mac and I believe the meals were just her way to keep an eye on the two of us. We have been known to get into great mischief together on our mountain trips, shopping excursions, or while planning clandestine adventures together in our offices or my artist's sunroom. My stories of bringing Mac kicking and screaming into the 21st Century with a new digital camera and teaching him how to use a computer delighted all his sons, much to Mac's chagrin. Still, there is much laughter and merriment at every meal, so perhaps that's also part of the trade. Friendship, laughter and love—isn't that what life and Christmas should be all about? Donna and Mac also have a very active role in my western novel, *Hunt the Hunter,* which was great fun to write.

I've been blessed with two lovely daughters (this book is dedicated to them). Their mother, **Diane d. Spalsbury**, (who believed in my writing but must have wondered) is a close and cherished friend, a lovely woman, a super mother, terrific cook and a darn good gardener. We might not have gotten everything right during the years we were together, but we got it right when we made our beautiful daughters. Though we now journey on different paths, she will always be one of my best friends, a close confidant and fan, just as she will always be the loving mother of our daughters.

Estella de la Rosa is Diane's mother. She is a beautiful, gracious, sociable and elegant woman. When I write about a truly magnificent woman, she comes to mind. Her other four daughters were a wonderful part of my life for 20 years as they grew to adulthood. They were, and are, a rich part of my life and my stories. Estella's daughters are all grownup, yet I still see them when I can. They and their husbands—**Judy** and **Neal Daily, Carol** and **Joe Jones, Ellen Segur, Sue** and **Mike Wiltz** —bring me much joy and laughter when we are together.

My mom, **Marjorie Spalsbury**, read many of these stories as I wrote them. Her favorite was *The Last S-2.* I wrote some of these stories on her front porch in Logan, Ohio, while visiting her on various summer breaks. Funny, she would say with a twinkle in her eye, how our family escapades appear throughout your stories. I miss her and that front porch. We don't have many front porches in California. I find that rather sad. Fortunately, my sister, **Dina Metzler**, who still lives in Logan, built one on the front of her house and even included an electrical plug for my computer. She's a good little sister!

Sandy L. Aldinger, my other sister, is the beautiful, foxy one. She's the ballroom dancer with the great legs, but that did her no good when she was younger. She had to put up with a mischievous and ornery big brother and not the sweet and innocent person I grew into. (That should evoke hilarious laughter from my sisters.) That she still loves me after the jelly sandwich in her face and assorted other misdeeds that a big brother can do, is a tribute to her patience and family love. Her tolerance of my many foibles, such as raising snakes and lizards in my bedroom— this was bad enough, but salamanders in her bed (how on earth did they ever get there?) and salamanders swimming in the washing machine (maybe they wanted to take a bath?)—is legend in the family. Her daughter, my niece, **Terre Buckles**, hasn't seen too much of that side of her uncle's orneriness, which is a good thing because I wouldn't want any of that to rub off on her two children, **Peyton** and **Seth.**

Sandy's son, my nephew **Brian Buckles,** and his wife **Mary Beth** live in Dana Point, California, a beautiful city along the coast. Brian now towers over me, but I still call him my 'little nephew' and he patiently bends down and gives his uncle a gentle hug. To eat dinner on the beach with them and watch the sun set is a special treat I never tire of.

Dina A. Metzler is my delightfully wonderful baby sister and an extraordinary seventh- and eighth-grade history teacher. (Anyone who teaches in the public schools is under-paid, under-appreciated and must have the patience of a saint! Sorry for the editorial comments, but as a college professor who is still teaching teachers how to teach, I hear firsthand the impossible difficulties they must face daily.) My sister helped edit an earlier book I wrote on using multimedia tools in the classroom, and I dedicated that book to her. What I said then still holds true today: As a teacher she makes a difference to her students every school year; as a friend she brightens my spirit with her phone calls, her wild sense of humor and our times together; as an editor she's one ornery woman who chuckles greatly at my mistakes; and as my sister she fills my heart with love.

Her husband, **Barry A. Metzler,** (known to use the handle BAM-3) when he's not being a vice president of a bank or having serious earthy conversations with his golf clubs, is an amazing creator of magical beer gardens. He tolerates my non-beer-drinking ways in his beer garden, and has on occasion even allowed me a glass of wine or two, although not without a few derogatory comments about my choice of drink or the color of my socks. His most serious complaint, however, is how he's never gotten even with me for waking him out of a dead sleep while napping on his sun porch and scaring the tar out of him in a way that I felt was most clever. I'm sure there must be a story in that!